DEATH
WILL GET
YOU SOBER

ELIZABETH ZELVIN

DEATH
WILL GET
YOU SOBER

Thomas Dunne Books / St. Martin's Minotaur

New York

This is a work of fiction. All of the characters, organizations, and events portrayed in this novel are either products of the author's imagination or are used fictitiously.

THOMAS DUNNE BOOKS.
An imprint of St. Martin's Press.

www.thomasdunnebooks.com
www.minotaurbooks.com

Design by Dylan Rosal Greif

Library of Congress Cataloging-in-Publication Data

Zelvin, Elizabeth.
    Death will get you sober / Elizabeth Zelvin. — 1st ed.
      p.   cm.
    ISBN-13: 978-0-312-37589-8
    ISBN-10: 0-312-37589-1
    1. Alcoholics—Fiction.   I. Title.
    PS3576.E48D43 2008
    813'.54—dc22

                                   2007050682

First Edition: April 2008

10 9 8 7 6 5 4 3 2 1

To Brian, always,
and to recovering people everywhere,
whose courage and honesty are a constant inspiration

ACKNOWLEDGMENTS

Heartfelt thanks to the Guppies who read all or part of the manuscript and offered support, encouragement, and tips on query letters, synopses, agents, and killing your darlings: Janet Bolin, Leslie Budewitz, Carolyn Chambers Clark, Judy Clemens, Cindy Daniel, Krista Davis, Kadi Easley, Daryl Wood Gerber, S. W. Hubbard, Catherine Maiorisi, Thelma Straw, Denise Tiller, and others too numerous to mention. Special thanks to my blog sisters on Poe's Deadly Daughters: Sandra Parshall, Lonnie Cruse, Sharon Wildwind, and Julia Buckley. Thanks, too, to Elaine C. Johnson, first reader of the first draft, who's known me since we were eleven; to Jay Mulvaney, whose unsolicited kindness got my manuscript to St. Martin's; and to the late Barry Roff, Ph.D., who gave me a job on the Bowery.

DEATH
WILL GET
YOU SOBER

ONE

I woke up in detox with the taste of stale puke in my mouth. Out of the corner of my eye, I could see twinkling lights. This had happened before as I came out of a blackout. I rolled my head heavily sideways on the pillow. The light came from a drooping strand of blinking bulbs flung over a dispirited-looking artificial pine. A plastic Santa, looking as drunk as I remembered being when I went into the blackout, grinned at me from the treetop. I had an awful feeling it was Christmas Day.

The ward was quiet, but from my other side came the weak sound of coughing. I rolled my head the other way. That hurt. A skinny black guy lay huddled in the next bed, shaking the mattress with his puny but convulsive coughs. I waited for him to get it down to a wheeze.

"Hey there."

"Yo," he said. "Know where you are?"

"Not a clue," I admitted. "Detox for sure."

"It ain't Paree," he agreed. His cackle shook the bed and started him wheezing again. Between gasps, he said, "You're on the Bowery."

"Oh, great," I said.

"Merry Christmas," he said, and laughed so hard, he coughed up blood. I didn't need a degree from Harvard Medical School to diagnose TB. I hoped he hadn't been lying next to me long and that they'd move him out soon.

The next time I came to, an even skinnier guy lay in the next bed. The smell of his cigarette woke me. Long and white as a skeleton, with sunken cheeks and shadowed eyes, he looked like someone the Headless Horseman might enjoy chasing. I mentally named him Ichabod. Ichabod lay there sucking up smoke. It sounded like he was working on a case of emphysema. So far, nobody in that detox was built like Santa Claus or breathed silently.

As I lay there, not doing much but breathing along, a small, pale female hand stuck a paper cup of juice under my nose. A sweet, cool voice commanded, "Drink!" To my roommate, she said, "Put that out, sir! You know better. And offer one to the new man."

Looming above us, she bored into him with a gimlet eye until he stubbed out his smoke on a plastic pill bottle and offered me the pack. I thought I was hallucinating because she seemed to be dressed like a nun. But I never said no to a cigarette.

"Thanks, bro," I said, taking two. "And thank you, sister. You're an angel."

"It's for later," she snapped. "Smoking room only."

Ichabod laughed until his dentures popped. When the nun trotted off to get him some water, he said, "Your first time here, huh? That's Sister Angel."

Sister Angel moved so quickly that she was back before I could ask him to explain. With her fresh pink skin and retro habit, she looked like the result of a penguin's night on the tiles with a particularly clean pig. After handing Ichabod his water, she turned on me. Her round blue eyes bulged slightly.

"How are you feeling?" she demanded.

"Just fine and wonderful," I said with weary irony. To tell the truth, I felt like hell. My mouth tasted like a garbage scow, my memory was on lockdown, and I bitterly regretted not being dead by thirty, the way I'd always thought I'd be.

The next time I surfaced, Ichabod had vanished. The guy in the next bed now couldn't have been more different. Well fed. Groomed, even. I decided that it would be a good idea to make friends. Not only did he look like a fellow who had at least one whole pack of cigarettes but he probably smoked an expensive brand and might consider it noblesse oblige to give a few away. Except, of course, that at the moment, he was puking his guts out. Sister Angel held the basin.

"Hi," I said. "I'm Bruce, and I'm an alcoholic." This is how people introduce themselves at AA meetings, of which I've been to a few in my time. He looked like a guy who might appreciate irony.

"Gggggaaahhhh," he said. "Jesus Christ. Oh, Christ, my head."

I knew how he felt. There's a very specific kind of headache that you get only when you're in withdrawal and puking at the same time. It feels as if somebody has inserted a particularly sturdy crowbar in between two neurons in your brain that are extremely close together and is using the lever principle to pry them apart.

Sister Angel held a damp cloth to his forehead. Now she straightened up and let go of the basin, which she had been steadying against his knees.

"Don't drop it, now. I'll go wet the cloth."

Half-falling out of bed as he sat up, he did almost drop the basin. I decided it was not quite the right moment to bum a cigarette. He retched, but nothing much was happening anymore. He lifted his head very, very carefully and gave me a sickly half smile.

"Hi, I'm God." He paused, either enjoying the flummoxed expression on my face or forgetting where he was going with the remark. That happens frequently when you're detoxing. Then he added, "Alcoholic."

It wasn't much of a résumé, but it told me he wasn't a virgin. He'd seen the inside of more than one AA meeting. Probably dozens, if not hundreds. You can't mistake that perky introduction. It would make you feel like an asshole the first time you raise your hand and say it, except that the first time you're usually shaking. If you're not crying.

Anyhow, this yo-yo made quite a first impression. *Hi, I'm God.* Maybe this wasn't detox after all, but the loony bin—all right, in-patient psych unit—a place I had so far managed to avoid.

"Are you delusional, or should I be genuflecting?" I guess my skepticism showed.

"Godfrey Brandon Kettleworth the Third," he amplified. He rolled his bleary eyeballs up past exhausted lids and threw his hands in the air in an "I surrender" gesture. "Blame my parents."

"What are you in for?" Joke.

"Ninety days with time off for good behavior?" A wit. Maybe I would have to forgive the guy his Harvard education. Contrary to legend, not too many déclassé rocket scientists end up on the Bowery. It was Princeton, he told me later. Whispered. Little boys grow up, but we never get over wanting to be cool. Ivy League was not cool on the Bowery.

By evening, Godfrey's guts were behaving a little better. After lights-out—did I mention being in detox is humiliating?—we exchanged some basic information. Preferred brand of gin—Tanqueray. Favorite Scotch—Chivas Regal, both of us, though he had probably been able to afford a lot more of it than I had. What bars we drank in. He had started out on the Upper East Side at the Bemelmans Bar in the Hotel Carlyle and worked his way down to some dive on Tenth Avenue in Hell's Kitchen. All right, fashionable Clinton. New York, always reinventing itself. Hi, I'm Clinton, I'm a grateful recovering neighborhood. Compared notes on what the hell we were doing in a place like this. He couldn't remember, either. Kindred spirits.

TWO

"You'll never guess who called me today," Jimmy said. Big and blocky, with a square, cheerful pink Irish face, ice blue eyes surrounded by laugh wrinkles that almost hid their glint of intelligence, and a small rosebud mouth like Henry VIII's, he clung to the rail that surrounded the ice rink at Rockefeller Center. He wore a puffy red down L.L.Bean parka and a violently colored fuchsia wool watch cap and mittens, obviously hand-knitted with great effort. Behind him soared the towering RCA building, with the giant Christmas tree, studded with red, green, blue, and yellow lights, standing sentry before it. "Hey, if you're going down, you don't have to take me with you."

He teetered on rented skates, the back edges of his blades banging against the low wall, as his girlfriend, Barbara, clutched wildly at the front of his jacket. Her thick brown hair, dancing with static, frizzed up around her head. Her teal-and-violet parka and turquoise accessories, knitted by the same inexpert hand, only emphasized the contrast between them. She was small and olive-skinned, with the long, slim nose and rounded cheeks of a Barbra Streisand who ate too many bagels. Even when not on skates, she appeared to be in perpetual motion.

"I'm stable, I'm stable!" she said, letting go her grip on his jacket and windmilling frantically. "Let me guess. Bill Gates? Bill W.? No, he's dead. The Pope?"

"Are you break-dancing or what? Nope. You're out of guesses. Bruce."

"Talk about a voice from the past," she said. Her voice trembled between wistful and excited. "Was he drinking?"

"Nope again. Are you ready for this? He's in detox. Aw, pumpkin, I know it's shocking, but you didn't have to sit down."

Barbara tried to glare up at him from her seat on the ice, but instead she began to laugh.

"Ow, my butt hurts. Good thing I'm well padded. Here, doofus, give me a hand." She extended a woolly turquoise paw. "How did you feel—hearing from him, I mean? What did he say? Where was he—what detox, I mean? Do you think this time he might finally have hit bottom? Are we talking to him? Can we go and see him? Did he say when he was getting out?"

Jimmy pulled her easily upright and stabilized her balance by putting his arms around her in a bear hug, his back braced firmly against the rail so they wouldn't skid and go down again. Barbara nestled happily against his chest.

"Whoa, there, peanut," Jimmy said. "One question at a time."

Barbara shook her head, her curls brushing his chin.

"One day at a time I can do when I work my program really hard. One question at a time? I don't know, honey, that's a tough one. Don't torture me, just tell me everything."

"He's down on the Bowery—woke up there Christmas Day." His arms tightened as she began to shake with laughter. "Stop that, it isn't funny."

"Oh yes it is." She caught a tear on her mitten as it rolled down her flushed cheek. "I'm sure he appreciates the irony—and maybe it'll even motivate him to stay sober. It could hardly get any worse, could it. So where is he? My old place on the Bowery or the other place?"

"Your place. And don't squeal like that. I know you're still in touch with the staff down there, but do you really think it's a good idea? No, don't answer that. I can see that you do. Will you think twice before you go barreling down there? You don't want to embarrass him, do you?"

"Nice try, sweetie, but forget it. You alcoholics don't embarrass worth a damn compared to us codependents. And I have so much recovery, I won't even blush when I call up Charmaine—you remember her, the head nurse—and invite her out to lunch. Actually, I haven't been down to the Bowery since I worked there. I hear it's gentrifying rapidly, and I've been wanting to go see for myself. From flophouses to fern bars, can you believe it?"

Jimmy sighed deeply, sending a puff of frozen breath out into the air above her head. She flung an arm around his neck, pulled his head down, and rubbed her cold cheek against his.

"Seriously, baby," she said, "I know it's hurt you to see him go on drinking all these years since you got sober. And you've been so good. You haven't gotten caught up in his bullshit, but you've been there for him the few times he's reached out. If there's a chance that this time he means it, we've got to help. Come on, skate with me. I promise I'll stay on my feet."

She hooked her arm through his and they moved slowly onto the ice, joining the families of tourists circling around a central knot of serious figure skaters in pert little miniskirted outfits.

"I want to help. You know I do," Jimmy said. "I told him fifteen years ago I wouldn't enable him but that anytime he wanted to put the bottle down, I'd be right beside him. Hell, I've missed him.

We've been best friends since we were eight years old. It's just—you do have a disease of helping, petunia."

"Oh, I do," she said. "What do you think I've been working on all these years in Al-Anon and therapy? I promise I'll maintain some boundaries. I won't screw it up."

Jimmy turned his head to give her a quick kiss, endangering their precarious balance.

"I appreciate that, pet," he said. "I know how hard you try. It's just—you know, I can't help thinking if we don't screw it up, maybe Bruce won't screw it up this time, either."

THREE

Sister Angel clanged a lugubrious bell. Some convent from before Vatican II must have had a yard sale. I threw away the stub of my cigarette and emerged from the stuffy little smoking room. The patients, many of whom had spent some time as guests of Uncle Sam, called it "the Gas Chamber." After two days, I knew the drill. The staff didn't count on us to make it to an AA meeting once we left the detox. So they brought AA to us. A few of the guys already sat in a circle of butt-destroying folding chairs. At almost every meeting, one collapsed under someone's weight. My new friend Godfrey tilted his backward against the wall. He looked ultracool even in the Fifties-sitcom pj's they made us wear. He was probably the only guy on the Bowery with a bathrobe from Pierre Cardin. Or at least the only one who'd bought it new. You'd be surprised what you can get from the Salvation Army.

"Take off your sunglasses, Godfrey," said Sister Angel. Her voice held a note of resignation. She said it a dozen times a day. She had made it clear that in this detox, he would not be known as God.

He waited a few seconds before removing his shades, casually, as if it was his own idea. He jerked his head at me. I ambled over and sat down next to him. Sister Angel put down the bell and clapped her hands for silence.

"Who's the speaker?" I muttered.

"Some poor bastard from outside," Godfrey said out of the corner of his mouth. Sure enough, one guy wasn't wearing pajamas. He had a square red Irish mug, watch cap, blue jeans, plaid flannel shirt, and big clumping work boots with a little snow still melting off them. White Christmas. In two days, I had almost forgotten there was such a thing as weather.

One of the counselors led off, an African-American dude with a better hairdo than Bo Derek. Medium tall, sleek, and glossy, he had a bodybuilder's biceps, abs, and pecs. Besides the fancy cornrows, he sported enough tattoos for a one-man show and a diamond chip in one of his bicuspids.

"Hi, I'm Darryl, and I'm an addict. Let's start the meeting by going around with first names only."

"Used to deal," Godfrey murmured in my ear. He meant drugs, not poker.

"I'm Bob, and I'm an alcoholic."

"Mike, alcoholic."

"My name ees Hieronimo." A stocky little guy with a heavy Puerto Rican accent.

Mike leaned over and muttered, "Why you're here."

"Drinking. I am here for drinking. Drinking and drinking, drinking all the time."

"*Basta,*" Mike hissed. Another big red-faced Irish guy, he knew a little Spanish, like most New Yorkers. A regular melting pot, detox.

Godfrey leaned toward my right ear.

"I'm God," he muttered under his breath, "and I'm an arrogant son of a bitch."

I agreed with him. Instead of saying so, I hissed back, "Don't let Sister A. hear you. Isn't there something else I can call you?"

"Later." He waited till the antsier guys squirmed with impatience. Then he drawled, "Hi, I'm God . . . frey."

When everyone had spoken up, the visitor took his watch cap off and scratched a little, like a dog settling down. The top of his bald head faintly reflected the red exit sign over the door.

"My name is Benny, and I'm an alcoholic. I'm here to tell you what it was like, what happened, and what it's like now."

All drunkalogues are the same. I drifted in and out. Godfrey dozed. He woke up when Benny's story about how he'd bottomed out got a laugh.

"I got out of here five years ago on New Year's Day. The only reason I didn't go right into the nearest bar was that I slipped on some ice and lost all my change down a grate."

He waited till the chuckles died down and everyone had finished shaking their heads over an all too familiar experience before he went on.

"I've been sober ever since, one day at a time, through the grace of God. I spent the holidays with my family this year. I had maxed out my credit with them, puking on their carpets, insulting their in-laws, stealing from their wallets, breaking promises to their kids. My sister and I used to be really tight. She looked out for me until she couldn't stand it anymore. Last time I saw her, she told me I could never come home again and if the booze killed me, I'd be doing the family a favor."

Godfrey had started to smirk, but at some point during that last speech the expression froze and lay forgotten on his face. I would ask him later what had jerked his chain. Or maybe I wouldn't.

"The best present I got this Christmas was a hug and her forgiveness," Benny ended. Tears stood in his eyes. He wasn't Tiny Tim, but I felt like crying myself.

Meetings close with everyone standing in a circle and holding hands. Have I mentioned recovery can be embarrassingly corny? Sister Angel bustled up to glare at Godfrey until he took his left hand out of his pocket and grabbed my right.

"God grant me the serenity . . . to accept the things I cannot change . . . courage to change the things I can . . . and the wisdom to know the difference."

The Serenity Prayer is so good, it's hard to make fun of. As soon as it ended, we dropped one another's hands like they were burning coals and did our best to make our getaway. One of the counselors blocked us. Boris was a Russian immigrant four inches taller and twice as wide as Godfrey. They both towered over me. I'm the compact, wiry type. I used to say it didn't cost much to give me a full tank of high-test. Boris used to put away two liters of vodka a day. He gets it that alcoholism is a disease. My best friend Jimmy's girlfriend, Barbara, who's a counselor herself, says most Russians think it's something prosperity will fix. They think *capitalism* will fix it.

"Everybody stay put." Boris had a booming basso voice like the guy in the opera. "There's something the whole community has to talk about." All of a sudden, we were a community. We sat down. Did we have a choice?

The head counselor, an old white guy named Bark, took over.

"There have been a few incidents of things going missing lately. Money and small items. Not just from staff but some patients' belongings, too. This is not okay."

A few guys exchanged furtive glances. Some looked hostile. Several looked bored. A couple, only a day or two off their last fix, were nodding out. To lift cash and watches or whatever, jewelry maybe, from desks, lockers, maybe pockets, you have to be awake. These guys were crashing.

"Patients' belongings," I murmured. "Gee, I guess I didn't have my stock certificates on me when I went out to get blitzed on Christmas Eve."

For all I knew, my buddy had reason not to find it as ludicrous as I did to think of any of us owning stocks. But he was cool. "Yeah, I guess this accounts for our cash-flow problem."

"I know you've all survived on the streets. So have I," Bark rasped. He'd smoked three packs a day for a hundred years. When he could get them. "We all know the code of the streets. When I was living in a box, I thought a pint of Thunderbird was the best thing in the world." That got a laugh. "And I thought squealing on a buddy was the worst. But this detox is not the streets. If you know something, if you see something, tell your counselor. Or confront the thief, because he's screwing you. He could be stealing your last chance."

I would not have made a money bet on anybody coming forward. The code was no squealing. I also noticed that although they talked about the community and had the staff there as if the warning was for everybody, they were talking at us patients. Bark added that the thief or thieves would be prosecuted if found. That kind of took the shine off the appeal to our higher selves. After that, they let us put away the chairs and go to lunch.

In this no-frills detox, Sister Angel handed out chores as if they were penances. That afternoon, Godfrey and I drew a couple of hours of Hail Marys scrubbing the floor in the patients' lavatory.

"Five bucks to a pack of Marlboros you've never done this before," I said.

"You'd lose," he said. "I was in the army. Got to Nam for just long enough to start enjoying the drugs," he drawled, "and then the war was over."

"I lucked out for once. Too young. Didn't your family try to get you out of it? Or at least out of getting drafted?"

"Not a chance," he said. "Even then they considered me a lily of the field: I toiled not, neither did I spin. You know the saying, God doesn't do windows?" His mouth twisted. "They had the connections, but their idea of tough love was not lifting a finger to get me out of it."

"The family called you God?"

"Only in moments of exceptional sarcasm. Otherwise, it was Godfrey or, more often, Guff."

"Guff? As in bullshit? I won't comment, but what a setup."

"My dictionary says 'insolent talk.' Believe me, I've heard all the cracks," he said. "That's not how it started, though. My sister Emmie called me Guffy when she was little." His grim face softened. "She couldn't pronounce Godfrey."

"I like it. Okay if I call you Guffy?"

"Guff will do." The caustic tone back in his voice, he added, "I doubt anyone here knows what it means."

I let that one lie and asked him what happened after Nam. At twenty-five, he told me, he came into a big trust fund. He'd been squandering it ever since. Hot and cold running booze and pharmaceuticals, with an occasional side trip to AA and a series of detoxes and treatment programs spiraling downward from Betty Ford to the Bowery.

"Speaking of toiling not," I said, "I need a smoke."

Guff banged the scrub brush smartly against the side of the bucket and tossed it in. Water went splashing. The prevailing atmosphere of ammonia—where we'd already scrubbed—and urine—where we hadn't—swirled into my nostrils and throat when I made the mistake of breathing.

"Is the coast clear?"

I stuck my head out the bathroom door and looked both ways. No staff in sight. We had kept the door to the stairs that led up to the roof unlocked with paper shims and wads of chewing gum. The roof, though windy, was a lot nicer than the smoking room.

We sheltered in the lee of one of those giant oak water barrels that perch on New York rooftops. A gray mist had settled over the city. The quiet, empty streets and softened contours of the buildings looked kind of peaceful. I took a long, hungry draw on my cigarette.

"The coast is clear." Guff cracked about an eighth of a smile. His eyes remained sad. "We used to say that when we were kids."

"You and your sister?"

Guff sucked up smoke. The tip of his cigarette glowed like Rudolph's nose.

"Sisters. Emmie's the baby. Lucinda and Frances are older." He spoke on the inhale, then blew out a perfect smoke ring. Terminally cool. "Lucinda's an intellectual. Mind like a steel trap that could take a wolverine. Eats a bowl of graduate students for breakfast every morning. Frances is so WASP, she's got a stinger in her butt. Faculty wife, but she does the charity circuit, too. Carries on the family tradition."

"Champagne for poverty?"

"Right." Another smoke ring. "Thinks Thunderbird is a car. No use for me, of course. Don't waste your quarter." I assumed he was referring to the proverbial one phone call you get when you're arrested. No point calling someone who won't make bail if you need it, or at least come down and pick you up.

"Emmie's different." He managed to send the next smoke ring straight up, so it hovered over his head like a halo. "She would have hung on if the others hadn't gotten to her. None of them speak to me now."

"What, no enablers?" There's usually someone who'll rescue you time after time, hoping you'll change. Letting them be controlling is a small price to pay. You just have to lie a little harder and stash the booze somewhere inventive. "Nieces and nephews who'd do anything for Uncle Guffy?"

His lips tightened. "No," he said shortly. Oops. Slammed door. We all had a few, or we wouldn't be on the Bowery. A pigeon— New York City wildlife—fluttered onto the low parapet around the roof. It flapped, cooed, strutted around for a while, and took off again. "Except my grandfather on the Brandon side. You could say he's been enabling me. He's been dead a long time, so he can't get on my case about how I spend his money." As if to demonstrate what a big spender he was, he threw his cigarette over the edge. It made little sizzling noises in the damp air all the way down to the street. Conspicuous waste. Nineteen out of twenty of our room-mates downstairs would have snuffed the butt and put it in their pocket for next time.

"Let's go."

Silently, we picked our way among the mysterious excrescences that dot city rooftops like mushrooms, then plodded down the stairs to finish cleaning the bathroom.

FOUR

Charmaine, the nursing coordinator, looked exasperated. As far as I knew, it was her habitual expression. But then, I was always right in front of her when I saw it.

"For someone with no intention of staying sober," she said irritably, "you know an awful lot about sobriety. Where do you think that's going to get you?"

"Now you ask what am I going to do different this time."

It wasn't very nice of me to tease her. But if I couldn't drink, I had to do something not to die of boredom. As Charmaine glared at me, a hubbub broke out down the hall. I heard a burst of angry shouting, peppered with those explosive f's and k's that occur when someone uses the *F* word several times in a sentence. Charmaine bounced up out of her chair, ready for action if needed. I followed her down the hall. The noise equivalent of a couple of sumo wrestlers shook the walls of Darryl's office.

"Out! Get the fuck out of my fucking office and don't come the fuck back until you can fucking behave like a fucking civilized human fucking being." That sounded like Darryl on a tear all right. Not so much of the grateful recovering at the moment. Guff strolled nonchalantly out the door. Why was I not surprised? I expected another furious roar to follow him out, but more of a sullen whine emerged. "And I expect you to fucking be on time for your fucking appointment this afternoon." Game, set, and match to Guffy.

Unfortunately, Charmaine turned around and saw me hovering behind her. She marched me straight back to her office to finish our interview. So I didn't get to hear Guff's side of it till later.

"The man's an asshole," he told me.

"You mean you don't like his sobriety," I said. An AA way to register disapproval without actual name-calling. Step Four was taking your own inventory, not someone else's.

"I mean the man's a jumped-up, undereducated heroin addict who wouldn't be in a position of authority if it weren't currently politically fashionable to kowtow to ethnic and racial minorities." His voice dripped contempt. He didn't give a damn about Step Four.

Whoa. Nasty streak. It made me uneasy.

"I don't think you can say that." In this detox, WASPs and even white working-class boys like me formed a distinct minority. Politically incorrect could get you stomped.

"Watch me." His tone was uncompromising.

"Don't be a fool, man. You don't want to antagonize the guy who gets to watch you pee in a cup, do you?" After we'd been good for a few days, they might let us out on pass. But they would breathalyze us and check our urine for drugs when we got back. No asking a buddy on the outside to lend you a little jar of clean piss, either. One of the counselors would watch you perform.

"Let him stay off my back, then. The loathsome little twerp."

But Darryl wouldn't leave Guff alone. His legitimate job was to needle, chivy, manipulate, emotionally disarm, and forcibly educate us into staying clean and sober. On top of that, he was tough, mean, and just as arrogant as Guff. Godfrey hadn't exactly become the Dalai Lama in three days of sobriety, either.

As luck would have it, Darryl led therapy group the next day. Just about everybody hated group. Not only did we have to sit in a circle and share our feelings but they expected us to interact. If we didn't, Darryl would go after us personally or get the group to do it. It was risky to let yourself get vulnerable. Guff made the mistake of admitting he'd had some losses and disappointments so painful that the bottle came as a relief. Even, he said, when the bottle was Thunderbird or Ripple. Darryl pounced on him.

"Maybe our friend from uptown here can share with us what it's like to be down-and-out. Maybe some of the homeboys can identify with the terrible life he's had." He bared his teeth in a wolfish sneer. The diamond chip glinted in the light. "Nome sane?" he demanded. "Do you know what I'm saying?" boiled down to two syllables on the street. Darryl used it almost as frequently as the *F* word.

Guff clenched his fists. He looked ready to start swinging, but he held on to the rags of his temper. If he got physical with Darryl, he'd get eighty-sixed in no time. And it was still midwinter out there.

"Whatsa matter, white boy? What you know about losing shit? You make me sick, rich boy, nome sane? You never gonna stay clean. Go back uptown and diddle your little friends. You know they say some people too fucking smart to recover? Well, Mr. Goddamn, you just might be one of them."

Next to me, I could feel Guff shaking with the effort not to react. Surprise kept the rest of us silent. Patients lost it all the time. But for a counselor, this attack was over the line. It was—I hate to sound like a counselor, but—inappropriate.

Darryl kept goading him. "Not such a smart-mouth now, huh? Still as sick as your secrets?" The AA phrase was supposed to encourage honesty. From Darryl, it came out a taunt.

"You b-bastard," Guff spat out. "Who are you to talk about down-and-out, you hypocritical pimp? Your losses, Mr. Candy Man? Don't make me laugh! Why don't you tell your brothers here about your bank accounts? The only way you'll lose is if all your customers get clean. As long as some of us still need to score, you're all right, Jack. Nice gig—counselor." He got up so abruptly, his chair fell over. With a disgusted growl, he stalked out of the room.

After group, I looked for Guff. I asked a couple of the counselors if they had seen him. Bark was meditating on the racing page in what must have been an out-of-town paper, Florida or California, at this time of year. Boris was communing with a little red-and-gold painting or icon of some kind that looked too good for the Bowery. Both looked startled when I popped my head in. Neither had seen Guff. I finally found him in the little laundry room both staff and patients used. He sat on a mound of dirty sheets, sulking. I tried to snap him out of it.

"Don't let him get to you, man. The guy's an asshole."

"If he gets in my face again, he's pulp."

"Hey, one day at a time." I kept my tone light. "If you've got to kill him, wait till next year." In fact, I doubted they would throw him out on New Year's Eve. Turning us loose on Amateur Night would be like handing us the bottle themselves. "At least wait till Check Day." What everybody here called "Check Day" passed for a holiday among the guys who got welfare, Social Security, or a VA pension.

"You do have a check coming in, don't you?"

Guff said nothing. I took it for a yes. Some of the family money obviously still clung to him.

"Don't let him screw up your three hots and a cot." The amenities provided motivation to come to detox even if you didn't really want sobriety. "Say the short Serenity Prayer." This was an in joke. The short Serenity Prayer goes "Fuck it."

Guff sat there pouring a cupful of laundry soap from one plastic container to another and back again.

"And he'd better stop needling me about my name."

In AA, they talk about the unreconstructed alcoholic as "His Majesty the Baby." That's just what he sounded like. I guessed petulant was better than ready to kill.

"He says I have more grandiosity than any client he's ever met. Ha! That's a good one, coming from him."

I hated to agree with Darryl about anything.

"Maybe you just have more class than any client he's ever met," I said.

"I'd rather be me than the fucking Jack o' Diamonds of the Bowery," he grumbled.

He had simmered down some more by the time Sister Angel marched in with a fresh load of laundry. She opened up the washer as it ground to a halt, releasing a cloud of steam. It was like being in a Turkish bath. With a nun.

"Come on, Guffy," I said. "Just forget it. Come have a cigarette." Sister Angel looked keenly at his thunderous face and whipped out her pack. "Thanks, Sister." I took two. I stuck one in my breast pocket and the other behind my ear. Guff took one. I told you he didn't belong on the Bowery.

At three o'clock in the morning, wide-awake and restless, I decided to wash the street clothes I'd come in wearing. If I was a good boy, I'd be going out on pass on Check Day. I bundled up my things, which still smelled of my lost Christmas Eve, and made my way to the laundry room. Clutching the big mound to my chest, my chin and nose holding it in place, I tripped over what I thought was a heap of sheets and towels until my shins made contact with something solid. I stumbled and came down hard. What I'd taken for a pile of laundry was a human being. It startled me, but I didn't freak out until I saw his face. His glazed eyes stared and his mouth hung open. He looked both astonished and very dead.

FIVE

I saw Barbara before she saw me. She bounced out of the elevator, talking a mile a minute. I might have known she'd show up.
I hung back behind a pillar, watching her.

She had hit rush hour. The elevator was packed with guys coming back from pass. She stood out among them. The older white
guys had bulbous red noses, broken-veined cheeks, and the filmy
eyes that said cataracts. The black guys were mostly younger and
very street, with hairdos ranging from shiny bald to massive mats
of dreads. Many of them carried the scars of knife wounds. A
few, the kids, were pierced in a variety of interesting places. Not
one man in the elevator had all his teeth. Barbara came from the
kind of home Jimmy and I had seen only on TV, where all the
kids had orthodontia. But she looked surprisingly comfortable. I
suddenly remembered she'd done an internship here. Oh, I was
in for it now.

I had almost worked up to revealing myself when little Hieronimo appeared at her elbow.

"Mees Barbara, Mees Barbara!" He jumped up and down trying to get her attention, his quiff of oily black hair bobbing.

"Hello, Hieronimo. How are you doing?"

She'd probably been his counselor at least once. She ran into former clients in alcohol and drug programs all over town. Hieronimo had been in detox sixty times. He helped keep the revolving door oiled and spinning. I'd heard him swear this was the last time. But we all said that. In the meantime, he lived on Social Security and some relatively harmless little hustles.

"I am good. I am doing very fine."

Barbara sniffed the air like a bloodhound. Counselors never took your word for it. If anyone on that elevator had smelled of alcohol, she'd have known.

"Mees Barbara, can I ask you a question?"

"Sure, Hieronimo, how can I help you?"

Hieronimo launched into a long story about his benefits. The bureaucracy had streamlined some procedure. As always, it improved nothing and confused the people it was supposed to help.

"They give me the paper for the new program," he told her in bewildered tones. "They say not to worry, they grandfather me in. Can you explain me thees, Mees Barbara? My understanding ees not good. I don't even got a grandfather."

"Hey, lady." I pushed myself off the side of the pillar. "My understanding is not good, either, but don't I know you?"

"Bruce!" Barbara squeaked. She threw herself on me and gave me a rib-crushing hug. I was glad I had on my freshly laundered sweatshirt, though I wore the bottoms of the undignified detox pajamas.

Barbara sniffed a couple of times. Checking for scent, damn her. She looked first at the pajamas, then down at my feet. I'd forgotten about the paper slippers.

"Well, well. Happy New Year!" She grinned widely.

I did my best not to look flustered. Keeping Barbara off balance is both an art and a necessity.

"Happy New Year to you, too." I sounded more sardonic than I felt. Okay, so I was glad to see her. "I know you knew I was here, because Jimmy tells you everything."

"Only what he knows will interest me." She hugged me again.

I squeezed back. Every time Barbara and I got within hugging distance, I could see her wondering if I remembered the one time we'd ended up in bed together. I think she just wanted the three of us to love one another. Knowing Jimmy, she should have known better. My excuse was the usual. Barbara probably hoped I'd been in a blackout at the time. And Jimmy didn't know. Best for all concerned. Her feelings for me were about 90 percent sisterly these days. Mine for her were purely brotherly. I think.

Hieronimo still stood there looking bewildered.

"Go see Bark, son," I advised him over Barbara's shoulder. "He'll straighten you out."

"How are you doing, baby?" Barbara asked when Hieronimo had strutted off like a bantam cock. "In detox on the Bowery over Christmas, that's got to be some kind of record."

"Not my best Christmas," I said ruefully. "How's the big guy?"

"He's good. Santa brought him some new toys for his time machine, and he's hardly been up for air since." Jimmy's passions were history and computers. "Have you gone out on a pass?"

"Not yet. I'll call Jimmy. Or I might go see Laura." Laura was my ex-wife, of whom Barbara was not very fond. It had gotten worse since she'd learned how to diagnose bipolar disorder, borderline personality, and anorexia.

"Decisions, decisions. Go to a meeting or get laid for New Year's. Hmm, which one will you choose?"

"Sometimes I think Jimmy is right when he says you'll say anything. Sometimes it's not as endearing as you think it is."

Barbara clapped a hand over her mouth.

"I'm sorry! There I go again. Jimmy thinks mentioning anything personal is like going out without your underwear. You know how Irish Catholic he can get. And sometimes I go all Jewish and over-compensate."

Now I felt guilty.

"I'm sorry, too. I didn't mean to zing you. I'm glad you came to see me."

"I'm really here because I have a lunch date with Charmaine."

Yeah, right.

"But can we go into a corner and talk for a few minutes?"

"I bow to the inevitable."

"Anywhere but the smoking room."

We ducked into the laundry room. The load jouncing around in the washer made it a little noisy, but nobody would bother us for seventeen minutes.

"So tell me what happened."

"I don't know what happened. I was in a blackout, I woke up here."

"And how are you feeling?"

"Fine."

"Come on, Bruce, this is me. Cut the crap. This has got to be a new low for you. Is there any chance at all you've finally hit bottom?"

"If scolding ever got an alcoholic sober, you'd be out of a career."

"I know, I know. It just exasperates me to see you throwing your life away."

I decided to change the subject.

"Hey, guess what. I found a body."

"What?"

"Fact. An old guy dropped dead right here in this laundry room the other night. I found him."

"What on earth were you doing in here in the middle of the night?"

I looked at her reproachfully. "My laundry. Have a little faith."

"Where have I heard that before?"

"Oh, Barbara, Barbara. You know me too well." That wasn't too manipulative, since she knew I knew she was a sucker for flattery. Besides, it was true.

"Okay, okay. I'm sorry. Go on. Were you upset?"

"More taken aback, I guess. I just came in to do my wash and stumbled over a corpse."

"Oh, poor Bruce!"

"I'd say poor Elwood."

"Elwood? I think I knew him. Elderly gent from Alabama, they called him Mudbone?"

"That's right."

"I did his psychosocial once. It took three hours because he'd lost his dentures and I couldn't understand a word he said."

Homeless chronic alcoholics tend to mislay their teeth. In Elwood's case, the condition had exacerbated an already-impenetrable rural drawl.

"Sweet old man, though. What happened? Did somebody kill him?"

"They only kill people on the stairs." I wasn't kidding. The dark stairwell had a reputation. "He had cancer. Rumor has it that he begged them not to send him to hospice because this detox was the closest thing he had to home and family."

"Jeez. Talk about a fate worse than death."

"It made me think. I know it's down to me or old Jack one of these days. Believe it or not, I don't want to die."

"So what are you going to do different?"

"I'm not sure yet. You know treatment programs haven't worked for me. There's one temp agency that hasn't thrown my file away. I figured I'd call them. I can work a few days a week, and it'll leave plenty of time for meetings." I had temped doing office work on and off for years, but I wasn't the world's most reliable employee. I'd managed to burn a lot of bridges. Dumb luck that one still held up. My Plan B in the past had always been to tap Jimmy for a loan. That, I did mean to do differently. But I didn't want even to mention it to Barbara. No point in her getting mad about the past.

"And at the meetings," she prodded, "what are you going to do different? Coming late, leaving early, and standing in the back schmoozing and drinking coffee hasn't worked for you, either." She reached out and rubbed my arm a little. She said it because she cared, not just to bust my balls.

"I'll get a sponsor."

"It can't be Jimmy."

"Yes, dear," I said with just a little snap and crackle.

AA sponsors have long-term sobriety and a built-in bullshit detector, which I knew I needed. I had always been an outstanding bullshitter. It's not that Jimmy didn't see right through me, but we had too much history together.

"He'd be happy to go to meetings with you."

"Kill two birds with one stone, huh?"

"You know how hard it is to get Jimmy away from his computer," she said. "And he can always use a meeting."

"Bless your codependent little heart. You're not still afraid he'll drink again after all these years, are you?"

Barbara grinned. "As he points out to me, how do I imagine he could forget, with me talking a blue streak about it all the time?"

"You're a good soul, Barbara."

"Why, thank you," she said, pleased. "And I'm there for you, too, if you ever want to talk or anything. You know we both love you."

Impulsively, I held out my arms. She locked her arms around my waist and snuggled her face into my sweatshirt.

"Mmm, you smell like clean laundry." She did the bloodhound thing again. "And shaving soap and just a little smoke."

"You don't like smoke."

"Better than the unbearable reek of alcohol seeping out through the pores."

"Amazing what a difference a few days off the stuff makes," I admitted. "I'm a new man."

"You're good to hug, too. So's Jimmy, of course."

"But different," I pointed out. I'm compact. Jimmy is a big tall guy with the density of a firm mattress.

"Mmm. Hugging Jimmy is like hugging Santa Claus." She gave my ribs a squeeze. "You really don't deserve these nice hard muscles, considering your lifestyle." She squeezed again and let me go.

Laughing a little, I popped my head out the laundry room door. I could see Charmaine coming down the hall, her irritable voice heralding her arrival.

"I think your date is here," I said.

Bark, the head counselor, trotted after her, working hard to keep up with her brisk pace.

"Please!" Charmaine snapped. "Sister Angel is muttering about a blessed release and the hospice is whining about what should they do with his paperwork now that he isn't coming after all."

Barbara and I exchanged a complicit glance. They were talking about Elwood.

"It's sad to see the old ones go," Bark said. "I used to drink with Mudbone. He was the last. No one left now remembers when I lived in a box."

I knew by now that Bark had been on the Bowery forever. He'd started drinking during the Korean War and lived in a cardboard box for at least a quarter of a century before getting sober—to his own surprise, as well as everybody else's.

Charmaine's voice softened more than I'd thought it could. "You've been sober a long time."

Barbara stepped out and greeted Charmaine with a peck on the cheek and Bark with a quick hug. I hung back, trying not to fraternize with the staff.

"You're amazing, Bark," Barbara said, "one of a kind."

"Right," the old man said dryly. "They don't make drunks like they used to anymore."

"Ready to go?" she asked Charmaine. "With you in a sec." She swung back into the laundry room, one hand on the door frame.

"You take care of yourself," she admonished me. "Don't you dare go AMA before you're discharged, and don't get into any trouble." She meant leaving against medical advice.

"Me?" I projected injured innocence. "Trouble? This is detox. A bunch of guys in their jammies and not so much as a can of Bud Lite. What could possibly happen?"

SIX

Along with Barbara's visit, Elwood's death kind of broke up the long, timeless days for me. Although it was hardly a blip for the detox as a whole, I couldn't stop thinking about the old man. No matter how bad a drunk you are, most of the people you trip over aren't dead. I thought about stuff I usually made sure I avoided, like pain and loneliness. I wondered if he had had time to feel relieved that he wouldn't have to go to hospice. I wondered if I'd been too flip with the baby cops who'd come and taken a per- functory statement. I even wondered if he'd really died of natural causes. Maybe he had seen the sneak thief or known somebody's secret.

New Year's Eve came quicker than I expected. We celebrated with an extra meeting. Recovering alcoholics don't make New Year's resolutions. We've all been on the wagon and fallen off too many times. If we choose to stay sober, we do it one day at a time. That feels a lot more tolerable than forever. If you make ninety days, they give you a little pin with a camel on it and the number

24, because a camel can go twenty-four hours without a drink. Jimmy had a camel. I didn't.

After New Year's Day came Check Day, and Guff and I both got our twenty-four-hour pass. He asked me what I planned to do.

"I thought I'd call my friend Jimmy, go to a meeting." I wasn't sure whether I was lying or not. Mostly I just wanted to walk around. Breathe some air that didn't smell of ammonia. Smoke a pack or two without anybody glaring at me. Throw the butts on the sidewalk if I felt like it. Eat a cheeseburger. "What about you?" Maybe he'd ask to hook up with me. I wasn't sure whether or not I wanted that, either.

"Oh, this and that." He gave the bed he was making a final thwack and stuffed a few small items in his pockets. "See a few people, rattle a few cages."

It didn't sound like he needed my company. Mostly, I felt relieved. I'd call Jimmy. No, I wouldn't. Maybe I would. I knew what he'd say if I did: "Let's go to a meeting."

Lying awake in bed the night of January 3, I thought the day hadn't gone badly. I had woken up that morning in Laura's loft in SoHo, a nice change from the detox. We'd made love. To tell the truth, though I would never admit it to Barbara, I think she's almost as crazy as Barbara thinks she is. I did manage to get a divorce. Okay, she got a divorce, but I didn't fight it.

Still, Laura and I knew each other's bodies. It's so simple to go to bed with an old lover. The way people adopt a road, I'd long since adopted the path of least resistance. So for better or worse, my ex-wife and I put it on rewind for a few hours. It was a relief in more ways than one. My mental checklist for sobriety: One, don't drink. Two, go to a meeting. Three, see if I can still get it up. I could.

Seeing Barbara was weird, but nice. Jimmy lucked out with her. I usually got the girls. Jimmy had feared he would end up with one of those Catholic girls from Queens who wouldn't wear patent-leather shoes because they might reflect up their dress. Barbara's smart, she's funny, she can talk the hind leg off a donkey, and she's crazy about Jimmy. I enjoy her little foibles and the way she tries to take care of me, an uphill task if I ever saw one.

Guff and I got back at about the same time. He was still the closest thing I had to a friend in the detox. His ugly side hadn't turned toward me yet. No one else was exempt. Guff didn't worry about getting knifed, because he didn't plan to stick around on the Bowery.

I couldn't curb my curiosity about him. He had a presence. You couldn't ignore him. I wanted to hear more about his family. What hadn't he told me? Why had they stopped speaking to him? Why did he clam up? I asked how his day out had been.

"Interesting. Made a few overdue calls. Annoyed a few people." He smiled rather nastily.

Dinner featured mystery meat, as usual. A culinary arts training program that served as work release for felons did the detox catering. I'm not making this up. Everyone kept more than usually silent during the meal. It had been a stressful day for some. Three guys hadn't made it back. They were out there copping drugs or in a doorway with a bottle. Two more had tried to get back in but had been kicked out as soon as the Breathalyzer lit up on them. Those were the Strike Threes. One or two more would most likely get thrown out when the lab results came back in a day or two. I didn't see any empty seats, though. Business in these places always booms after major holidays. Especially New Year's Eve. Now, there's a holiday with no traditions whatsoever. If you don't count getting blitzed and counting backward from twelve.

A video provided the evening's entertainment. Big thrill. Fore-play consisted of the usual squabble between what the guys wanted and what the staff wanted. That meant something with a lot of noise, automatic weapons, explosions, and at least one car chase, versus something silly and harmless that they thought might make us laugh, like *I Love Lucy*. Even drunks on the Bowery laugh at Lucy.

I had seen too many movies and TV shows on acid to find whatever they chose anything but boring. Instead, I hung out in the smoking room, trying to decide what I wanted to do when they discharged me tomorrow. The lady or the tiger? A meeting or the nearest bar? By 9:30, I hadn't even figured out if AA or the booze was the tiger. I went and lay on my bed, staring at the ceiling until the movie ended and the guys started drifting in. Just after lights-out, about 10:30, I heard the small sounds of Guff undressing and getting into the bed next to mine. He called out a gruff good night. I mumbled one back without opening my eyes.

I couldn't sleep. Alcoholic jet lag. My old sleep pattern, up all night and zonked all day, wouldn't do if I stayed sober. About half an hour passed. Then I heard Guff get out of bed, presumably to go to the bathroom. I must have dozed and missed him coming back, because later I heard him get up again. When he came back, I propped myself up on one elbow. It never got really dark in the ward. The unshaded windows looked out on streetlights and neon signs outside the stores and bars across the street.

"You okay, fella?"

"Terrible cramps." He sat doubled up on the edge of the bed, looking kind of greenish, though some of that was the light from the nearest sign. Beads of sweat glistened on his forehead.

"You want me to get the night nurse?"

"No, I'll be fine," he said, gasping. "Just want to lie here."

I lay back down. For the next hour, I heard him thrashing around, trying to get comfortable and obviously failing. The bed, old-fashioned metal springs with a cheap hard mattress over them, squeaked every time he rolled.

"You want me to call the nurse?" I peered over at him. He looked lousy.

"No. I don't know. Something I ate? Feel like shit. Bathroom. Help me get up?"

I sat up and swung my legs onto the floor. I had reached over to take his arm, when he suddenly dropped his head over the side of the bed and vomited onto the floor. I leaped back, swinging my legs back up onto my bed just in time. He started jerking around. It looked like he was convulsing.

"I'll get the nurse." I rolled off the other side of the bed, away from him. My voice surprised me by sounding scared.

His convulsions got noisier. Heads lifted from pillows all down the row of beds. I hadn't made it all the way to the nursing station when the night nurse, a pint-sized Filipino named Sylvia, hurried to meet me. Sister Angel trotted up right behind her.

Someone turned the lights on. Sylvia and Sister Angel bent over the bed.

"Hold still, Godfrey," Sister Angel said. "Let Sylvia take your vitals."

Sylvia did her best to take his temperature, pulse, and blood pressure. But he couldn't hold still for long enough. His chattering teeth sounded as loud as a jackhammer drilling in the street. I sat up on my bed, trying to stay out of the way. Someone mopped up the vomit, which I appreciated. Guff promptly heaved again, but this time Sister Angel held a basin in the right place.

"Here!" Sylvia snapped, her eyes falling on me. "Come and help me hold him."

"Me?"

I took a couple of gingerly steps toward them. At her direction, I put one arm around Guff's shoulders, half-propping him against me. My other hand clasped his upper arm. It felt strange to hold him. He felt hot and cold, damp and dry at the same time. I could feel the muscles underneath his thin pajamas. It seemed unreal, almost like an out-of-body experience. The hubbub swelled to a crescendo all around me. Yet at the same time, all the sounds seemed to come from far away.

I don't know how long it went on. It felt like forever. Every once in awhile, Guff would gasp out a few words, most of them incomprehensible. Once, he called for brandy in a loud voice. His breathing sounded terrible. It came in irregular gasps with jerky pauses between them. Then everything stopped. The weight of him fell back onto my chest and shoulder. My arm buzzed with pins and needles from being in one position so long.

"Let him down!" Sylvia ordered. "Gently, just ease him down. Hurry!"

She slammed the palms of her hands down on his chest a few times.

"Are you all right? Are you all right?"

He didn't answer. Couldn't answer.

The whole thing had a ritual quality to it. She leaned over him as he lay flat on his back. She lifted his chin up and back with her fingers, putting her ear to his lips and nostrils. She squinted down along his chest, checking for the rise and fall as air went into his lungs. She looked grim. No breath. Clamping her hand over his nostrils, she inhaled deeply. Then she laid her mouth across his and blew a long breath out. She did it again, the ear, the mouth, a breath, sighting along his chest. At the same time, her fingers groped at the side of his neck. She shook her head abruptly, as if a fly were buzzing around her ears.

"No pulse, and he's not breathing. I'm starting CPR. Angel, call nine one one!"

Sister Angel tap-tap-tapped away. Sylvia got me and a couple of the other guys to move him onto the floor. She knelt beside him. I shoved my bed back to give her room. She whipped an alcohol pad out of her pocket, ripping off the paper with hands that trembled slightly. Quickly, she wiped down the whole lower half of his face. I wouldn't want to do mouth-to-mouth resuscitation in the age of AIDS. The pump they were supposed to use was probably in a drawer in the nursing station. There was no time.

First, she did the two breaths again. Then she wiggled her knees around a little, positioning herself a little farther down his body, with her knees wedged up against his ribs. She was so little that she had to tilt forward to get her short arms right over the middle of his chest. She positioned herself with elbows locked, thumbs clasped, fingers splayed out, the heels of her palms digging in right around his diaphragm. Her lips moved as she counted in a half-voiced whisper, keeping the rhythm steady.

"One and two and three and four and five and six and seven and eight and nine and ten and eleven and twelve and thirteen and fourteen and fifteen."

She slid up his side just far enough to do another two breaths. Her cheek lay against his face as she checked for breathing again. If his chest had been moving even slightly on its own, she would have seen it. She went right back into the chest compressions, arms rigid, elbows locked, thumbs hooked together, palms pressing down.

"One and two and three and . . ."

She kept going and going. Sweat poured off her face, raining down onto her hands as they dug into his chest, trying to force life back into him. Every once in awhile, she looked up briefly, her eyes scanning. Sister Angel hadn't come back. The street outside lay quiet.

It must have been two in the morning when we finally heard sirens. Sister Angel led them in. The three EMS people and four or five cops overflowed the small space around Guff's bed. They quickly rigged a folding screen and went in with their defibrillators and oxygen, or whatever it was.

It didn't work. For the second time that night, everything stopped. The techs folded the screen back and came out looking grim. No more guff from Guffy. God was dead. I hoped his Namesake had a sense of humor.

SEVEN

The next morning, I got discharged. It felt anticlimactic. I was so depressed that I walked past I don't know how many bars and liquor stores without even thinking about going in. Eventually I reached a subway station. I let my feet carry me down the stairs. I wasn't in the mood to jump the turnstile. The wrinkled dollar bills I found in my pocket looked as if I'd put them through the laundry. I probably had. I bought a MetroCard, hopped the first train that came along, and went home.

Home was a fourth-floor walkup in an old-law tenement on Second Avenue. It was located just a little too far north to be on the fashionable Upper East Side that the old Yorkville neighborhood where Jimmy and I grew up had morphed into, and a little too far south to be considered Spanish Harlem. I had a railroad flat. One room led right into the next.

I used the room looking out on Second Avenue as a living room. The decor consisted of a battered couch, a faux-leather recliner with a temperamental mechanism, and a TV with a few knobs missing. I'd salvaged all of them from Dumpsters. The room doubled as a storeroom. That is, cartons I'd never gotten around to unpacking teetered in unstable piles. I didn't have a clue what was in most of them. Alcohol hadn't done my memory any good.

The other end room was the bedroom. A king-size mattress took up most of the floor space. A lot of crumpled clothes, clean and dirty, lay strewn all over the bed and on the narrow strips of floor. Sorting and folding, like giving up alcohol, was one of those things I was always going to get around to later.

A variety of candles with their bottoms drip-melted onto equally unmatched saucers provided ambience. Two speakers, not much bigger than cigarette boxes, that plugged into my Walkman added sound effects. Every once in awhile, I brought home a woman who wanted romantic, and that was it. Hey, candlelight, music, a snifter of fine brandy—what more did she need? Okay, a tumbler full of anything 86 proof or better. It went with a Don Juan somewhat the worse for wear who suspected that his liver was beginning to affect his capacity for sexual athletics. A passed-out Romeo who might or might not remember her name in the morning. Or, if she left before morning, that she'd been there at all.

The middle room must have been one of the last kitchens in New York with a claw-footed bathtub in the middle of it. Too chipped and stained with rust to be worth anything on the market, it probably should have been in a museum. I had rigged a curtain all around it and stuck one of those handheld showerheads with a flexible cable onto the faucet so I could take a shower in it. But I couldn't leave anything on the stove when I took a shower. At least I had a clean kitchen floor. After every shower, it was mop or wade.

I felt an urgent need to soak. Instead of showering, I tossed things around till I found a stopper for the tub and a couple of towels that might have been clean. I ran the water hot enough to fog the windows in the other rooms. Then I rolled up another towel to use as a pillow behind my neck, lay back, and stretched out until my crossed ankles were resting on the rim of the tub, letting the Bowery steam out of me.

I was so spaced-out that the water cooled off some before I thought to scrabble underneath the tub for the pack of cigarettes and box of kitchen matches that I'd stashed there. As I fished around for the Baggie I kept them in, my fingers touched something smooth, cylindrical, and metallic, and then, when that started to roll, something smooth, cylindrical, and glass. Beer can and liquor bottle. More than one of each, by the ensuing clinking and rattling. Moment of truth. I grabbed a bottle by the neck as it rolled out from under the tub. Empty. I leaned farther over the side like a shipwrecked man in a lifeboat trying to catch a fish with his bare hands. Beer can. Empty. Another bottle rolled just beyond my reach. Discount bourbon. I couldn't always afford top shelf brands. This one had a couple of fingers in the bottom.

I hung there by my armpits, my bare butt sliding around a little in the enamel tub, up to my hips in tepid water, thinking about it. Well, not exactly thinking. More of a vegetative state. Was it worth the effort? I had once cracked an ankle chasing a bottle out of that tub and onto that floor. Not that I considered the pros and cons. When my armpits started to hurt, I slid back into the tub and stretched out again. I hooked my toes around the tap and ran a little more hot water in. Of such small, mindless decisions is sobriety made. One moment at a time.

If Christmas Day counted as my first day sober, I now had eleven days. My brain still felt a little foggy. But if I stayed sober, my mind would get sharper, my digestive tract would get less acidic, and I would have a lot more energy than I did at this moment. On the downside, I would get to feel all my feelings and remember all my mistakes. Except for those I'd made in a blackout. Blacked-out memories were gone forever.

I wished I couldn't remember Godfrey dying in the next bed. I'd seen more than my share of dead people. You do when you've been skating on the edge of the abyss as long as I had. Stumbling over poor old Elwood had been almost par for the course. Not much difference between a passed-out drunk and a corpse—just a few cubic inches of air. And he'd been on his way out anyway. Once I got over the sheer surprise of it, I'd handled it okay. But Guff's death weighed heavily on me. I'd never before been right there at the moment when somebody I knew switched off.

What the hell had happened? He'd been fine the day before. He'd still seemed okay when he got back from his pass. Though I know from my own experience that anyone can be fooled, I thought he'd been clean. His shades might have hidden glassy eyes or pinpoint pupils. The whole detox had gotten used to Guff wearing them practically all the time. I couldn't even remember if he'd had them on. Surely a staff member would have checked his eyes when he signed back in. Wouldn't they?

If he'd been high, why had he come back? For a habitual addict of any kind, it takes a lot of chemicals to overdose, believe me. Guff hadn't looked high at all. He'd seemed satisfied, even a little smug, about whoever he'd seen or talked to. His family? He'd said he didn't have any contact with them. But he might have gotten in touch with them. A lot of the Twelve Steps are about coming to terms with the harm you've done and making amends.

On the other hand, a lot of people say the steps are consecutive for a reason. Even if I decided to try sobriety for a while, it would be a long time till I'd expect myself to apologize systematically to the many people I'd pissed off. Guff had hardly been any further along. Though he and I had gotten along just fine, I had begun to get the feeling that he could be a vindictive kind of guy. And there was a lot I didn't know about him. He'd mentioned his sisters and their families. Who else had he been close enough to hurt? I knew he'd been in and out of AA the way I had. That meant he'd met hundreds of people from every possible background. They were all supposed to be anonymous.

But people are only human. All sorts of things happen in AA. Men hit on women. Some men hit on men. People loan one another money, even get involved in business transactions. And not everybody manages to zip the lip as firmly as they're supposed to about whom they've seen at a meeting and what they've heard them say. Especially if they relapse.

The water got closer and closer to cold. I heaved myself up and out of the tub. I pulled the plug and wrapped a towel around my waist. The refrigerator stood only a few steps away. Being interested in food was another thing that came back gradually. And having enough forethought and disposable cash to stock the refrigerator took more sobriety than I had had in awhile. I opened the door and gazed in.

I saw about what I'd expected: some bread so moldy it was well on the way to penicillin; a plastic container whose contents had sprouted what might prove to be the cure for cancer; a wedge of mummified cheese; a couple of shriveled limes—I vaguely remembered Laura going fancy on me with tequila last time she'd come over, which was months ago—and, of course, a couple of six-packs. I stood there looking at them for a long time. Then I swung open the freezer door. Oh shit. A Ziploc bag with a little packet wrapped in aluminum foil in it, what was left of a gram of cocaine. Now what was I going to do with that? Flush it? Sell it? Say the hell with it and use it?

I stood there with both doors open long enough for steam to start rising from my body as the cold air from the fridge and freezer hit my skin, still relatively warm from the bath. My mind was a complete blank. My hand went tentatively out toward the baggie a couple of times and then pulled back, as if I were a marionette on strings. I needed a drink. Funny, huh? I wanted a drink to relieve the anxiety I felt about my conflict over whether or not to do the coke. I figured if I was going to pick up, maybe I should just get it over with.

I didn't know which way I would go until I slammed the white enamel doors. The phone had to be around here somewhere. My cell phone lay on the floor near the tub, but I knew that was one bill I hadn't paid for months. I didn't think my regular phone service had been cut off. My old black clunker had a long cord. It could be anywhere. I finally dug it out from under a stack of sections of the Sunday *New York Times* that I had meant to read or put out for recycling someday. I dialed Jimmy's number. I figured I'd give it four rings and then hang up.

He answered on the third ring. I could hear a variety of sounds in the background. A sports commentator and crowd sounds must be football on TV. The tripping rhythms of Irish instrumental music, a jig or reel, were radio or a CD. On top of that, what any friend of Jimmy's would recognize as simulated black-powder rifle fire from his Civil War reenactment Web site boomed out. Jimmy was a great multitasker. Great. I had a task for him.

"Hey," I said. "It's me. I'm home. I need you to come over and throw some stuff away for me."

He arrived half an hour later with two shopping bags full of groceries and a couple of giant dark green garbage bags. He went for the refrigerator first, sweeping the six-packs still linked together in their plastic collars into one of the bags. I wondered how long it would take him to think of the freezer. Nanoseconds. Into the garbage bag. He didn't have to turn around to read my reluctance to throw out the money it represented. Crack was cheaper than this coke, but even I wasn't that much of an idiot. He scooped up cans and bottles from the floor and dumped them in, too.

"Forget the money," Jimmy said as the empties crashed and tinkled. "It's like the money over the bar. It's gone."

I wasn't in the mood for a lecture, so I started telling him about Guffy. Jimmy was a good listener. He also knew I already had his sobriety lecture on my hard drive, as he would have put it.

"A little charismatic, a little caustic. Sounds like you with a pedigree," Jimmy commented. "What did he look like? I might have seen him at a meeting."

"Tall, blond. Aristocratic. Snotty-looking bone structure, good skin, great teeth. You'd probably remember. Someone who said 'Hi, I'm God, I'm an alcoholic' would stand out."

"You know what? I do remember." Jimmy named a meeting in a church on Fifth Avenue, across from the park, that got a lot of carriage trade. Anyone who thinks alcoholics are a bunch of lowlifes should check that meeting out. Even in the age of animal rights, at this time of year there would be enough fur coats in there to stock a boutique. "A couple of years back, they made a big fuss about his name. A few people got all worked up about it at a business meeting. They took a group conscience."

Business meetings are where AA members who happen to be control freaks get a chance to use *Robert's Rules of Order.* They take more time than anyone who isn't a control freak wants them to.

"Who won?"

"He did. I sat through a few impassioned speeches about how there's no requirement to have any particular beliefs. He pointed out that it actually was his name. Godfrey, right? It's coming back to me. Some of the folks at that meeting didn't like your friend at all."

"Just because of the name?"

"No, I vaguely remember some ongoing animosity. I steered clear of the whole thing." Avoiding gossip and criticism is supposed to be good for your sobriety. Also, Jimmy wasn't that interested in twentieth- or twenty-first-century people. "After a few months, he stopped coming to that meeting, and that was the end of it."

"Would you remember who they are? The guys who didn't like him?"

"If I think about it, probably. Why?"

"I don't know. It's just bugging me. There was no reason he should have died. I have a feeling about it." I handed Jimmy another garbage bag.

"You have a feeling? Tell me about it." No question, living with Barbara has had an impact.

"I don't know how. I'm only eleven days sober."

"Asshole," he said affectionately.

"Creep." We had been doing that routine since we were eight.

But I meant it. Not that Jimmy was a creep. That Guff's death bothered me. Not just uncomplicated mourning, as Barbara called it, but the puzzle of it. I couldn't figure it out. Had he overdosed on some drug he'd taken while he was out? Could something he'd eaten have killed him? Had he had some kind of medical problem I didn't know about? I certainly hadn't heard the staff talking about anything like that. They'd seemed as surprised as I was. People die for all kinds of reasons. Guff could have gotten beaten up on the subway. I'd known a guy that happened to. He'd died of a brain hemorrhage a CAT scan hadn't detected. But Guff hadn't come back looking damaged. Besides, if he'd had a random confrontation, he would have mentioned it. A fight with someone he knew, though, he might have kept to himself.

"They'll do an autopsy, won't they?" Jimmy tied off the top of the first bag expertly and heaved it in the general direction of the door.

"I'm not sure. They send him to the morgue without his designer label, they don't think of arsenic and old lace. Did Barbara tell you about the old guy I found?"

"The one with cancer? Yeah. You gotta watch where you put your feet, fella."

"Hey, I was doing my laundry. Being a good boy for once."

"Grandmother, what a big halo you have!"

"Yeah, yeah. About Guff, though, the doctor probably just signed the death certificate. If we want to know for sure, I know how we can find out."

Jimmy caught the gleam in my eye.

"Oh no." He waved his finger at me for emphasis. "Oh no, you are not roping Barbara into this."

"You know she'll love it. She loves snooping. She'll thank me."

"That's just what I'm afraid of."

"All she has to do is get the head nurse or Sister Angel talking a little. She gets them complaining about the paperwork, they'll open right up." I was on a roll. "And she can check Guff's chart. Death certificate, labwork. They urined all of us when we got back that day. Barbara could find out about the lab results. They'd grab her if she offered to work a night shift."

Jimmy groaned.

"What if I say don't ask her, as a favor to me? Please?"

I grinned. Jimmy knew better than I did that Barbara could outdo the Energizer Bunny when she got going.

"Come on, big guy. Do you really think she'll wait to be asked?"

EIGHT

Going to meetings didn't pay the rent. I needed a job. Jimmy didn't need any help being a computer genius. So I drove up to the Bronx with Barbara a few days after New Year's. She thought her hospital might be able to use a peon with a college degree. Well, not exactly a degree. More like a résumé with a few exaggerations and a couple of outright lies. Alcoholics lie. Recovering alcoholics tend to stop lying when they work the steps. But I figured I had a grace period. Besides, the trip uptown gave me an opportunity to run my ideas about Guff's death by Barbara. No doubt she saw it as an equally golden opportunity to unveil her plan for my continued sobriety.

I hadn't counted on the fact that Barbara listened to the radio when she drove. She had it preset on a country station in New Jersey. Pretty funny, Barbara going for an art form that consisted almost entirely of stories about alcoholism, infidelity, and domestic violence. But she knew all the words. She even sang along.

Nor had I counted on my own fuzziness at 7:00 A.M. It had been so long since I'd gotten up early that I'd forgotten how at that hour my brain resembled a stack of IHOP pancakes. The few thoughts that trickled through the fluff were thick and sluggish as cheap syrup. Her heater was on the fritz, so it was cold. We both could see our breath. I kept my hands in my pockets. Barbara had thick mittens on and had to concentrate to compensate for the clumsiness of her steering. So we rode mostly in silence, apart from the yodeling and steel guitars.

"You can come up to my unit first," she said during a lull, when she had turned a particularly obnoxious car commercial down to barely audible. "There'll be coffee and doughnuts at the staff meeting. There are always doughnuts in a hospital."

"Like police stations." I'd seen more of those than hospitals.

"You'll have to leave, though, when we start to discuss clients. I'll get someone to show you where the Human Resources office is. They don't get in till nine anyhow."

Fine with me. The idea of hearing what the professionals thought of guys like me gave me the creeps. Barbara's unit was outpatient, not detox. But it was still too close for comfort. She went back to Nashville and I retreated into my own not particularly cheerful thoughts until she turned in at a set of massive gates at the entrance to the hospital campus.

"That's it? Looks more like an Art Deco hotel than a hospital."

"It's the balconies," she said. "It was built as a TB sanitarium back in the Thirties, when the only remedies they had were fresh air and sunshine." She maneuvered expertly between two gas guzzlers with vanity plates parked way too close together. "Let's make a left here, maybe it's not too late to get my favorite parking spot." She added, "Oops! Now what?"

A hospital security guard barred our way, holding up a big gloved hand, palm out. Barbara rolled down the window, stuck her head out, and called, "Good morning! What's the problem?" To me, she added, "Only an idiot makes enemies in the parking lot."

The guard strolled up to the car. He was securely wrapped in heavy fleece-lined leather. A bright red-and-green scarf circled his neck at least three times. It looked like his elderly mother had knitted it for him for Christmas.

"Sorry, miss, you'll hafta wait. We just found a body in the Dumpster over there." With the chattiness of a born gossip in a job that probably lacked excitement most of the time, he added, "I always say they got some nerve leaving it there permanent like. Takes up half the spaces in that row."

"I know just what you mean," Barbara agreed. "How many times have I been late because I had to circle around and around looking for an empty spot? But how awful!" She meant the body. "Who was it? Do they know?"

"An old guy, musta been out there all night. He musta climbed in there, looking for a place to sleep, maybe. One a them homeless. They're everywhere these days. Covered with vomit. Nearly upchucked my own breakfast when I went ta take a look."

Thank you for sharing, as they say in AA.

"Not a patient. Had his clothes on anyhow."

"He could have been one of our outpatients," she told me. "Our clients don't wear hospital gowns." To the guard, she said, "Do you know if they've identified him?"

The guard snorted. "Think them high-and-mighty cops are gonna tell us?" Hospital security ranked lower on the totem pole than the NYPD, and it obviously rankled.

"Stank a booze all right." The guard answered her next question before she asked it. "Pee-yew. I don't envy the guys who gotta cart that meat away."

A Mercedes with M.D. plates blatted a demand for attention.

"All right, all right, there, hold your horses!" He swaggered away to engage in a tiny power struggle with the driver. Dr. Big couldn't see why he should have to wait like us mortals while the ambulance loaded up the dead man and took him away.

Barbara grinned when security won.

"Only an idiot or an arrogant doctor," she said.

The meeting had already started when we finally got there. A burly, silver-haired, hawk-nosed guy who looked like a kindly banker and talked like a movie mafioso seemed to be leading it.

"Carlo, the head counselor," Barbara murmured in my ear. "Drug addict, been in NA for decades, used to be a loan shark."

Carlo stopped talking and raised an eyebrow.

Barbara waved a casual hand at me.

"My friend Bruce. He's going down to HR as soon as they open. Okay if he stays till we get clinical?"

"Sure. Hi, Bruce. Have a doughnut," he added genially.

I nodded my thanks. Someone handed me a jelly doughnut and a Christmas napkin. Someone else kicked a chair my way. Barbara had already found a seat. She inched it over so I could squeeze in next to her. Locating the coffee urn across the room, I poured a stiff one for each of us before I sat. I sipped mine gratefully. With luck, I might even wake up soon.

"Okay, people," Carlo said, "we've got an audit coming up next month. Supervisors, you'd better do a spot check of everybody's charts. If there are too many gaps, we'll form a chart review committee to check every chart."

This was evidently unwelcome news. Groans resounded all around the room, and three people sought consolation by taking another doughnut. Barbara took advantage of the ensuing pause.

"Do you guys know they found a dead man in the parking lot?"

More groans. Several people offered tales of woe involving parking, interrupting one another and, in a couple of cases, spraying powdered sugar all over their front. I could see how Barbara felt at home here.

"Forget the parking, guys. I was thinking—could he be one of ours?"

A slightly shamed silence fell.

"He is one of ours." A severely dressed woman in her forties stood in the doorway. She had a British accent and the face of a well-bred horse.

"Dr. Arnold. Unit chief," Barbara whispered. "Brilliant neurologist. Knows all about addictions. Looks scary, but she's a pussycat." Dr. Arnold stalked over to the coffee table and plunked down a large box of Krispy Kremes. I shrank down in my chair like Frodo hiding from the Eye of Sauron. I didn't want to get kicked out just when it was getting interesting. Luckily, Dr. Arnold's attention immediately shifted to the group.

"A client? Who was it?" someone asked.

Barbara's running commentary got softer, hardly more than a warm breath in my ear. "Sister Perseverance. Nursing nun, been here even longer than Carlo. They call her 'Sister Persistence.'"

In turn, I put my lips to Barbara's ear.

"Not to her face, I assume."

"Persy, I'm sorry," Dr. Arnold said. "It was Nick."

"Oh no!"

"What a shame!"

There was a general outcry. The dead guy, Nikolai, was a Russian immigrant who had been in and out of the clinic for years. They thought he must have crawled into the Dumpster either with or in pursuit of a bottle of vodka and gotten too sick to climb out or shout for help. Or he might have passed out and gotten sick later on. Security guards patrolled the grounds at night, but they'd missed him. They had a lot of territory to cover. Security was understaffed, like every other department in the hospital.

"We won't get autopsy results for a while," Dr. Arnold said. "We all know how it is around the holidays."

"The staff are as bad as the patients," Sister Perseverance sniffed. "It should be a holy time. There's altogether too much whoop-de-do in this hospital."

Barbara snorted a little coffee out her nose at that one. A couple of other people snickered, but quietly.

"How many Christmases had Nick spent in this program?" someone asked.

"Fourteen, I believe," said the nun.

Barbara whispered, "They don't call her Sister Persistence for nothing."

"And damn few of them sober," Carlo said.

Dr. Arnold frowned at him. "And some of them were sober. Give yourself—and Nick—credit for that."

"He had cirrhosis," another woman said. "Even if he'd stayed sober, he couldn't have lasted forever." Liver damage past the point of no return. I'd been lucky so far. It could have been me.

"Did he have family?" someone asked.

"No," Carlo said. "A sister in Brooklyn, down around Sheepshead Bay, died a couple of years ago. He lived in an SRO."

A welfare hotel. Poor Nick. What a depressing life. What a lonely, humiliating death. I was almost glad that Dr. Arnold noticed me at that point and kicked me out. Barbara told me later that I hadn't missed anything. Silence had descended, and then the whole group sought comfort by finishing off the doughnuts.

NINE

Barbara had the rest of my day all planned. Rather than let me go back to Manhattan after I filled out the job application, she pointed me at a lunchtime AA meeting within walking distance of the hospital and ordered me to go to the Bronx Zoo in the afternoon.

"Panda therapy?" I inquired.

"There are no pandas at the Bronx Zoo," she said.

"Gorilla therapy, then."

"It will do you good. Just do it."

It was cold at the zoo, and a lot of the animals that were usually outside were inside. But to my surprise, I enjoyed it. I spent a long time gazing at the gorilla. I couldn't decide if he was sad or pissed off, but he looked like he needed a meeting. When Barbara got off work, I met her at the hospital and we drove downtown, past a helluva lot of commuter traffic going the other way, to their apartment on the Upper West Side.

It was the first time I had been invited to their place in years.

They may have thought I hadn't noticed, but I had. Jimmy would talk to me on the phone for hours, or he would meet me at a meeting, and Barbara would meet me for coffee anytime. But neither of them wanted to be around me when I drank. Jimmy knew my altered states on everything from 'ludes to speed. He could always tell. So I hadn't been there in a very long time.

They lived in one of those prewar buildings that had never had any pretensions to being classy but was built for solid comfort and never came anywhere near going downhill. A genuine live elevator man ran the elevator. All Albanians, Barbara told me, because the current super was Albanian. The guy who was on when we got there had limited English and a terrible sense of humor. I guess he told us an Albanian joke. He wouldn't open the elevator door until he'd reached the punch line. Talk about a captive audience. I didn't understand a word he said, but he found himself excruciatingly funny. We had to wait politely until he stopped laughing and slid open the cagelike grille to let us out.

They had a nice apartment. Half of the living room housed the computer and the rest of Jimmy's high-tech home office. The other half was crowded with overstuffed furniture in the saturated colors Barbara liked—rich gold and rust and peacock blue, with a riot of fat little cushions in shades of crimson, orange, and rose. Floor-to-ceiling bookshelves lined the walls. Books were piled everywhere in disorganized heaps, Jimmy's history and military and computer library crammed in with Barbara's counseling texts and psychology books, mysteries, and the more readable kind of classics. Tumbling and meandering around and over and between the books were the toy soldiers that Jimmy had collected since he was a kid and the cuddly stuffed animals that Barbara always fell in love with in the store and just had to rescue and take home. About the clutter, Barbara would say, "I know, I know, we flunk feng shui. But we like it this way." Jimmy would say, "What clutter? I know where everything is."

When we walked in the door, Jimmy had an old Planxty album playing, and he was fighting the Battle of Antietam on his Civil War reenactment Web site on the computer. The Web is Jimmy's time machine. He can tell you the name of Robert E. Lee's horse and what Ivan the Terrible ate for breakfast.

"Hi, pumpkin." Barbara went around behind him as he sat at the computer. Jimmy always sat at the computer. She leaned over and kissed the back of his neck. "Look who I brought home with me."

"Pumpkin yourself. Hey, fella." Jimmy greeted me as casually as if I had never been banned. "I'm starving," he said. "You guys want to eat?"

Like many New Yorkers, none of us cooked. I had solved the problem for years by not bothering much with food. Jimmy and Barbara ordered out. Less than half an hour later, we sat in the kitchen, working our way through a big container of guacamole with a huge pile of blue-corn tortilla chips and some very spicy burritos.

"How'd the job hunt go?" Jimmy asked. He lost a chip in the guacamole, fished it out, and licked his fingers.

"I'm not sure," I said.

"You did fill out an application?"

"Yes, Dad, Mommy made me promise."

"Stop that!" Barbara threw a chip at me.

"No food fights, guys," Jimmy said mildly. "She only wants you to be happy." Then he grinned like a wolf.

I smiled back reluctantly. "I know you two mean well."

Barbara mimed getting stabbed.

"Ooh, that hurt."

"So stop nudging," I said, giving it the New York Jewish pronunciation. "After your boss kicked me out, I hung around the corridors, watching all the little worker bees going to and fro. The job that looked the most fun was pushing a cart filled with vials of blood up and down the halls, like a Good Humor man for vampires. And that's setting the bar very, very low."

"Glad to hear you didn't say the pharmacy."

"I'm not stupid. I know 'people, places, and things' are out." If I really meant to stick with this recovery thing, a job involving access to pharmaceuticals would be a lot more fun than I could afford to risk.

"What about a desk job? You can do computers, and you have plenty of office experience. Human Resources? Billing? Medical records?"

I put my head in my hands, clutched a couple of fistfuls of hair, and groaned. "You mean I do have to die of boredom to stay sober? I've done that kind of job as a temp, but full-time? Permanent? I did consider it. For about ten seconds. I took one look around that Human Resources office and my heart sank like the *Titanic*."

Barbara shot Jimmy a conspiratorial look. Jimmy raised his eyebrows, tilted back in his chair, and flung up his hands in an "I give up" gesture.

"Speaking of not getting bored," she said, "we were thinking—"

"We, white man?" Jimmy said. But he sounded resigned.

"No, seriously, Bruce. We were talking about your friend. I know you liked him. And I know you're upset."

"You think I need closure?" I asked innocently. It looked like Jimmy hadn't told Barbara I wanted us to look into Guff's death. That way, he kept the leverage of magnanimously supporting her desire to snoop.

"Yes," Barbara said firmly.

"Gee, Barbara, I don't know. It's not really our business. And we're not experts." Then I relented. I might joke about what Barbara would call "the process." But I had liked the guy. It had shaken me to watch him die. Especially not taking the edge off it with booze or drugs. And something just felt wrong. "I thought you'd never ask."

Before I left that night, the three of us talked it through as far as we could without further information.

Guff had come back to the detox on time and apparently clean. He'd given in his urine without any stalling or kvetching, as Barbara put it. He might have OD'd, but I couldn't see how. Guff had eaten whatever they'd served for dinner, along with me and everybody else.

"It's not as if the cook was out in the woods picking poison mushrooms that afternoon," Barbara said.

"So whatever killed him was something he took or got hold of while he was out," Jimmy said.

"Seems so," I said.

"Remind me again," said Jimmy, "I keep forgetting. Why is it our job to figure it out?"

"Because if we don't," said Barbara, "no one will. Dr. Bones will sign the death certificate and that'll be it." His name wasn't Dr. Bones, but that's what they'd been calling the docs in detox since 1967.

"It's still none of our business." Jimmy made a stern face that didn't impress either of us. "Bruce, your job right now is to stay clean and sober. And Barbara, yours is to live my life—I mean your own life."

"Good one, Jimmy." I grinned appreciatively.

"Very funny," Barbara said. "Anyhow, we already agreed doing this will help Bruce stay clean and sober. Oops." She clapped a hand to her mouth. She did that a lot. Jimmy called it her "Tenth Step Twitch." "When we were wrong, promptly admitted it."

"Ohhhhh," I drawled, "this is my therapy. But you weren't going to tell me. 'Don't drink, go to meetings, and investigate a murder.'"

Having made her amends, Barbara moved right on. As we all knew, she'd say anything.

"The best reason you might actually make it this time is that you have real feelings about this. You cared about Godfrey, and it hurt you when he died."

"So it's deerstalker hats for three," Jimmy said.

"He needs closure," Barbara said.

"And here I thought you were motivated by sheer unholy curiosity."

"I was," said Barbara with her usual devastating frankness. "But Bruce hasn't let himself feel anything for years. If finding out why Guff died keeps him interested in staying sober, we have no choice. Or rather, we have choices—we always have choices—but we choose to take this to the limit, if I have anything to say about it."

"Thank you for sharing," I said. "Why don't you just cut me open and display my bleeding heart?" But she was right.

"Okay, okay," Jimmy said, "I'm for truth and justice and Bruce having feelings, too. But I'm still not sure why we think Guff was murdered when the professionals don't."

"Think about it," Barbara said. "It's not an English country house weekend in a murder mystery. Everybody expects drunks on the Bowery to die. No one will go looking for evidence of murder, and if they did, they wouldn't run around like Lord Peter Wimsey, hunting down appropriate suspects. They could lose the paperwork. They could lose the corpse, for that matter. You know what the city bureaucracy is like. Or if you don't, I do. I've worked in city hospitals, I have stories that could curl your hair."

"Let's see if I've got this straight," Jimmy said. "Bruce needs closure. You need to make sure he doesn't shut down emotionally."

"Also, I'm the only one who can get back into detox. I've been thinking about that, and I have a great idea. I'm going to call and ask for some per diem work—they always need counselors, and I can do a couple of night shifts at least. It'll be a great chance to snoop through the records."

"Great, so now we're raiding confidential records."

"You're not," said Barbara, "and I'm inside the confidentiality loop if I go back to work there as a counselor, even temporarily."

"Okay, that's why you're in. And I get why Bruce is in. But what about me? How come I'm involved in this?"

"Elementary, my dear Watson," said Barbara. "We'll need the Internet."

TEN

Barbara emerged from the subway into the dark. She paused at the top of the stairs to catch her breath. The steps at Broadway-Lafayette had to be the steepest in the city. Even climbing them every day as an intern had never improved her wind. Waiting for the green light so she could cross the broad expanse of Houston Street, she clutched her handbag, tucked up under her armpit in streetwise New Yorker style, and glanced from side to side. She had never feared the streets of New York, or its subways, at night, though common sense demanded that she remain alert and cautious. The flutter at the pit of her stomach came not from dangers without but from doubts within.

She had always had the habit of self-scrutiny. On first reading the Twelve Steps, she had been alienated, if not horrified, by what she still thought of as the God stuff, but she had thought the searching and fearless moral inventory sounded like fun. "No problem," she had told first Jimmy and then her skeptical sponsor. "I've been making lists of what's wrong with me my whole life." She had learned a lot since then. Recovery had taken her a lot further than the Bowery from her nice Jewish upbringing. Her mother, a strong personality and always a point of reference, had never said a prayer in a church basement or hugged a nun. Barbara grinned, thinking of tough little Sister Angel and crisp Sister Perseverance. Then, ever self-deprecating, she chided herself mentally for being so impressed with her own broad-mindedness. She wished that as she moved through her life, she could refrain completely from thinking, Look, Ma! as she met the people, took the actions, thought the thoughts, and felt the feelings that went so far beyond the compass of her upbringing.

"Progress, not perfection," she muttered to herself. Her mother would have derided these upbeat twelve-step slogans if Barbara had ever been so foolish as to use them in her presence. But Barbara had discovered that they could be remarkably profound when applied on a practical level. On the other hand, she still experienced moments when the fear that she was only kidding herself and, in fact, believed none of it stabbed her sharply.

So what was tonight's anxiety about? Fear of a murderer? If Godfrey's killer existed outside her imagination—and she had no illusions about whose imagination drove the three of them on this peculiar quest—surely he was long gone from the detox, if he had ever been there. The whole point of studying Guff's chart was to discover his world. So many of the clients in that particular detox had none beyond the Bowery itself. Barbara had sat through her share of case presentations and treatment-planning meetings as an intern. In the old days, that mythical creature who must never be called a bum—the old-fashioned chronic alcoholic on the model of Bark—had existed in the hundreds. She remembered taking notes: "On and off the Bowery for fifteen years. . . . On and off the Bowery for twenty-two years." That world hardly existed anymore. In any case, Guff had been an anomaly in that last-resort detox. From what Bruce had told her about his history, it might even have been a stubborn pride that brought him there, to helpers and companions his aristocratic family hardly knew existed except as the shadowy recipients of a dutiful charity.

What stuck in her throat and made her palms prickle with sweat under the heavy mittens she wore against the cold? The ethics of the situation, she admitted to herself—not the dead man's world, nor the mean streets, nor the detox itself, a health-care facility not so different from the one that employed her now, despite its quirkiness. It went against the grain, no matter how cleverly she rationalized it, such as saying that the limits of confidentiality become debatable when the client is dead. Or that unless they actually caught the murderer, she wouldn't tell anyone but Jimmy—who never talked about the living or anyone who'd died after 1945, or possibly 1899—and Bruce, who hardly counted, because he already knew.

Look, Ma, I'm so self-honest! She gave a short bark of laughter that sent what she hoped was a mouse rather than a rat scurrying for cover almost under her feet. Was she breaking confidentiality? Yes. Was she behaving in a professional manner? No. Was she willing not to do this, to let it go? No. For years, she had watched with an aching heart as Jimmy blew off the loss of the best friend he would never admit how deeply he loved. AA, usually so wise, had easy answers: Just don't drink and go to meetings. We're powerless over people, places, and things. Stick with the winners. He has his own Higher Power. Al-Anon, the twelve-step program for relatives and friends, couldn't fix it, either, just gave tips on how to bear it: Keep the focus on yourself. Detach with love. Barbara knew perfectly well the importance of attending to her own life, not to mention the grandiosity of dreaming she could mend what lay between Bruce and Jimmy. But if she could do anything at all to help this friendship heal—which could happen only if Bruce stayed sober—a tenet or two of the counselors' code of ethics seemed a small price to pay.

It had been easy enough to get both the official version of Guff's death and an invitation to work the night shift out of Charmaine. One phone call had done it.

"Hey, I hear you lost another patient," she'd said.

Charmaine had been off and running, not even asking how Barbara had heard the news. As she had told Bruce and Jimmy, people died in detox all the time. But even in detox, they usually didn't die right before your eyes, especially not the relatively young and healthy ones. Guff had been exceptionally healthy for a client on the Bowery, having had a lifetime of good nutrition and minimal exposure to HIV, tuberculosis, and the many other ills that haunted the poor and drug-addicted. So Guff's dramatic demise had been noteworthy. Charmaine had given theme and variations, with a long coda on how much paperwork such a death generated and the impossibility of getting the staff to stop gossiping and get on with their work. That had given Barbara the opening she needed. She'd offered to cover a night shift, pleading the expense of an ecumenical holiday season—both Hanukkah and Christmas— as her reason for taking on extra work.

"Bless your heart," Charmaine had said. "We'd welcome you with open arms. Sylvia was so upset, she's taking a few days off, and Darryl is out, too. He seems to have the flu."

"I know Sister Angel never takes a sick day," said Barbara, setting the hook.

"Bark and I are trying to get her to take some time off," Charmaine said. "She was up all night that night, doing a double shift. You know her. Evil is never off duty, so Sister Angel is always on."

"Sister Angel is amazing."

"So she is." A little tartly, Charmaine added, "Everybody says so."

"Sounds like you could use some time off yourself," Barbara said with sympathy.

"From your mouth to God's ear," Charmaine said. "Not that I'm likely to get it."

Charmaine, however, did not work nights. Sister Angel sat in the small glassed-in nursing station, doing paperwork, when Barbara stepped off the creaking elevator. The unit was dimly lit so that the patients, who had little enough privacy and all the discomforts of withdrawal, could try to sleep. For a moment, Barbara saw the nun, alone in the brightly illuminated cubicle, as a starship captain keeping watch in the night. Then the fancy vanished as Sister Angel bustled out to greet her—Look, Ma, I'm hugging a nun!—and exhort her to read or take or use anything she wanted, as long as she put it away in the same place afterward. As always, Barbara was surprised by how small and solid she was. Tonight, she wore one of the postmodern abbreviated habits. Barbara had seen her both swathed in full medieval regalia and shopping for secondhand dresses and silly hats in the antique clothing stores on Broadway. She had danced up a storm at the staff Christmas party the year Barbara interned. Sister Angel's order or community functioned very much in the world. She had her own apartment and seemed to be free to do anything she wanted, except, presumably, have sex. She exuded confidence, implacability, and conscience. And she was leaving.

"I'm just going off duty."

"I'm disappointed. I hoped we'd get to talk." On the other hand, it left Barbara free to take a leisurely look for and then hopefully at Guff's chart, which she had no earthly reason to be interested in. On the whole, she was relieved when Sister Angel gave her a brisk pat and a mild version of her famous glare, indicating that Barbara was there to work, not to talk, although she was too nice to say so.

She left quickly, not bothering with the elevator, but tap-tapping briskly down the stairs, completely unfazed by the dim light and whatever ghosts of violence haunted the stairwell. They wouldn't discomfit Sister Angel. They wouldn't dare.

Barbara stashed her handbag in a drawer that locked and went looking for the chart. The night nurse, a temp who knew little about the detox beyond what she needed to do her job, had wandered in and taken Sister Angel's place at the desk in the nursing station. She didn't find anything odd in Barbara's scurrying back and forth and flipping through the charts in every cabinet. The active files lived in the most accessible drawers, but because so many of the clients were recidivists, the inactive charts were almost equally important. Barbara stooped, squatted, and stretched while the nurse unself-consciously played FreeCell on the nursing station's computer. Occasionally, a client in pajamas wandered in, wanting a glass of juice or a pill or the answer to a question, but mostly the unit lay quiet.

She had been too overexcited at the prospect of this task to write down Guff's full name, and it took her half an hour of racking her brains, trying to remember if it began with a B or an H, to think of calling Bruce, who supplied "Godfrey Brandon Kettleworth the Third, like the kings of England," and pointed out that Kettleworth began with a K. It took her another hour to get through the many drawers of charts, which were filed not in alphabetical order but according to a code that the exasperated Barbara decided would have been challenging for military intelligence to crack and that had been instituted two years after her internship. She would have liked to take a look at Elwood's chart, too, if only for comparison, but she couldn't remember his last name, either. She decided it wasn't worth the energy to look into a death with no real mystery about it.

The search would have gone faster without the participation of the night nurse, who was bored enough to enter into the spirit of the hunt without asking any questions except whether Barbara had tried this unlikely location or that. Reluctant to alienate her or arouse any further curiosity, Barbara resigned herself to periodic smiles and thanks as the nurse helpfully spotted piles of charts on various desks, even though staff members were supposed to return them all to the chart room at the end of the day. In the end, she found Guff's chart not in the chart room but under a stack of folders on Sister Angel's desk.

Sister Angel's tiny office was minimalist—no computer, no bookshelves, no decor except for a crucifix on the wall. However, unlike the nursing station, it had opaque walls. Barbara locked the door—Look, Ma, I'm locked in with Jesus on the Cross, she thought irrepressibly—and settled down to read.

The chart had a heavy cardboard cover in an eye-zapping shade of lavender and was supposed to contain a written record of every single incident and bit of data relevant to Guff's stay. Each section was secured with long and wickedly sharp metal fasteners. Barbara knew from long experience that she would have to unfasten at least some of the pages and remove them from the chart in order to read everything. She reminded herself to put everything back in precisely the same order. She didn't want her presence to be noticed. One government agency or another audited the program at intervals, and every word written in the charts could and would be scrutinized. The detox could lose money or even its license if anything were found amiss. Staff did sometimes get sloppy, though. She just needed to be careful.

Guff's chart was thin and in excellent condition, which indicated to Barbara's practiced eye that he had never been in detox on the Bowery before. Some of the old-timers' files ran to three or four volumes, stuffed with paper and falling apart, documenting their many admissions. She opened the lavender cover to the face sheet, which held the basic information collected on admission. Name, Godfrey Brandon Kettleworth III, exactly as Bruce had told her. Domicile, an address on the East Side. Not homeless, then—if he'd really lived there. She jotted it down. Some of the men used a relative's address to collect their welfare checks or stayed intermittently on someone's couch but, in fact, lived on the street. Date of birth. Guff had been forty-seven: old enough for Vietnam, and he'd told Bruce he was a vet. Not too old to die young. Social Security number. Even the most brain-fried guys remembered that, Jimmy had once told her. She had found it true even on the Bowery. Jimmy claimed that he didn't need to know his because she was so codependent that she knew it as well as her own. This both amused and annoyed her, because it was also true.

The medical part of the chart came next. Barbara flipped quickly through the lab reports. To her disappointment, the last one filed dated from December 30, before Guff had left on pass. She scanned the sheet for street drugs or any other substance that would not have been prescribed. Nothing, at least through two days before New Year's. Medical history, including alcohol and drug treatment. No one who abused alcohol and drugs for long enough got off lightly, and Guff was no exception. He had been treated for hepatitis B, an alcohol-related liver disease, and had had a bout of pancreatitis, which she knew was not only life-threatening but extremely painful. He had broken a few bones, been wounded twice in Vietnam—scars noted—and passed through various detoxes a handful of times. Two inpatient twenty-eight-day rehabs, both expensive ones. He had completed neither. Treated for venereal disease in the early 1970s, probably another legacy of Vietnam.

Next came the psychosocial, many of its staggeringly intrusive questions prescribed by state regulations. This one ran eleven pages, two more than the one used at Barbara's outpatient clinic. "Are you sexually active?" "What is your sexual orientation?" "Have you ever experienced any kind of sexual dysfunction? If so, describe." "Have you ever experienced any kind of sexual abuse or trauma? If so, when? Describe. What treatment, if any, did you receive?" "Have you ever been the perpetrator of sexual abuse?"

Since stumbling embarrassed through her first psychosocial interview here, Barbara had learned some tricks for getting the answers. One was to put the questions in plain English. "Have you ever had trouble getting it up?" "Are you into men or women?" If you just read the questions off the page, you were dead in the water. You had to sound matter-of-fact, compassionate, supportive, and incapable of becoming judgmental no matter what you heard. Barbara reflected, not for the first time, that most counselors had more than their fair share of empathy as well as insatiable curiosity. They certainly didn't do it for the pay.

For many homeless alcoholics, the road to the Bowery led through crime, with or without discovery and punishment. Even the toughest clients were in a vulnerable state at the point of detox admission. Barbara had heard them reveal an astonishing amount of information. But many wanted as little as possible on the record. Guff had been either one of these or pure as the driven snow. No item on the psychosocial could be left blank. It was one of the regulations. But if the client wouldn't answer, there was a formula: the word *Denied*. All the sex and violence questions: Denied, denied, denied. She would have to ask Bruce if Guff had mentioned any significant history in those areas, other than the war.

Guff had not seen a psychiatrist. The service was too expensive to squander on clients who showed no signs of mood or thought disorders. Eleven pages of questions usually offered some clues as to whether the client was irrational or suicidally depressed. Darryl had done the mental status exam, which tested the client's cognitive functioning. Not every counselor believed that the mental status questions were a reliable guide to whether a person could still think rationally. Barbara smiled, remembering how Bark used to rant about the stupidity of the mental status. "When I lived in a box"—Bark always said "in a box," never "on the streets" or "on the Bowery"—"I didn't give a damn who the president was. That's no way to decide whether a man's got all his marbles."

Barbara flipped through to the family history. What made Guff different from the other drunks on the Bowery boiled down to money. A lot of money, from what Bruce had gathered. Family money made an excellent motive for murder. To trace Guff's activities on his last day, they needed as much concrete information as they could get about his family. Barbara scrabbled on Sister Angel's desk for a lined yellow pad and a pen, annoyed at herself for not thinking sooner about taking notes. She started scribbling as she read.

Father: Godfrey Brandon Kettleworth, Jr., investment banker, deceased. Died of a heart attack at age seventy-three. History of alcohol or other drug abuse or dependence, denied. Mother: Augusta Brandon. She wrote, "Guff's parents—cousins?" Fund-raiser, deceased. Died at age sixty-one, car accident. Took prescription pills for "nerves." That usually meant anxiety or depression. Darryl hadn't asked the next logical question, whether she took the pills as prescribed. It would be interesting to know if Guff's mother had abused medication. She could have been an addict, however respectable, and that, in turn, would have affected the whole family. Three sisters were listed: Lucinda Kettleworth, Emily Brandon Weill, Frances Augusta Standish. Lucinda might be single or too feminist to change her name. Emily had evidently married out of the WASP enclave. Frances must have married a Mayflower descendant. Bruce might know more about the sisters.

Guff wasn't the family's only substance abuser. Both grandfathers, a maternal uncle, and two uncles on the father's side had all had alcohol problems. He had also mentioned a couple of drug-addicted cousins. Guff's father might have been the family hero, the one who achieved while the others screwed up. And Guff was the only son. In a blue-blooded patriarchal family, he might have been considered a disgrace but still gotten all or much of the money. Barbara put down the pen, stretched her fingers, and rubbed at her scalp, wondering how on earth they were going to find out about the family finances. Even if they managed to track down and meet the sisters and other family members, the Kettleworths would not show them their income tax returns. Jimmy and his Internet skills would provide their best chance to learn what they needed. Jimmy took the honesty and integrity that AA considered essential to sobriety too seriously to be an actual hacker, but it was not for lack of ability.

Barbara skipped over the goals and objectives for the future that Guff was now not going to have and turned to the progress notes that documented every counseling session or activity, including medical care. Besides Darryl's, she recognized several distinctive handwritings, including Charmaine's and Sister Angel's. Sylvia had written a whole page documenting his death. Even in the computer age, those who worked in a health care facility of any kind became very familiar with the handwriting of everyone they worked with. All this documentation was how the team communicated. Everyone needed to know what was going on. As Carlo in the Bronx put it, "Everybody's job is harder if you write lousy notes."

This team's notes varied in both legibility and expressiveness. Boris spoke English fairly well but spelled creatively, and he formed some of his letters as if he did not quite believe everything he had been taught about the Latin alphabet. Darryl's writing looked as if he had some kind of learning disability. If so, he had done a good job of compensating well enough to pass the counseling credential exam. He knew how to write clinically, in that the

— 75 —

focus of most of his sentences was the client, not himself. As Carlo said, " 'The client opened up to me real good' is not a clinical note." But Darryl's anger and dislike of Guff, fully described by Bruce, came through. "Client is resistant to group process. Client still in denial about his addiction." The doctor, true to the profession's reputation, had an unreadable scrawl. Sister Angel had the clearest and most disciplined penmanship.

Barbara skimmed, not sure what she was looking for. Every note mentioned the drinking: either some detail of his patterns and the progression to high tolerance, withdrawal symptoms, loss of control, and the general falling apart of his life, or something he said that indicated how self-aware he was or how open he seemed to changing. But Charmaine and Sister Angel, especially, were interested in everything. Never married. No children. No current partner—in fact, he'd denied long-term relationships altogether. Why not? Barbara wondered. From Bruce's description, he had been an attractive guy. Charmaine wrote that he seemed attached to his nephews, and Sister Angel noted that relationships with his sisters' children needed to be explored further. "Resentments," she had written cryptically.

Educated at Princeton, majored in French. That would not have done him much good on the Bowery. Maybe his father had wanted him to be a diplomat. Did not graduate. No job history of any significance. Barbara wondered if that just indicated a family with plenty of inherited money or the usual story of the chronic alcoholic who never got his act together. She kept skimming. "Still v. guarded re sexual activity," she read. Barbara snorted. If she were a man who had had both his clothes and his major coping mechanism taken away, and a nun started quizzing her about her sex life, she would probably be less than forthcoming, too. On the other hand, she recalled that Sister Angel was very adept at getting all sorts of personal information out of clients. Colleagues, too, for that matter. She was a great listener. Barbara had told her one or two stories herself about which Jimmy had said later, "You told her *that*?"

Before she could read further, someone hammered aggressively on the door. She jumped. She did not want to get caught snooping into charts she had no business with, especially this particular chart.

"Hey, open up!" It was Darryl's voice. What was he doing here at this hour? She remembered with relief that she had locked the door.

"Just a second." She went on the offensive with a tone of slight annoyance, though to her own ears, her voice wobbled a bit around the edges. "Be right out."

She slapped Guff's chart shut and slipped it in on the bottom of the pile. A yellow sticky note she had missed before shot out onto the desk. Charmaine's writing. "Add death certificate, then file in- active." Damn. She had become so absorbed in the personal infor- mation that she had forgotten her primary agenda, to see the official cause of death. According to this, it would be a while be- fore that paperwork got into the chart. Unless she came back, she would miss the chance to see it. The inactive files consisted of floor-to-ceiling piles of very heavy boxes in a storeroom in the sub- basement, a dank and cavernous space that looked as if the Count of Monte Cristo might have tunneled through it. During her in- ternship, they had taken her down there once to help dust and haul before an audit. Normally, however, no one dared try to find anything once it had been filed in the subbasement.

She opened the door.

"Hey, since you're here, you might as well do some work," Dar- ryl said without preamble.

Yeah, and happy New Year to you, too, she responded silently. Barbara had always found Darryl scary and had no trouble believing

— 77 —

he had been a major drug dealer. "Guy down on the end there can't sleep, wants to talk."

"Sure, no problem." She really was here to help the clients. Sometimes that unpredictable window of opportunity when an alcoholic's pain got momentarily worse than his desire to drink came in the middle of the night. "Seize the moment."

"I'm not really on duty anyhow. Should be home with the flu. Not my client. And the guy doesn't like me much. Besides, I gotta check on something, need to see if the chart I'm looking for is in here. Don't see why Sister Holier than Thou can't put her charts back like she's supposed to before she leaves, nome sane?"

"No problem," Barbara repeated. It was her job, after all, and she did care about doing it. But Darryl was usually more of an "I'll do what I damn please. You got a problem with that?" kind of guy. Why was he explaining?

ELEVEN

Four dozen voices chorused, ". . . and the wisdom to know the difference." The meeting had started. To my relief, I had missed the hand-holding part. Call me resistant, but it still made me feel like a jerk.

It was my first real meeting since I'd gotten out. The mandatory meetings at the detox didn't count, in my mind. I looked around the room. About fifty people, of all shapes and sizes, perched on chairs too small for them in a church basement with inadequate lighting that made everything look even more dingy than it was.

"Tradition Three. The only requirement for AA membership is a desire to stop drinking," someone recited.

Did I really want to stop? I mulled it over. As I had learned in previous passes through AA, there's a big difference between going on the wagon and getting sober. When I went on the wagon, I knew I could fall off it whenever I wanted.

It's like the old joke among civilians who think alcoholism is funny. "Sure, I can stop drinking. I've done it a thousand times."

That's not sobriety. To tell the truth, my bowels turned to water when I thought of *never*. Never feel the fire of old Jack trickling down my throat and spreading flames through my belly. Never pick up a cold frosty on a hot summer day. Not a problem at the moment, in January in New York. Jimmy's uninvited voice commented annoyingly in my head: If it's not today's problem, don't worry about it. One day at a time. A corny concept, but it makes sense.

They tell you that if you're serious about recovering, you should sit in the front and raise your hand when it's time to share. I acknowledged my ambivalence, as Barbara would say, by making my way over to the table in the back, where a guy I knew from meetings stood guard over a mammoth coffee urn and several plates of cookies. Doing service, another thing they recommend if you really want to stay sober. We had never had a conversation of more than two sentences, but his face lit up at the sight of me.

"Hey, good to see you! Welcome back!" His friendliness made me want to snarl. Could I stay sober without giving up more attitude than I could afford to lose? Jimmy sober was still Jimmy. But he was such an odd duck that he'd be different from everybody else even if he lived in Nebraska. Who was I without my attitude? You know, the quality that makes comedians portray New Yorkers as saying "You got a problem with that?" every time we open our mouths. According to Jimmy, it's a kind of body armor. Trust him to find a military metaphor. The bitch of it was, he was right. The thought of being without it scared the hell out of me.

To my own surprise, I remembered the coffee guy's name.

"Gary. How ya doin'?"

The coffee tasted like piss, but it was better than I'd gotten in detox. As I sipped, he said, "I hear you just got out of detox."

Don't ask me how people in AA get to know things. As I said, it's an anonymous program. And most people do their best to avoid telling secrets and spreading malice at least. But the grapevine, even in New York, with its hundreds of meetings a week, still functions with impressive efficiency.

"Yeah, well, reports of my death have been greatly exaggerated."

Gary laughed, as if it had been me and not Mark Twain who'd made that one-liner up.

"I hear someone from the fellowship died." He sounded half sympathetic, half avid to dish the dirt. A stranger's tragedy is just another piece of gossip. Guff's death felt different because I'd known him. All right, I admit it, I'd cared about him. I had no desire to regale Gary with the details.

"Yeah. Died sober anyhow, as far as I know."

He nodded solemnly at that. I didn't even know if it was true. But I somehow felt protective of Guff's reputation. And just about anyone in AA would consider it a good epitaph, if not exactly good news.

"You were there?"

I made a face, conceding it.

"I heard it was that guy who called himself God. Big Waspy-looking dude? Not to break his anonymity," he added hastily.

Hypocrite.

"I guess he doesn't need it anymore," I said dryly.

"Ever heard him qualify?"

To tell your story at a meeting, you had to be sober for at least ninety days. I didn't know that Guff had ever made it for that long a stretch. Maybe after one of his times in rehab. Getting locked up was as good a way as any to get a drunk or druggie jump-started on sobriety. Though, trust me, it's easy enough to drink or drug even in jail if you want to.

I was tempted to squash Gossipy Gary, but I wanted to hear what he had to say. Guff's death troubled me like an itch under a shoulder blade—maddening and almost impossible to relieve. I wanted to know what had happened. Not to do anything about it. I didn't think that far. See? I could do one day at a time. Just to know. I looked encouraging.

"Trust-fund baby," Gary said. "When I first got sober, I used to get such a resentment at guys like that. They'd had it so easy. What did I care whether they got better?"

That had been my own first reaction to Guff. Less than two weeks ago. It felt like forever.

"A lot of people didn't like him. A couple of folks in this room right now made the mistake of getting into some kind of money stuff with him. Not dealing or anything, but you'd think people would know better than to bring financial relationships into the fellowship. Somebody always gets screwed, and then you've got more resentment than ever."

I looked inquiring, but he wasn't quite ready to break the anonymity of people who were alive and maybe present.

"People found him arrogant," he said instead. "And of course there are always some folks who have trouble with anyone who re-lapses."

Lord knows I'd had more than my share of relapses. Gary had forgotten that. He needed to put tactlessness on his fourth-step in-ventory, the list of his defects of character.

"Though there but for the grace of God . . ." Predictably, he of-fered another of those AA truisms that have the unfortunate merit of being true.

"No pun intended."

"Oh, right," he said earnestly. No sense of humor, either.

"You happen to know any women he was close to in the pro-gram?" I asked only because I really wanted to know.

Guffy and I had never gotten around to talking about sex. By the time they hit the Bowery, most guys aren't interested. Guff, though, hadn't been a typical Bowery drunk. He was just an alcoholic with no health insurance who ended up in a detox that took you in for free. Like me. I wasn't homeless anyhow. Was Guff? Maybe it's a class distinction. If a drunk who's broke and uneducated stays on a buddy's couch or in a girlfriend's bed to avoid actually being on the streets, he's homeless. But if Godfrey Brandon Kettleworth III says he's crashing in a relative's spare room on Park Avenue, he's domiciled.

Gary recalled my attention, indicating a woman up near the front of the room

"There's a woman your friend Godfrey thirteenth-stepped or something like it."

This is a relatively polite AA term for hitting on a newly sober member. It implies that the exploitive person has been in the program for a while and should know better.

"You sure it wasn't the other way around?"

"They were both in their first year," he said. "It was around the time I heard him qualify. Then after awhile, I noticed they were sitting as far from each other as possible if they showed up at the same meeting. Bunch of women always in a huddle around her, casting dirty looks his way. Hey, you know what they say: The first year, you should put relationships on the shelf. Keep the focus on staying clean and sober."

The speaker wrapped it up. A patter of applause broke out. Someone passed a basket around. "We have no dues or fees, but we do have expenses." People shifted in their seats and got up to use the rest room or grab a smoke outside. AA meetings used to be the smokiest places in town apart from bars. Now the area outside the door of an AA meeting tends to be the second smokiest place in town.

Gary made a beeline for the door, his pack of Marlboros already in his hand. The woman he had pointed out swiveled in her seat to talk to someone in the row behind her. To my surprise, I realized I knew her. Her name was Maureen. She had short spiky hair that I remembered as dark brown. Now she had it fashionably streaked with improbable magenta highlights. Small, with a slight, boyish figure, she had the kind of face you'd probably call cute if you could stand the word *cute*. We'd spent a week in detox together once. She'd stayed clean for a while that time, while I'd gone straight back out to the nearest bar. I made my way toward her.

"Hey, Maureen!"

Her face lit up in a big smile that I remembered as soon as I saw it.

"Bruce!" She gave me a big hug. Detoxing together was a bond. On the other hand, like most alcoholic women, she had had bad experiences with men. I mean very bad experiences, a lot worse than any kind of hard time I could imagine myself or Jimmy giving a woman.

"I call myself Mo now. Celebrated a year just a couple of weeks ago. How about you?"

"Oh, you know me. You're looking great. Really."

"I know." She did have an incandescent grin. "Haven't seen you around in awhile."

"Well, I'm here now. Listen, can I take your number?" It just popped out. Getting people's phone numbers is another of those things you're supposed to do. If you're going to pick up a drink or a drug in the middle of the night, you're supposed to pick up the phone instead. Everybody in the program knows how that is. There's always somebody willing to talk you through it. I had never made a habit of asking for numbers. I'd never actually called anyone but Jimmy. And no, I had never called him in the middle of the night instead of drinking. Yet.

"Of course!" Mo sounded delighted. She probably really was. She dug in a big bag, found a pen and a scrap of paper, and started scribbling. "I'm giving you my home, my work, and my cell phone. Call me anytime. Really. If you need to talk, I'm there."

I told myself that maybe I just wanted to make sure I could get hold of her to find out what had happened between her and Guff. I sure wasn't going to bring it up right there in the meeting. The break was just about over. No more talking. People began to take their seats, and a few eager-beaver hands shot up. Mo gave me another quick hug and sat back down. The person next to her had left at the break, leaving an empty seat. She glanced back up at me and patted it invitingly. I shook my head, squeezed her shoulder once, and wormed my way back through the rows of seats and out. I had had about all the recovery I could stand for one evening.

I had a date to meet Jimmy and Barbara at one of the ubiquitous Starbucks that had sprung up all over the city like fungus. Alcoholics loved them. We'll drink any kind of coffee that's not unleaded. Barbara had arrived before me. She sat at one of those little tables, her nose buried in a book.

"Hey, it's Espresso Bar Barbie."

In one economical movement, she stood up, closed the book, and swatted me upside the head with it—not too hard, though.

"If I've told you once, I've told you a thousand times: No Jewish girl who hasn't been surgically altered looks anything like Barbie."

"Yes, dear."

Jimmy arrived at that point and we got down to the serious business of ordering coffee. Jimmy picked the cups up at the counter and plunked them onto the little table, along with a couple of trees' worth of napkins and an AA meeting list. I glanced around at the crowded room with a quick left and right that struck even me as furtive.

"Jeez, Jimmy, put it away, will ya? We're in a public place. And trust me, just seeing you reminds me I should go to a meeting."

Jimmy grinned, picked up the fat pamphlet, and made flapping motions at me with it. He knew I didn't want to be conspicuous.

"Cut it out. I've got one, I've got one."

"Nobody's looking, Bruce," said Barbara. "And considering how many times you did it in the street and frightened a helluva lot of horses, it wouldn't ruin your reputation if anyone noticed you were sober."

"It?" I said.

"Whatever you did drunk," she retorted.

"You don't have to rub it in."

I can usually make Barbara feel guilty when she gets on my case. She knows she shouldn't, but she isn't very good at refraining.

"It's usually best," Jimmy advised, "to say 'Yes, dear' and be done with it."

"Seriously, Bruce, how are you doing?" Barbara asked.

"Aside from the recurring instant replay of my buddy choking himself to death and me being up in the middle of the night ready to kill for a drink, just fine and dandy."

Barbara put her hand on my arm. I decided it was too much effort to go on being caustic. Jimmy looked around at the coffee drinkers who thought it was cool to bring their laptops out in public. You could see him thinking, Amateurs! He made a sympathetic face at me.

"No one says it's easy."

"It was a shock."

Their concern, I must admit, was comforting. I felt a rush of what I hoped was grief and not just self-pity.

"Well, it was. It doesn't make sense."

"I got interrupted before I finished skimming the notes," Barbara said, "but I didn't see any indication that they thought he was poisoned or anything like that. It's not the first thing you think of when an addict dies, is it."

"I still don't believe he picked up. When he was discharged, sure, maybe, he might have, but on a pass? And then come back? For the luxurious accommodations on the scenic Bowery?"

"Did you look at the medical records?" Jimmy asked.

"Nothing current," Barbara said. "Hepatitis B and pancreatitis in the past. Wrong kind of tummy ache. Anyhow, active pancreatitis would have put him in the hospital before they got the alcohol out of his system."

"He had twenty-four hours out on his own," I said. "He could have gone anywhere, taken anything."

"I found an address," Barbara said. She dug some folded papers out of her bag and shuffled through them. "East Sixties."

"Expensive part of town." Most of the people I knew wouldn't even think of it as a residential neighborhood. "I could check it out. All I'm doing for the next few days is going to meetings."

"Sure you're okay?" Jimmy meant did I have any money.

"Fine for now. Really." And when I started to run short, I'd temp. It wasn't a long-term plan, but it had the merit of feeling doable. One day at a time. Damn it. Don't you hate it when the preachy stuff turns out to be right?

"If it's a relative," Barbara said, "you could certainly introduce yourself as a friend who was there when he died. Or no, maybe you'd better just have heard that he died. You don't want them to have a knee-jerk reaction to you as another drunk. You did say he'd alienated all his relatives, didn't you? So you'd better show up there looking squeaky-clean."

"What's the uniform? Pinstripe suit? Tennis whites?"

"No, you goofball. It's January anyhow. Just don't wear fuzzy white socks with your black leather shoes, okay?"

"No, ma'am." I grinned. Barbara had a theory about socioeconomic status and socks. I had heard it before.

"You're not going to be breaking the bad news to anyone close,

I hope," Jimmy commented. "If they notified anyone at all, it would've been whoever's at the address he gave, I should think."

"I hope not. That would be tacky, wouldn't it. And awkward for me. Not the kind of situation I'm dying to be in, especially sober."

"Maybe I should do it." Barbara looked stricken. "Maybe you shouldn't risk it."

"I'll be fine."

Barbara thought for a moment.

"How about this? Jimmy, why don't you do some on-line research first? Find out who lives at that address. In fact, let me give you all the names I got. Sisters. Find out where they are, what they do, what their financial position is." Barbara, like me, assumed that Jimmy could find out whatever he wanted to on the Internet.

"He talked about his sisters," I said. "The one he liked was Emma—Emmie."

"Emily," said Barbara, looking at her notes.

"I'm pretty sure he called her Emmie. She might not have been speaking to him. He said everyone in the family was pissed off at him."

"She'd still be upset that he died. Especially if she'd been mad at him. I know I would." Barbara riffled through her notes. "Did he talk to you about women?"

"Other than his sisters, no. I told him I was going to see Laura on my pass. But he didn't come back at me with any reciprocal confidences."

"According to his psychosocial, he'd never been married, wasn't in a relationship, and hadn't been with anyone for very long. Any chance he was gay?"

"No way. And why wouldn't he have told the counselors? They ask about it at least three times, the way they ask about everything."

"Just because everybody we know who's gay is out, it doesn't mean that everyone is out. Jimmy, if you were gay, would you want to tell a nun about it?"

Jimmy shuddered.

"I may be lapsed, but I'm still an Irish Catholic."

"That Sister Angel in the detox is not exactly your typical nun," I said.

Barbara grinned.

"Yeah, she's pretty cool, isn't she."

"Tough," I said. "Savvy. And gets the information out of you with a scalpel if she needs to."

"Besides," Barbara said, "she's not the only one who worked with him."

"If I was gay," I said, "I'd rather tell Sister Angel about my love life than some of the counselors there. You know Darryl?"

"He was the one who interrupted me while I was looking at Guff's chart," said Barbara. "I don't know what he was doing there in the middle of the night. Not exactly sweetness and light, is he. Did he give you a hard time?"

"I managed to stay away from him. He and Guff had one or two big blowups, though. Mutual antipathy, to say the least."

"Rumor says he was a big dealer. Do you think it's true?"

"Probably. He didn't do five years in the slammer for selling Girl Scout cookies. Doesn't mind talking about it, either. One of his routines is 'Done harder time than thou.'"

"Yeah, he was like that when I did my internship there. At the time, it kind of impressed me. You know, the glamour of living on the edge."

"I hope that's worn off, now that you're making a living off us bums and desperadoes," Jimmy said.

"The big question on the ward about Darryl," I said, "was, Is he dealing now?"

"A counselor selling drugs?" said Jimmy. "Now you shock me."

"It wouldn't be the first time."

"So Jimmy checks the Internet—"

"Family, finances, known addresses. I'll get on it tonight."

"Tomorrow morning," Barbara said. Jimmy would be up and on-line all night every night if he lived alone. "And I'll take the sisters."

"I met a couple of folks who knew him at the meeting," I volunteered. "This woman Mo, this guy Gary. I'll see what else I can find out. Hot on the trail of justice. And not even tanked."

"At least you won't get bored." Barbara always has to have the last word. At least she didn't say the rest of it. If I didn't get bored, maybe I wouldn't drink again.

I spent the next day making the rounds of temp offices. To my relief, not all of them remembered me. When I couldn't stand any more of it, I went over to Jimmy and Barbara's.

Jimmy greeted me characteristically.

"Did you know that Frederick the Great used a lot of snuff and got it all over his clothes? He wasn't noted for his personal habits. He wrote some nice flute music, though."

"Yes, dear." I used Barbara's line. Jimmy never wanted to live in this century. Sometimes we just had to let him be. Luckily, Barbara came bounding in before he told me even more about Frederick the Great than I wanted to know.

Barbara stays in this century, but she's a master of the blow-by-blow account.

"We had staff meeting today. Dr. Arnold brought Krispy Kremes again. Hey, has it ever occurred to you that if you cross potato chips—can't eat just one—with M&M's—melt in your mouth—you get Krispy Kremes?"

Jimmy and I gazed at her with wonder.

"Never," I said.

"She lives to digress," Jimmy told me.

"At least I take it one century at a time. And unlike some people, I never leave out the interesting parts. Now, be quiet and let me tell you. Two clients tested positive for hepatitis B, they're making us watch the hand-washing video again, and another client died."

I knew the important part of this was the client's death, but Barbara's style was contagious.

"Hand-washing video? You've got to be kidding."

"No, really, it's part of universal precautions. The hospital takes it very seriously, especially in the age of HIV. We have to watch it every year, I think it's part of the nursing curriculum, but Dr. Arnold makes us all go."

"A client died," Jimmy prompted. He had a lot of practice getting her back on track.

"Another old one, Daniel. He was Ingrid's client—she's the nurse from Nebraska who works in addictions because she has more alcoholic relatives than I have any kind of relatives—and Marian, the social work intern, was his counselor, she's never lost a client before, and she only has a few, so she got very teary. Carlo and Sister Perseverance had known him forever, of course, but they stayed calm about it—they've seen a lot of clients come and go."

"They're dropping like flies at your place, aren't they?"

"No more than down on the Bowery. And Nikolai and Daniel had both been beat up pretty badly by the disease. They actually put 'acute and chronic alcoholism' as the cause of death."

"And this is a good thing?"

"Not for poor Daniel, obviously, but it shows that hospitals and the medical profession are beginning to get it about alcoholism and addictions. They used to put anything but—seizure disorder, heart attack—because it was so stigmatizing, and that just fed the denial, which led to lack of funding, which led to not enough treatment and training for health professionals, most of whom—well, a lot anyway—come from alcoholic and dysfunctional families themselves."

"They do?" I'd never thought of that.

"Yeah. They're the family heroes and caretakers—they rescue and control anyway, so why not get paid for it? And if they haven't had treatment and aren't in program, they're going to ignore the signs and symptoms in the clients just the way they do in their own families. Carlo said he was a dirty old man."

She'd lost me.

"Carlo is a dirty old man?"

"No! He said Daniel was a dirty old man. Well, first he said he wasn't exactly a nice old man—you know, trying to get Marian to stop crying. He called her 'honeybun'—Carlo is hopelessly sexist, though I think he isn't really, he just likes to push our buttons. We usually let him get away with it. There's no point trying to get Carlo to pay attention to gender politics. He said Daniel was a great fanny patter. He called Sister Persistence 'cookie.'"

"Daniel called her 'cookie'? That sounds pretty out of line for a client."

"No! Carlo did—when he asked her if she remembered. Only Carlo would dare call Sister Perseverance cookie. Marian said he never patted *her* fanny. She sounded really put out about it. Students never get it that when clients make them the favorite, it's a manipulation."

"Then what happened?" Barbara's saga sure was a new slant on treatment for me.

"Oh, Dr. Arnold made him stop teasing before Marian really broke down and Sister Persistence murdered him. She reminded us that postponing the scheduled case presentations today would give us an unmanageable backlog in no time. So Ingrid and Carlo gave their presentations, and then we ordered out for pizza."

"What kind?"

"My favorite, mushrooms and—oh, you! Jimmy, tell us what you got on Guff."

"I looked up his address for you."

"In the East Sixties? Some comedown, dying on the Bowery. So did he really live there? Whose address is it?"

"I don't know if he lived there or was staying there or what. But the owner of the whole building is a Dr. Weill, which is the name of the sister that you gave me—Emily Brandon Weill."

"That's the one he got along with," I said. "Though I think he said there'd been some kind of rift. And she's a doctor?"

"No, it's the husband, if that's who he is. Dr. Samson Weill. I looked him up. He's a plastic surgeon. Publishes occasionally in medical journals, so he's not a quack. And he must make a bundle."

"If he owns a whole building in the Sixties, he must be loaded. Though she may have family money, too. Guff had a trust fund. I don't suppose you looked her up?"

"O ye of little faith. Wellesley, class of 1984, majored in anthropology. On the boards of several charities and her class reunion committee in the college alumni association. Alumnae. Three children, Brandon, Lucille Marie, and Duncan. All in private school." He named a well-known institution.

"That's the kind of place you register your kids for at birth," Barbara said, "if you have a lot of money and want to be sure they get into Harvard."

"Yeah, that fits. Lucille Marie rides horses, competes in horse shows—she won some kind of trophy out in the Hamptons three years ago—and Brandon, the older boy, plays chess, competitive chess. The little one danced in *The Nutcracker* this Christmas."

"A family of high achievers," Barbara mused, "and Uncle Guffy, the Bowery bum."

I couldn't let that pass.

"I beg your pardon!"

"I'm just saying how they'd think of it," Barbara protested. "You're not a bum. You just think not drinking is no fun."

"Isn't it?"

"And when you do drink, you can't function."

"Not so hot," I admitted. "Sounds like a bum to me."

"Are we having fun yet?" Jimmy chimed in.

"He doesn't mean that," Barbara told me. "He just says it all the time because it's in the ACOA handbook." There is no handbook for adult children of alcoholics. But I knew what she meant.

TWELVE

Barbara got off the crosstown bus at Lexington Avenue, shaking her head as she did every time over the inconvenient demise of the bus stop at Park Avenue. The Christmas lights strung overhead across Eighty-sixth Street every year had been dismantled, to her disappointment. But on Lex, shop windows still glittered, hoping to lure buyers for their unsold holiday stock. She had meant to take the subway down to the Sixties, but she decided to walk. The air held a hint of January thaw. The city smelled and looked less wintry than it had, if not springlike yet. All traces of the last big snow had vanished. Since the last act of even the most spectacular blizzard in the city consisted of raggedy mounds of blackened, icy snow, liberally stained with bright yellow dog urine, barring the egress of cars unfortunate enough to be parked on the street when it snowed, she wasn't sorry.

She window-shopped her way down to Seventy-second Street, content to look without covetousness. She and Jimmy had celebrated the holidays to satiation point. He had introduced her years before to the Christmases he'd never had: mysterious, artfully wrapped packages heaped under the tree, a fresh-cut evergreen bristling with tinsel and hung about with minor works of art, and peace, if not on earth, at least in the family. She had chipped in the secular Jewish American's Hanukkah: a menorah, a present every night for the eight nights of the holiday, and abundant potato latkes made from scratch, with the traditional blood sacrifice produced by knuckles scraped as the raw potatoes were grated.

Emmie's address must be between Lexington and Park. If she cut a block west to Park, she'd have to retrace her steps. She decided the change of pace was worth it. To her disappointment, the holiday displays on the parklike medians had also been removed. But the broad street with its massive residential buildings felt peaceful in spite of the flocks of yellow taxis zipping past. Without the distraction of commerce and passersby, she began to think about her mission and felt nervous for the first time. The gentle touch of butterflies fluttered in her abdomen. Worst-case scenarios played in her head. What if she couldn't find the house? What if nobody answered the door? What if Emmie slammed it in her face? It was absurd to let such minor social concerns frighten her, but what she called codependency magnified them to the point of dread. Anybody in Al-Anon would understand, but anybody outside it would think she was nuts.

A childhood incident suddenly flashed through her head. She had become almost apologetic because her family had been so loving. Her memories were so benign compared to those of Jimmy and Bruce and almost everybody she knew these days. But children didn't need trauma to agonize. She had been shy. Too shy to venture down the block alone to sell Girl Scout cookies to the neighbors, she had panicked at the thought of having to confess to her Brownie troop leader that she had sold none. So her mother had stuffed her into the cocoa brown uniform, clapped the felt beanie on her head, and escorted her from door to door. She couldn't have been more than eight years old, since Brownies "flew up" to become green-clad Scouts at nine or ten. Her mother had been part of the problem as well as part of the solution—a paradox that had recurred often in the many years since. She must remember to tell her therapist. She had a sudden visceral memory of the terror with which she had climbed each stoop and pushed the bell. When the lady of the house appeared—one of the not-yet-dying breed of housewives—her mother would push her forward and say firmly, "This little girl has something to say to you." Well, if she couldn't think what to say in her first attempt at sleuthing, she could always try asking, "Would you like to buy a box of Girl Scout cookies?"

She had no trouble finding the number. The block itself had a vast luxury apartment building on the Park Avenue corner, a high-rent florist at the corner on Lex, and a row of well-kept brown-stones in between, along with a trio of short, slim Federal-style architectural gems and a couple of broader white stone town houses. It was precisely the kind of street she liked to venture down from time to time, pretending for a brief period that her life had gone quite differently. The address she wanted was an impec-cable little carriage house three stories high, the brick sandblasted so that not one speck of urban grit adhered to it. The single en-trance sat level with the street: a heavy hardwood door gleaming with what might be hand-rubbed oil, and a brass knocker in the shape of a lion's head, bright with polish. The windows sparkled like a diamond-hung grande dame at a charity ball.

"I feel inferior already," Barbara said to the door, then glanced hastily around to make sure no one had heard. No one had. This kind of block discouraged pedestrians.

Through a diamond pane in the door, Barbara could see another door to the right and a flight of carpeted stairs going up straight ahead. Two brass bells, the lower one labeled DOCTOR'S OFFICE, glinted invitingly. Barbara rang the upper one.

The butterflies flapped alarmingly as she waited for some kind of response, half-hoping no one would come to the door. Afraid they wouldn't. Afraid they would. Afraid of whoever it might be. Afraid of making a fool of herself. Codependency really was irrational. Did she think she'd get demerits? What was the worst that could happen? Why on earth had she volunteered to do this? Why didn't she just walk away? She rang again.

Peering through the glass, she saw someone clattering down the stairs, or at least moving at a rate that would have been clattering if the carpet hadn't been so thick and the front door so heavy. It looked like a child—or rather, a young boy. He was tall enough to peer back at her, putting them eye-to-eye. She leaped back, thinking just too late that if there had been a stoop, she would have fallen off backward. Making eye contact through the glass from a slightly safer distance, she produced a sickly grin that she hoped made her look harmless. Two locks that sounded like they meant business clicked, and the door opened about a foot, leaving a heavy chain in place. The boy's face looked out at her. Oh help! she thought. Curtain going up.

"Hi. Do you think I could speak to your mother? Um, it's personal."

The boy looked at her, evidently trying, like any sophisticated New York child, to assess whether she might be a Jehovah's Witness. He appeared to be about fourteen, rather frail in build, with pale, smooth skin, very fine mouse brown hair, and dark brown eyes with startlingly long lashes. His small mouth was sculpted in an old-fashioned bow shape that made him look sweet and faintly epicene.

As he and Barbara stared at each other, a woman's voice wafted down the stairs.

"Brandy? Who is it?"

"I'm not sure, Mother," he called back. The term struck Barbara as oddly formal and very East Side. Anyone she knew would have said Mom or Ma. "Uh, wait a minute."

Barbara flapped her hands out to indicate she wasn't going anywhere. He ran swiftly up the stairs. After a period of whispers and muttering, he came running down again.

"What is it about, please?"

"It's, um, personal." She felt excruciatingly embarrassed. How did Lord Peter Wimsey do it? They probably took one look at his aristocratic face and told him anything he wanted to know. "It's, um, about her brother."

A look she couldn't read flitted across his face. He whirled and galloped up the stairs again. More muttering. Then a woman appeared at the head of the stairs. She must have sent the boy back in. Barbara heard the upper door close. The woman descended the stairs at a dignified pace. From four steps up, she looked at Barbara inquiringly.

"May I help you?"

"Mrs. Weill?"

She had the same fine hair and sweetly sculpted mouth as the boy. She wore a white silk blouse that looked like it wouldn't dare to show a stain or wrinkle and a beautifully fitting charcoal gray suit in a soft, finely woven wool from undoubtedly expensive sheep. Diamond studs, big enough to emit a significant twinkle but not big enough to call vulgar attention to her ears, framed an oval face touched with perfect, almost imperceptible makeup. Her well-sculpted legs were swathed in equally near-invisible panty hose, her feet clad in black leather pumps that looked as if they would rather have died than become scuffed. Barbara marveled not only at the outfit, but that she had evidently put it on just to hang out at home. When Barbara hung out at home, she wore sweats and bunny slippers. Thoroughly rattled, she had only one coherent thought. If she didn't say something fast to explain and justify her presence, she would sink through the sidewalk and into the ground right there on the spot.

"Mrs. Weill, I'm so sorry to bother you. I was—that is, I'm a friend of your brother." Well, she could have been. And Guff wasn't around to contradict her. "I hope you don't mind. If I could just talk to you a few minutes? I'm really very sorry." Always sorry, Barbara thought, whether or not it's appropriate. Sorry when somebody steps on my foot or cuts me off in traffic. Emmie Weill looked a little puzzled but not unapproachable or too terribly surprised. Belatedly, Barbara realized that for once her apology was appropriate. She had just offered the woman condolences for her brother's death. "I'm *very* sorry about Godfrey, very. Oh, I'm Barbara Rose."

"That's very kind of you. Would you care to come in, Ms. Rose?" She slipped the chain off the door.

Yes! "Thank you so much." Barbara took a giant step across the threshold before she could change her mind. As they climbed the stairs, it occurred to her that if Emmie knew Guff had been in and out of AA, she was likely to think Barbara was probably a fellow alcoholic. And how do you feel about that? she asked herself, posing the counselor's favorite question. Like most clients, she found it hard to answer.

Ten minutes later, she sat perched on the edge of a tapestry-covered wing chair, sipping tea—Earl Grey with lemon—from a translucently thin porcelain cup. In the other hand, an inch or two below the cup, she held a saucer. Barbara could not remember the last time she had had tea in a cup that had a saucer. She would have liked to turn it over and read the label, but she had higher priorities than satisfying her curiosity. For whatever reason, Emmie was willing to talk to her, and she didn't want to screw it up.

"Guffy was always wild," Emmie said. "Even as a child, he seemed to have no brakes. He was always going too far, dreaming too ambitiously, taking too many chances. He discovered drinking in prep school, and I'm afraid he started going too far with that immediately. Unfortunately, the family didn't have the means to stop him."

"You mean he had his own resources?" Barbara probed delicately. If she knew one thing from reading too many novels, it was that the upper classes considered it rude to talk openly about money.

"Well, yes," said Emmie apologetically, as if it were Barbara who was bound to think her rude. "I'm afraid there was a great deal of bitterness in the family about that."

" 'Bitterness'?"

"Guffy was my grandfather's favorite, and my sisters were afraid that he was squandering resources that they felt should eventually go to them. Guffy was unlikely to marry, you see, so of course he had no direct heirs."

"And you?" Barbara asked gently. Why was Guff unlikely to marry? Could he have been gay after all? Or did she mean because of the alcoholism? Alcoholics did marry, as 28 million children of alcoholics could attest.

"I didn't care about that," she said passionately. Her eyes filled with tears. "It was wrong of them to put pressure on him like that! Even if he did threaten to—but I'm sure it was only teasing. He knew how to agitate them, and I'm afraid it amused him. But it was wrong of them to give up on him. I couldn't bear to turn my back on him completely. He had done some things that were unforgivable. Utterly unforgivable. My husband forbade me to see him again. I knew—for the children's sake—but—I'm sorry." She dabbed at her eyes with a handkerchief edged with lace. Probably handknotted by arthritic little old ladies in some French village, Barbara thought. I feel guilty, she added mentally, so I try to distance myself by making smart-ass comments in my head.

"It must have been hard for you." It wasn't difficult to project what one school of therapy called "unconditional positive regard." Emmie was obviously a nice woman, and she was in a lot of pain.

"The first time he tried to stop drinking, he invited me to a family weekend at the facility. It was a lovely place, in Minnesota."

Barbara nodded. Minnesotans in recovery called their state "the treatment capital of the United States."

"They said I had to stop enabling." Barbara had heard this many times in her counseling career, in tones ranging from indignant to self-flagellating. She had said it herself when Jimmy first got sober. "I only wanted to help him!" Emmie sounded distressed and frustrated, although her voice was so gentle that the words lacked force, like a spent wave on a beach. "I only wanted to see him! He was my brother, and I loved him. And now he's gone!" She blew her nose hard on the elegant handkerchief. The tears ran freely, and so did her mascara, not lightening her lashes appreciably but leaving, Barbara thought distractedly, what Jimmy called "little Boris Karloffs" under her eyes.

"Emmie," she said impulsively, "would you like to go to a meeting?"

THIRTEEN

It was three in the morning, and I wanted a drink. I sat on the kitchen floor with a bag of potato chips and a box of Oreo cookies in my lap. I thought maybe I could resist the booze by substituting junk food. Now I couldn't stop eating, but I still wanted a drink. One, and then another and another and another. I was doing what I was supposed to do. I went to a meeting every day. I even sat down and listened a lot of the time. I admit I hadn't raised my hand to speak yet. It just wouldn't go up. One of the temp agencies I'd visited had said they were quite sure they'd be able to call me with something within a day or two. So I didn't have to worry about where the rent or my cigarettes would come from. I even made an appointment with the dentist. Recovering alcoholics always say their teeth were fine until they got sober.

Tonight, I had reviewed my whole life. I couldn't do that when I drank, and I didn't enjoy it now. It made me feel bleak. For a guy my age with the brains I'd like to think I have, I hadn't accomplished much. Nor was I eager to change. I'd rather scream and bang my head against the wall. I could think of nothing but that caressing slither of liquid fire running down my throat and my esophagus. What a dumb thing to be enslaved to! Fermented grain. I ask you.

It had worked better when I didn't need so much of it. When I didn't have anything to lose except a few years' time that I would probably have dicked around with anyway, the way most young guys do. Lately, booze had taken me not to Pluto but to Purgatory: a nasty, boring vestibule to Hell. Pain had faded to dullness and futility. I wanted out. I wanted a drink with an agony of desire. Now.

How could I stand the boredom of sobriety? I couldn't even stand the boredom of being a drunk. When someone in the meeting said in chipper tones, "Hi, I'm Pollyanna, I'm a grateful recovering alcoholic," I wanted to barf. I had to admit that Jimmy seemed pretty happy. I had watched him closely for the past fifteen years, trying to decide if what he had was worth shooting for. But Jimmy is the right kind of terminal loner. He's 100 percent content with his own company at any time. He finds so many weird things interesting and amusing. And he isn't even alone. He has Barbara. He has the many millions of people who use the Internet. He even has all the people in history who are just as vivid to him as if they weren't long dead. I'd never stayed sober long enough to confirm it, but I had an awful feeling I was the wrong kind of terminal loner. That would be the kind who experiences loneliness as a black and endless void reeking of despair.

I'd always said my buddy Jack Daniel's kept me from ever being lonely. But who was I kidding? Oh, right. Myself. Denial, that well-known river in Egypt. Denial is to alcoholism as pustules are to the Black Plague. Unavoidable. As I sat there on the floor with crumbs all over me, an empty bag and an empty box spilling out of my lap, and physically, emotionally, and spiritually nowhere to go, I felt a wave of sheer terror wash over me. I've never felt anything quite like it. Then it felt as if something really big and dull and heavy that existed both inside of me and all around me, as big as the whole damn universe, went *thud*. A hand that didn't feel like mine reached out to the phone, which was miraculously within reach. Somebody else's fingers dialed Jimmy's number. And a voice that wasn't mine said, "Jimmy? Hey, man. I think I just hit bottom."

Jimmy thought a recovery job would do me good. He didn't consider finding Guff's killer a job, either. Barbara, on the other hand, thought a toe in the corporate world might lead eventually to a whole foot or even a leg in the door of Guff's family's business. My first temp job took me way downtown to Wall Street. It was mostly typing and filing, though they love to have a guy around to make the coffee. I decided to hit a meeting on my lunch hour. A church or two survive among the temples to Mammon. As every recovering alcoholic knows, every church comes with a basement. And every church basement is honeycombed with meeting rooms that can be rented out to fill the clerical coffers. Did you think AA meetings take place in crypts? That we drink our coffee and tell our sordid stories perched on stone sarcophagi?

The first step of AA says we are powerless over alcohol and, by implication, everyone and everything outside ourselves. After a long morning in a busy corporate law office, I needed a reminder that I was powerless over temperamental partners and frenzied associates. I also began to appreciate another spiritual slogan you hear a lot around the rooms: "This, too, shall pass." One reason I had put up with temping for so long was my continual desire for whatever was going on to pass. Another was that I was too unreliable for a permanent job.

I slipped into a packed room about fifteen minutes late. It looked even more crowded because everybody was bundled into their outer clothes. This church seemed to be economizing on fuel. It was a more than nippy day, with temperatures in the twenties. I spotted a narrow slot between two women who looked as if the space they took up might be 50 percent feathers. Slithering into it, I found the one on my right was my friend Maureen. Mo. She gave me a sidelong look and a brief smile and returned her attention to the speaker.

"So after spending eighty thousand dollars on law school tuition, here I am working as a paralegal in the same firm where I once dreamed of making partner, and you know what? I'm grateful."

I heaved what turned out to be a loud sigh. I couldn't help it. Mo stuck out an elbow and nudged me sharply in the ribs. This taking sobriety seriously was uphill work. They tell you to "identify, don't compare," but sometimes it was really, really hard. Jimmy always said that if I started showing up on time for meetings, I would hear the beginning of the speaker's story, the part about all the stupid things he did while he was drinking and drugging. Maybe he had a point.

The happy paralegal wound up his qualification. I wondered what firm he worked at. Maybe I could temp there instead of where I was, a place more notable for scowls and snarls than expressions of blissful gratitude.

Everybody patted their hands together in polite applause, much of it muffled by gloves and mittens. I managed to space out through all the shares. It wasn't a long meeting. Because everybody was on their lunch hour, people came and went constantly. Now the room was emptying out. Mo turned to me.

"Time for coffee? My boss is out this afternoon, so no one's watching the clock on me for once."

"Sure. I'm temping, so they're paying me by the hour, and my minutes come pretty cheap."

Wall Street becomes one big wind tunnel in the winter. We walked briskly to the nearest place, the kind of cafeteria where you can get a latte and a gourmet sandwich for more than you really want to pay. The amenities included paper plates, no service, and Formica tables filmed with spills and crumbs from the previous occupants. Mo grabbed a table and used a handful of paper napkins to wipe it off while I got us coffee. Real drunks don't drink latte.

Going out for coffee after a meeting is a big tradition. You're supposed to learn to socialize without booze or your drug of choice. You're supposed to stop isolating and build a social network. You're supposed to have a normal conversation. You have to live one day at a time. But you don't have to keep saying it like a parrot. Jimmy has great sobriety, and he's just as likely to tell you the difference between an arbalest and a trebuchet as "Let go and let God."

"Speaking of God," I said to Mo. "Not God God. God the guy." From what I could tell, if anyone had tried to stop him from using the G word as his AA name, they'd failed.

Mo looked uncomfortable.

"You knew him?" Stalling.

"I was in detox with him." I went for shock value. "I was there when he died."

"Such a sad thing," she said flatly. Flat wasn't at all like the Mo I knew. She was usually more like all lit up or in the depths of despair. Maybe she had bipolar disorder, like Laura. Manic depressive. Maybe she was on too much lithium.

"I heard you were an item."

"With God? Hardly!"

"Someone you had a resentment against?"

"I said my share of prayers for his health and happiness," she said.

You're supposed to pray for anyone you resent. You ask a Higher Power to give them all the good things you want for yourself. But you don't have to mean it. On those terms, even I might try it some time. You've got to love AA.

"Can I ask you something?"

She looked wary.

"Did you by any chance see him recently? Since New Year's?"

"I've got to get going." She stood up and gathered her things together. "It was nice talking with you. Good luck with your sobriety."

Well, that was a big success. I guess I needed some more practice in socializing.

"Can I phone you?" I called after her.

But she was already gone.

Jimmy and I sat in a meeting on the Upper West Side, not far from his apartment. We were in the front. He got me up there by telling me the meeting started fifteen minutes sooner than it really did and getting there before me. He spent most of the extra time reminding me that I was a recovering alcoholic with about two minutes of sobriety, not a private eye. I needed to put first things first. Another slogan.

"Closure!" I seized on one of Barbara's favorite words. "I need closure on this business in the detox so I can move on." With more sincerity, I added, "You weren't there, Jimmy. I saw the guy die. Hell, I liked him. I think about it when I can't sleep, and I'm sleeping lousy. I can't imagine why I haven't gone back on the sauce yet, except that I don't want to hear what you'd have to say about it."

"That never stopped you before."

People drifted in and came up to say hello. For someone who

never came out from behind his computer, Jimmy knew everybody. And then the meeting started, and we couldn't talk.

The speaker that night was really funny. The room rocked with laughter as he recounted one hilarious near-death experience after another. Trust me, if you were a recovering alcoholic you would know this is not an oxymoron. At one point, I went off into a reverie about being the one up there getting the laughs. I sure had the material. When I was a kid, for a while I wanted to be a stand-up comic. But when I grew up, my drinking put the kibosh on the standing up part of it. Jimmy must have remembered, because he leaned over and whispered, "This could be you."

"Right," I whispered back. "I've already got the stories; all I need are the ninety days."

"And there I was," the speaker said, "with my two-hundred-dollar pants on one side of the sliding doors and me on the other." Everybody roared. And that wasn't even the punch line.

He finished to prolonged applause. Then came the break. I turned to Jimmy. Jimmy nodded at the speaker, what you could see of him through the crowd surrounding him. He said, "His name is Glenn. Go up and get his number."

I made a "Who, me?" face at him. It didn't do any good.

"You know you need a sponsor. It can't be me, and you're not going to be able to work with someone you think is a gloomy Gus or a Big Book thumper. You've got to start somewhere. Having someone's phone number doesn't commit you to anything. It might even keep you from waking me up in the middle of the night sometime. Go on. You don't have to have a conversation. Just get the number." He gave me a little shove.

I got the number. Then the meeting started again. I felt I'd earned a cup of terrible coffee and a few Oreos. Anyhow, one of Jimmy's friends had taken my seat. Jimmy looked around for me until he made eye contact. He stuck out his index finger, made a circle in the air above his watch with it, and pointed at the door. In other words, meet him after the meeting. I stood up straight and saluted. Then I slumped against the back wall, sipping at the toxic muck in my Styrofoam cup. At least it had caffeine in it, so it trumped detox coffee.

After the meeting, Jimmy made his way through the chattering crowd, detouring around hugging couples and groups trying to decide where to go for coffee. He reached me just as Glenn, strolling past, caught my eye and asked if I wanted to join a bunch of them at the coffee shop around the corner.

"Go," said Jimmy in my ear.

"You coming, Jim?" Glenn asked.

"Not tonight. Bruce will; we just need a minute." Glenn moved on as Jimmy turned to me and added, "I told Barbara I'd be back right after the meeting, but I want to give you something." We went with the flow, literally, moving with the current of people out the door, past the clot of smokers, and onto the sidewalk. "I knew you and Barbara were not going to be talked out of this, so I did a little research for you." He handed me a couple of index cards on which he'd scrawled a list of Internet addresses.

"URLs," Jimmy said. "I found them for you, but you, my son, are going to do the reading. You said your friend had a trust, and now that he's dead, he also has an estate. First, you're going to see if he had a will. If he did, you're going to see what's in it, who benefits from his death. If not, we're still going to be able to figure out who inherits. And then there are the terms of the trust. Someone scoops the pot on that, too; that kind of money doesn't just disappear if the beneficiary dies."

"I don't have to do any hacking?" I asked suspiciously. "One, you know I don't know how. And two, I'm damned if I'll go to jail for playing sorcerer's apprentice. Especially, as you so neatly put it, with two minutes of sobriety."

"Nope. All this stuff is public record now that he's dead. Well, I did get a little creative. I wanted to see if I could check out how much bread we were talking about. You don't want to know what I did and how I did it, and I didn't even write it down. The less lyin', cheatin', snoopin', and breakin' the law I do, the less amends I have to make. But we're talking a couple million bucks easy. More if the economy improves, since some of it's definitely invested for growth. More than enough to motivate anyone who was up for it if Guff kicked the bucket. So the next step is to find out who that was. Or who-all they were, as the case may be."

"Are you volunteering me?" I didn't really mind. For someone who I knew didn't want anything to do with it, Jimmy had already done a lot. "Two million sounds like a lot of money to me." A lot of bottles, a lot of grams, a lot of ounces or vials or tabs. Or on the other hand, a lot of living that Guff would never get to do.

"One step at a time, bro." Jimmy clapped me on the shoulder. He nodded toward the direction he would be going, away from the coffee shop.

I guessed I was committed to meeting Glenn and his friends. The thought of even beginning to get to know somebody new well enough to maybe ask him to sponsor me gave me a flutter in the gut. It made me a lot more nervous than the idea of plunging into cyberspace to look for a possible killer. I'd known Jimmy forever. We had a friendship I didn't have to work at. We were in each other's bones. As for Guff, well, we'd washed up together on the same spit of an island. Fellow survivors for a while. I guess when you're clinging to a life raft, trying to keep the water out of your nose for one more breath, you don't worry about what kind of impression you make. It's okay if your underwear is ripped. Or gone. But here I was on dry land, in more ways than one. And the only other friend I'd ever had, not counting women, was booze.

"Oh, by the way," said Jimmy, turning back. He screwed up his face in a lopsided Columbo leer, just good enough that I got it. Jimmy and I had watched a helluva lot of TV together over the years. "Barbara's met the sister. Better than met." He beamed with what would be uxorious pride if those two would ever say the hell with it and get married. "She took her to a meeting."

"An AA meeting? I don't get it."

"Nope." Jimmy grinned. "An Al-Anon meeting. They'll be telling each other their life stories in no time."

It took me five days and more hours at the downtown law firm than I would have chosen to spend. I couldn't do anything personal on the Internet while the lawyers, the paralegals, or the full-time secretaries were around. I needed the job, not just for use of the computer but for the nice paycheck that went along with it. One of the best things about temping is that you don't stand or fall by how you get along with any one set of people you meet along the way. But I couldn't afford to alienate the agency that had sent me there by getting kicked out or complained about. There were plenty of temp agencies, but not that many that thought Bruce Kohler was not only a crackerjack word processor but a reliable guy.

Shorn of the legalese, the information I found about Guff's estate meant the family got the money. The sister Barbara had met, Emily Brandon Weill (Mrs. Samson Weill), and her son Brandon both figured in the trust, which came from a grandfather, Maxwell Brandon, Guff's mother's father. Guff's parents were cousins. His father's father was Godfrey Brandon Kettleworth Sr., so the Brandon connection on the paternal side went a generation back. Guff's paternal great-grandmother had been a sister of Maxwell, the one with the big bucks. It was confusing, and I got confused. I used up many pieces of paper making little diagrams to keep it all straight.

Luckily, the office had stocked its computers with fancy programs for making graphs and charts. Afterward, Jimmy told me he had state-of-the-art genealogy software on his computer at home. But hey, he wouldn't want to spoil my fun. I know the way his mind works. He thought exercising my brain would speed up the recovery of my faculties as the neurons dried out, or whatever it is they do in early sobriety.

Emmie's two younger children weren't mentioned. They probably hadn't been born when the trust was established. The will might have covered unborn children, but it didn't. Maybe the whole gang of them figured Guff would straighten up once he'd sown enough wild oats. Something they feed wild horses? I was a wild barley man myself.

The other two sisters also benefited. Frances was the one in Ohio. I found the address. Her last name was Standish. The husband seemed to be a history professor, and she figured in various social pages as Mrs. Henry Standish. The WASP charity circuit might be the only place in America, barring maybe a down-home church or two, where married women still tote around their husbands' names. Or am I being provincial? They say New Yorkers don't have the foggiest idea what America is really like.

Frances, out there in the heartland, had two sons, Charles Gregory and Robert Miles. Jimmy pointed out that that could have been either a literary reference or an actual claim of descent from the historical Miles Standish. The original Standish must have married somebody after the legendary John Alden, as Jimmy put it in his inimitable style, "copped this broad Priscilla from right under Miles's snoot." He was kidding when he used the word *broad*. Otherwise, Barbara would have sicced her coven on him. Er, her women's group.

The third sister was Lucinda Kettleworth. Same last name as

Guff's. Unmarried, or married without changing it. Either way, she didn't have any kids. At least the trust didn't mention any.

Guff did have a will. The beneficiaries were the same, except Emmie's two younger children, Lucille and Duncan, were mentioned by name. With the possible exception of Emmie, none of these people had been speaking to him. He'd told me so himself. He might have intended to change his will. I remembered his saying he'd made a few calls on that last day out. He probably wouldn't have gone to the attorney whose name I had here, since he figured not only in Grandpa Brandon's trust and Guff's will but on every family document Jimmy had found. Guff would have wanted a lawyer who was in nobody's corner but his. No new will had been executed. The one that was now in probate was eight years old, made when Emmie's youngest was a baby. But what if he'd taken steps toward changing it and mentioned it to the wrong person? That would be anyone who could expect to get cut out.

On the other hand, Emmie was the only one he was speaking to. So Emmie was the relative he was most likely to have visited that day. I wondered how her husband was fixed for money. And how badly, comparatively speaking, he got along with Guff. It was also possible that Guff had deliberately visited one or more of the relatives he resented most to tell them they could kiss his money good-bye. Or on the other hand, he could have gone in a conciliatory frame of mind and then quarreled with them. As far as I knew, he'd been planning to stay sober. He'd known you weren't exactly supposed to cling to being a son of a bitch if you wanted it to work. But he still could have gotten mad all over again. That might have made him want to lash out at them. He could have told them what they'd lose. Would it have made someone want to kill him? Someone with the same crappy impulse control as an addict and with immediate access to some kind of poison?

It couldn't have been the sister in Ohio. Were her sons in New

York? What did they do? How prosperous were they? Had Guff said one was a lawyer? I wasn't sure. Barbara had mentioned a study that proved alcoholics remember only 10 percent of what they hear during the first week of sobriety. One of the Standish brothers might be broke. He might be a perennially out-of-work actor moonlighting as an underpaid waiter. New York was full of those. Or a stockbroker whose firm had gotten busted by the SEC.

I couldn't help wondering if there were any other addicts in the family. Whether it's alcohol, gambling, coke, or heroin, there's nothing like an addiction to make money flap its flimsy wings and fly away. In Debtors Anonymous, they saw high finance as just a socially acceptable form of gambling or compulsive spending. And if they still had debtors' prisons, kids with college loans would waste away in those long before they could get their first job. Jimmy knew all about debtors' prisons. The bottom line: Even the rich, like Guff's family, were not immune to need or greed. The annotated bottom line: Would they kill to keep it?

FOURTEEN

"**Eugene of Savoy**," **Jimmy said.**

"Yes, dear," Barbara said.

I stayed out of it.

"Military genius. Louis the Fourteenth wouldn't give him a commission, so he went over to the Hapsburgs and spent the rest of his career whipping Louis's ass all over Europe. The fucking duke of Marlborough gets the credit for Blenheim, but he wouldn't have won without Eugene."

"Yes, dear."

Jimmy gets so excited when he talks about history. Luckily, Barbara thinks it's cute, even when she pretends to be—or actually is—bored. I'd been picking up information cheap when it interested me and letting the rest roll off my back for many years. Take what you like and leave the rest, as the program says.

"There's hardly anything written about him in English," said Jimmy, scrolling down what looked like an endless list. "Maybe I should write a book."

It took awhile, but eventually she got him into the present century, and then we were able to pursue the topic of our own personal little mystery. Barbara, blast the girl, thought it was highly amusing that Jimmy had gotten me to do the scut work of scrolling through the fine print on endless pages on the Web. I had spent a lot more of my life than Jimmy avoiding anything that might remotely be called boring. Not that I felt bored these days. Barbara thoroughly approved of how emotionally engaged I was, and even Jimmy was impressed. I knew because I eavesdropped. I went to the kitchen for a glass of club soda. It still seemed peculiar to me to open a refrigerator, especially mine or Jimmy's, and not see any beer. When I came back out, they were talking about me.

"Jimmy, do you think Bruce is different this time around?"

"What do you mean?"

"You know—he cares more. Have you noticed how he calls him Guffy when he's feeling tender toward him?" I hadn't realized I did that, but she was right. "Seeing him die like that really rattled him. And look at the way he's taking on these assignments you've been giving him. Maybe he's really getting it this time. Maybe he's finally going to get sober for real. What do you think?"

"I think," said Jimmy severely, "you need to stop daydreaming about Bruce's sobriety and get on with your own life. Isn't that what you're supposed to have learned in Al-Anon?"

"It's not as simple as that," Barbara said indignantly. "You alcoholics are lucky. You put a cork in the bottle, and that's that."

"Yeah, right."

"I didn't mean that it was easy. Would you really want me to give up managing other people's lives completely?"

"Yes."

"And then what would I do for fun?" she demanded. She came up behind him, flung her arms around his neck until he squawked, and dropped a kiss on the top of his head. One thing about Jimmy spending all his time at that computer, he was a sitting duck when she needed him to be. Before they could turn it into a necking session, I shoved off the doorway I'd been lurking behind and propelled myself into the room.

"Fun?" I said. "Did I hear fun? Are we having any yet?"

"We were about to," said Barbara, "but never mind."

"You must have had fun," Jimmy told me. "I gave you all those Web sites to check out."

"Your fun is my damn homework," I growled.

"You did it, then." Barbara sounded surprised. I was surprised myself. I was becoming quite the busy beaver. "What did you find out?"

I slung myself onto their old leather couch and stretched out full length. I'd spent many a night passed out on it before Jimmy stopped drinking and decided he'd better draw some boundaries.

"For one thing, I've located the Standishes. The Ohio sister's sons."

"Guff's grown-up nephews. Where are they?"

"In New York."

"Great!" Barbara crowed. "Did you find out what they do?"

"One is a stockbroker who was interviewed in one of those online magazines a couple of years ago, talking about the joys of day trading."

"I knew it!" she said triumphantly. "In other words, an upmarket gambler. Too much is not enough. And the other?"

"An attorney."

"What kind?"

"Corporate. Big downtown firm."

"The kind of place you might wangle a temp assignment," Barbara said thoughtfully.

"Oh, thanks a heap," I said. "Feel free to auction me off."

Barbara ignored my feeble rebellion.

"Do they live in Manhattan?"

"Nope, one in Westchester, the other out in Nassau County. Larchmont and Garden City." Both high-rent suburbs. Expensive lifestyles. Prone to embarrassment by a black sheep uncle, maybe.

"Genetics being what it is," Jimmy pointed out, "one or both of them might be functional alcoholics themselves. Four martinis with lunch and knock back a few more before you go home, but your employer still thinks your performance is great."

"Or the day trader could be doing coke," Barbara added. "I'll get Emmie Weill to tell me about them."

"Are you pretending to be that woman's friend?" Jimmy demanded. He was so upset, he took his hands completely off the keyboard.

"I'm not pretending," she protested. "Her alcoholic brother just died, she's hurting, I took her to a meeting. What was I going to do?"

Jimmy shook his head. "You're the one who's always talking about boundaries."

"I know, I know," Barbara admitted. "But how are we supposed to find out anything without getting to know any of the people involved? Besides, Emmie really likes Al-Anon."

"So you're really just doing a good deed." Jimmy shook his head. "I don't know, petunia."

Petunia? Since I'd started spending more time with them again, I had an inkling that Jimmy and Barbara talked an awful lot of baby talk together when nobody was around. Sometimes it slipped out in public. Maybe they didn't consider being with me "in public." The thought cheered me considerably. Anyhow, Barbara rolled right on.

"It's a great place to hear that it's possible to love someone without going down the tubes with them. Emmie seems to be one of those codependents who can always find someone who needs rescuing. She's like a magnet for other people's pain. She's told me a lot about Guff's great promise as a kid and his road to destruction, all the way to the Bowery and then the morgue. She also talks a lot about her older son, they call him Brandy. She worries about him because he's become very withdrawn."

"How so?"

"Isolated, uncommunicative. Not into sports, not interested in girls."

"Maybe he's drinking."

"He's fourteen!" Barbara protested.

Jimmy and I looked at each other. We had been fourteen when we chugged those first two bottles of Colt 45 that changed our lives forever.

Barbara went on talking about Emmie and her family.

"According to her, Brandy was Guff's favorite when he was younger, but they hadn't been close in recent years. She also went on about her husband, who isn't any kind of addict, as far as I can tell from what she says, but he sounds a lot like someone with a narcissistic personality disorder."

"And what's that in plain English?" I asked. "I can never keep them straight."

"A self-centered bastard who thinks the world owes him and who's never going to change."

"Oh, that," I said. "I know what those are."

"Meanwhile, back at the detox," Barbara said, "I finally saw the death certificate."

"That's good news, isn't it?" I sat up. Jimmy tilted his chair and peered around the computer to get a little closer to the conversation.

"It is," she said. "I had to do some fancy dancing to check Guff's chart again. But it was worth it. I guessed right: Dr. Bones signed it. It said acute gastritis and heart failure, which doesn't tell us anything. His family certainly hasn't questioned it. Emmie's made it clear that the rest of them didn't want to think about Guff once he started deteriorating physically, emotionally, and socially. And once he was dead, they just wanted him hustled out of the way."

"With dispatch," Jimmy said.

"Funeral?" I asked.

"He was cremated. Emmie confessed that she had the urn with his ashes in it up in the back of her closet, behind the hats, because her husband didn't want to see or hear about it. She seemed very embarrassed. I was glad she didn't offer to show me."

The family had refused an autopsy, though we didn't know who'd spoken most loudly against it. Maybe Emmie's husband, maybe someone else. We kicked it around for a while. If someone in the family had poisoned Guff and had the slightest doubt about whether they'd gotten away with it, that person would have jumped at the chance to make sure no expert examined the body. And the whole family went right along with it. Anyone who had no hidden agenda must have figured that the less known about Guff's condition at the end, the better. And cremation was the flambé on the cherries jubilee, so to speak. There went any evidence of poison. To make it even easier, Guff had specified in his will that he wanted to be cremated.

"Just as well," said Barbara. "Emmie says she was the only one who wouldn't have minded ending up next to him in the family mausoleum. Speaking of family, I still haven't met her husband."

"The plastic surgeon?"

"Yeah, Dr. Samson Weill. And I can't ask to meet him."

"Why not?" I asked.

"Anonymity," Jimmy said, looking at me as if I should have known.

"She's a program friend," Barbara added. "You know in AA or Al-Anon, it's just not done to be curious about each other's outside lives."

"So maybe you shouldn't have taken her to program," Jimmy said. "Not that I want to say I told you so."

"So don't," Barbara snapped. Visibly reining herself in, she said, "If she'd had an alcohol problem, you'd have offered to take her to a meeting. You know you would have, Jimmy."

"Yeah, I would have. Sorry, peach."

"It would still be a good idea to meet the guy," I said. "Get a sense of what Dr. Samson Weill is like."

"I have an idea," said Barbara. "Cut it out!" she added as we both groaned. "But I swore these words would never cross my lips."

"What words, poppet?" Jimmy asked. "Have I heard this one before?"

"I don't think so," she said. "It was my first act of moral courage, back when I was a fifteen-year-old Jewish girl in Queens. All the girls were doing it. I had to choose between being who I was—cultural pride, I guess—and the kind of looks the girls' magazines said would attract men. And I swore I'd never even say it, no less do it."

"What?" we asked simultaneously.

"Gentlemen," she said, "I am about to consider getting a nose job."

FIFTEEN

It took Barbara a week to get an appointment and seven minutes in the doctor's waiting room to confirm her diagnosis: Dr. Samson Weill was an egotistical bastard. He had all the earmarks of narcissism. Although his personality was hell on everyone around him, it felt just fine to him. Along with several other deeply embarrassed patients in his waiting room, she listened as, from behind the closed but not adequately soundproofed door of his office, he verbally annihilated his unfortunate secretary. She had allowed a patient into his presence before double-checking on that patient's insurance status. Barbara, ever the counselor, decided that the secretary's self-esteem would be in dire need of reconstructive surgery by the time he was through. She doubted that Dr. Weill kept staff for long.

As the abusive tirade rolled on, she sat meekly, hating herself for failing to rise and storm the arrogant son of a bitch's office. She wondered if the other waiting patients, all women, felt the same. When the doctor had roared himself to a standstill, the hapless secretary came stumbling out of his office holding an inadequate clump of tissues up to her face. She had a streaked blond fluff of shoulder-length hair and a face that would have been pretty if it hadn't been puffy from crying. An open white lab coat failed to hide a well-filled stretchy red top, a little black skirt that was both too short and too tight, and too much cheap jewelry. She looked very young.

The waiting patients tactfully kept their eyes cast down at the floor or glued to their magazines as she blundered across the room toward the coat closet. She snatched a faux-fur leopard-print coat from the closet, dropping several wire hangers on the floor in the process. Sneaking quick peeks as she pretended to read a month-old issue of *Vogue*, Barbara noticed that additional heavy wooden hangers were securely fastened to the metal bar they hung from, as if the doctor were afraid his patients would walk off with them. Anal retentive bastard, Barbara thought. The secretary fumbled with the coat for an endless couple of minutes before she succeeded in poking both arms in the sleeves, dropping gloves, tissues, and a bright red scarf in the process. Finally, she got herself out the door, no doubt heaving a sigh of relief.

Barbara hesitated, uncertain as to whether or not to follow her. Her plan had been to tell the doctor that she wanted to buy herself a more shapely nose. She would then engage him in a conversation digressive enough to lead to his late brother-in-law. With luck, she would get a sense of whether the doctor hated him and how likely it was that he had poisoned him. Barbara had great confidence in her powers of digression. She planned to back out before the point of actual surgery. But who was more likely to talk freely? An angry egomaniac just past volcanic eruption, or a disgruntled employee? Barbara patted her nose. Why even pretend she wanted to trade it in? Most of the women her age whom she knew who had had nose jobs in their teens had ended up with identical, unmistakable little pinched-off snouts with too much nostril showing. She hadn't even seen Dr. Samson Weill, but she had seen enough. She grabbed her bag and ran after the secretary.

At least she was easy to follow, thanks to all that leopard and red. Barbara caught up with her at the corner of Lexington Avenue.

"Uh, excuse me."

The young woman turned and looked at Barbara dully. Smudged makeup gave her the look of a raccoon with a hangover. Her nose ran copiously in spite of the fistful of sodden tissues she kept dabbing at it.

"Excuse me," Barbara repeated. "I'm sorry." Barbara told herself to get a grip. "Sorry to bother you. I was in there just now." She jerked her head back toward the doctor's office. "I was so mad at how he treated you that I decided I was damned if I'd go to him, so I came out to see if you were okay."

The young woman's face turned brick red. Evidently, she hadn't known everyone in the waiting room could hear him.

"Look, I'm really sorry." Barbara reached out and put a hand on her faux leopard-skin arm. "He has a very loud voice, and everybody in there thought he was being a real pig."

"Thanks." Her voice came out in a pitiful little wobble. "Thanks, that's nice of you. I don't know what to do."

"That's okay," Barbara said meaninglessly. "Look, I'm sorry, I don't know your name." Hard to believe, she thought, how firm and decisive I can be, sailing into a crowd of Bowery drunks and junkies with a clipboard. It must be the clipboard. She had always carried one, adopting it the first day of her internship on the advice of Sister Angel, who had called it "Dumbo's magic feather."

Still sounding embarrassed, the young woman offered her name. "Marlene."

"Look, Marlene, would you like to go for coffee? I think there's a place right around the corner." She smiled warmly. "I'm a good listener." That's true, she thought. And when I'm listening, I'm not apologizing.

"It's on the next block," Marlene said, her voice small and childish. Regressing, Barbara thought with professional acumen. She put her hand on Marlene's elbow to steer her. The secretary trotted along obediently beside her.

Once they were settled in a padded vinyl booth, it wasn't hard to get her talking about the doctor's family. Barbara had a steaming cup of coffee in front of her. Marlene had ordered hot chocolate topped with marshmallows—comfort food—and she fiddled with her spoon as she talked.

"She's a lot nicer than he is. I wouldn't mind if she came downstairs more often, but I don't blame her for staying away. He's got quite a temper. She's such a . . . well, a lady. She never sinks to his level. She does a lot of smoothing down, though. She's good at letting him have his way."

"A case of the yes dears?" Barbara suggested.

Marlene sniffled, blew her nose, and smiled for the first time.

"There's also a drunken brother-in-law. Her brother, not his. That poor woman, what a family. The drunk was in there"—she meant the office—"right after New Year's."

"Looking for a handout?" Barbara prompted, hoping to keep her going.

"It sounded more like he was threatening the doc."

" 'Threatening'?"

"I couldn't hear it all," she said ingenuously, "just mostly the doctor's side, and when he was yelling over the doctor's voice. Something about money, something he would sign or wouldn't sign?" She shook her head.

"When was that?" Barbara kept her tone as casual as she could. "After New Year's, you said?"

"It must have been the day after," Marlene said. "I had the holiday off." She had been busy taking the holiday decorations in the waiting room down when the doctor bellowed at her to bring in a pot of coffee.

"I'm surprised he gave him that much." Marlene sniffed again. "I've heard him telling the wife that he doesn't want her brother going near the children. The brother behaves a lot better than the doc does, if you ask me. So what if he drinks? The doc keeps all sorts of pills in his desk drawer and pops them whenever he feels like it. The pharmaceutical reps are always bringing samples, you know, and if they don't, he writes the scripts himself. Valium, codeine, Fioricet. Guess who has to go all the way to Madison to pick them up. On my lunch hour yet! God forbid I should run his errands on his time."

"The Valium doesn't calm him down any? You'd think it would."

Marlene giggled. "Actually, it does. The way he went off today, a little something from the pill drawer might have improved the situation. Same when the brother-in-law was here."

"He had one of his outbursts with the brother and still gave him a cup of coffee?"

"It was funny," she agreed. "Usually, the next step would be to throw him out. But he managed to calm himself down that time. Maybe he did open up that drawer. He made a big fuss over giving the brother-in-law his coffee just the way he liked it. He had me running back and forth with cream and sugar. That powdered stuff is good enough for me and the patients! But oh, no, it's got to be real half-and-half, and he sees him all the way out afterward with his arm draped around his shoulder as if they were the best of friends. The patients waited fifteen extra minutes for their appointments, but that's no problem as far as the doc is concerned. Speaking of which, I'd better be getting back."

"Are you sure you'll be okay?"

"No problem, this happens at least once a week. I go back, we make like nothing happened. I'm leaving, don't worry, but not until I get another job. Gotta pay down those credit cards. So I'm letting the doc cover my Christmas. And the time I spend going on interviews." She shrugged herself into the leopard coat and applied another coat of lipstick. "Thanks a lot for the coffee. Are you coming back for your appointment?"

"You know what?" Barbara massaged her nose reflectively. "I think I've decided to stick with the face I've got."

SIXTEEN

"**So what do you think?**" Barbara asked us. "Was it worth it?"

We were on our way to a meeting. Two meetings, in fact, that met at the same time in the same church and drew a lot of couples in recovery. Families, even. They had an Alateen meeting for the kids. I couldn't imagine what our lives would have been like if Jimmy and I had known about Alateen and been able to talk frankly about our drunken dads.

"To know if it's worth it, you have to know the price," Jimmy said. "What did your little talk with Marlene cost you?"

Barbara laughed.

"Just the arm and a leg they charge for two coffees—not even Starbucks latte or espresso, just plain old greasy-spoon joe in a thick white mug—in the East Sixties."

Jimmy draped his arm around her shoulders.

"I'm glad it didn't cost you your beautiful nose."

Barbara snuggled up to him with a little wriggle as they walked.

"The most wonderful guy in the world—he thinks my nose is beautiful. No, I got to keep my Ashkenazic schnozz."

"Your nose is beautiful," Jimmy said stoutly.

"And my mother thinks I should have picked a nice Jewish boy. They all go for blondes with thighs like Emmie Weill's and no nose at all."

"You've seen Emmie's thighs? When did this happen?"

"No, but I can tell. It's genetic."

"You always say I have no nose," said Jimmy fatuously.

Barbara reached up to caress his minimalist Irish snoot.

"You have a *good* no nose. Those shiksas have *bad* no nose. Noses."

"When you folks are quite through being terminally cute," I said, "maybe we can talk about what Barbara learned that's relevant to the murder."

"Okay, okay," Barbara said. "I wrote it all down afterward so I wouldn't forget." She fished in her bag and brought out a little lined notepad with a spiral binding. She flipped through its dog-eared pages. "Here it is. January second, Guff dropped in on Dr. Weill, who gave him a cup of coffee. Dr. Weill keeps psychotropics in his desk drawer. Marlene mentioned Fioricet and Valium. Fioricet is a headache pill with a barbiturate in it. Suggestive, isn't it?"

"Barbiturates can be lethal combined with alcohol," Jimmy said. We alkies know all about it. Ask us anything.

"The doctor could have hoped that Guff would drink," he added.

"But he didn't," I said. "Because if he had, they wouldn't have let him back into the detox, at least not without a fuss."

"I still think it's stupid," Barbara said, "to throw people out for noncompliance. They never want to take the revolving-door guys, even though those guys are their bread and butter. But I digress."

"When do you not?"

"Smile when you say that."

"I *am* smiling," Jimmy said.

If I had a dollar for every time I've heard the two of them do that routine, I wouldn't have to temp.

"Back to the murder, guys?" I pleaded.

"Valium by itself won't kill you," Barbara said, switching gears effortlessly. She'd had lots of practice.

"But it's cross-tolerant with alcohol," Jimmy said.

"Addiction docs know this," said Barbara, "but did Dr. Weill? He might have hoped it would trigger cravings and then relapse. If Guff got drunk, he wouldn't be organized enough to follow through on any plan he might have had to change his will, or whatever it was he threatened to do. My guess is that he would have cut the Weills off from any money he controlled, or at least tied it up so that Emmie but not Sam could get at it. But as a way of killing someone, it's a nonstarter."

"And Guff didn't drink that day," I said.

"That leaves codeine," Barbara said. "Marlene mentioned codeine, too. I'm not sure how much codeine is too much and or what's the worst it can do. I'll have to look it up. Or ask the psychiatrist at work. In any case, too much codeine for a chemical dependent might be a lot more than too much for someone nonhabituated, like me. How many pills can you dissolve in coffee with the recipient sitting right there? Unless Guff went out for a minute, to use the rest room, maybe, which Marlene would, naturally, not have mentioned to me."

"We've still got a lot of unanswered questions," Jimmy said.

"But more information than we started out with. And I managed"—Barbara grinned—"to do it without having to confront the doctor and get myself yelled at. And I saved my nose."

At the church door, we separated. Jimmy and I made our way to the big room where maybe a hundred alcoholics were celebrating one more day of sobriety. At the Al-Anon meeting, Barbara's luck held. Not only did she find Emmie there but Emmie actually raised her hand and shared. That is a big deal for a newcomer. I still hadn't done it myself, in spite of much prodding—they called it "encouragement"—from Jimmy. Barbara told us later what Emmie had said. Barbara thought murder trumped anonymity among the three of us. But Jimmy going along? Amazing. I guess he wanted me to stay sober so bad, he was willing to sacrifice even his beloved twelve-step principles. Humbling.

According to Barbara, Emmie said it was hard not to blame herself—not for her brother's death, but for the aftermath. She had let the family tidy him away because she couldn't bear the scene she knew her husband would make if she protested. The doc had been the most vehement in wanting to keep things quiet. It was exactly the information we'd wanted, and Emmie had actually told the whole meeting this. Evidently, Dr. Weill was averse to any noise he didn't make himself. She said enough to make it pretty clear that it was he who'd pushed the hardest to refuse the autopsy and whisk Guff right to the crematorium.

Now he had convinced the rest of them to put off any kind of memorial service indefinitely. That didn't make them guilty of anything but misplaced embarrassment. Like the rest of us, Guff must have been a lot more embarrassing when he was alive and drunk. But it sure sounded like Emmie's husband was the bad guy who didn't want any light at all cast on this unexpected death. Nobody gives advice at an Al-Anon meeting, as Barbara keeps telling us. But after the meeting, Emmie got a lot of sympathetic pats and murmurs and a few hugs from people who had learned the hard way that blaming yourself for everything doesn't help and isn't even good for you.

Emerging from our own meeting, Jimmy and I threaded our way through the crowd of mingling AA and Al-Anon members and moved as casually as we could toward Barbara. We figured out who Emmie was because Barbara hovered within six inches of her and warned us away with her eyes. Emmie looked fragile and lady-like and haunted.

It was an East Side meeting. Barbara had already told us that if Emmie was at the meeting, she would offer to walk her home. It was only a few blocks. So we trailed discreetly behind as Barbara waited for her outside the door and fell into step beside her. Once the crowd from the meeting dispersed, the streets were quiet. By stretching our ears just a little, we could hear their conversation.

"I hope you don't mind my asking," Barbara said. "I don't want to pry."

"The reluctant crowbar," Jimmy muttered to me. We went into what would have been a fit of the snickers if we hadn't had to keep quiet.

Barbara ignored us.

"How come your husband minded so much about your brother?" she asked. "Were they close? Had they been seeing a lot of one another right before or anything?"

Emmie was new enough to the program that she didn't realize that Barbara was not what she called "recovery side up" when she got gratuitously nosy.

"They never liked each other." Emmie sighed. "I wanted so much for them to be friends. But each thought the other was arrogant and prone to take advantage of me."

They had that right. We could see Barbara nod encouragingly and hear her zip the lip.

"Once Guffy's troubles got really bad, Sam didn't want anything to do with him. He didn't want him near the children, either. He and Guffy had one altercation that frightened me. I know it was about Brandy, my son, but neither of them would tell me what was said. Sam just insisted that he didn't want any of us communicating with Guffy in any way. I asked my son if he knew what they could have been talking about, but he said he had no idea." She sighed again. "Actually, he shrugged and went into his room. He didn't slam the door—that's not his way—but he closed it in such an excluding way. My little boy. He used to tell me everything."

Her voice faded off into a depressed murmur, and we missed the next couple of exchanges. Then she spoke more loudly.

"So of course I didn't tell him."

"Tell who, Brandy?"

"No. Sam."

"Tell him what?" Barbara asked. She pitched her voice to make sure we could hear. Emmie automatically increased the volume, too.

"That Guffy came by that afternoon," Emmie replied. "The day before he died."

"So the two of you had a chance to talk?"

"And had a cup of tea," Emmie added. "I had made fresh scones, but he said he wasn't hungry."

That struck me as sad. Guffy's failure to seize the moment and enjoy a final scone stood for all the failures of omission and commission of a lifetime.

"And he was sober," Barbara said. There are worse epitaphs than "He died sober."

"Yes."

Good. We'd needed that confirmed.

Emmie turned to Barbara impulsively. For a moment, it looked as if she might hug her. "I'm so grateful to you for introducing me to the program. I didn't understand before how important that was."

She paused and drew a sobbing breath.

"Crying," Jimmy mouthed at me.

"At least he wasn't drinking when he died. The children got to see him sober one more time. They were running in and out. Duncan, the little one, doesn't remember Uncle Guffy as he used to be, before all this started."

Ouch. I'm afraid I skipped the stage when anyone could overlook my drinking.

"Even Brandy said good afternoon," Emmie said. "He was a little sullen, but at least he was civil. I didn't know how much it would matter. I wasn't sure, after Guffy left, whether I ought to warn the children not to say anything to Sam. In the end, I left well enough alone. Now I wish they could somehow have had one last time together. Maybe they would have made peace."

The tears got away from her and started rolling down. We saw Emmie reach into her buttery kidskin Coach bag for a delicate little white handkerchief. No red bandanna up her sleeve for Emmie.

Barbara made soothing program noises.

"You did the best you could at the time. We're powerless over other people. This, too, shall pass."

It may be hard to believe anybody finds this trite stuff comforting. But people do. *We* do.

"The most important thing is that you loved him. And I bet it meant a lot to him that you didn't turn your back on him. You accepted him. He knew you loved him."

As we all walked on in silence, I thought about what we had heard. It seemed Guff had visited both his sister and his brother-in-law the day he died. First, tea and scones with Emmie and the kids. Then, on his way out, coffee in the doctor's office. And neither husband nor wife had told each other that the family black sheep had stopped by.

SEVENTEEN

"I'll make amends to Emmie as soon as this is over," Barbara said. "I'll never interfere in anybody else's business again."

Yeah, right.

"I'll never get anywhere near another murder."

Now, that I could go along with. I hadn't exactly planned on this one.

"I'll be really nice to Emmie, with no ulterior motive whatsoever, as long as she goes to Al-Anon. And if she quits the program, getting out of her life will be part of my amends."

"I know you will, pumpkin," said Jimmy soothingly.

Barbara can be a real fruitcake, but she tries very hard to work the steps.

"We still know next to nothing," Barbara said, "about Guff's other sisters."

Lucinda, the one who was still using her birth name, lived in New York. I found out the low-tech way—by looking her up in the phone book. She lived way west in Greenwich Village.

"How do I find out what Lucinda's into?" Barbara demanded.

Jimmy, hunched over the computer as usual, didn't even lift his fingers from the keyboard.

"Google her."

"Duh," Barbara said. "Shove over, let me do it."

"Just a second," Jimmy said, his fingers flying. "Let me finish this and save. Okay, here."

"Here's a bio," Barbara said about two minutes later. "Lucinda Kettleworth. Wow. Lucinda's been a busy girl. She's a tenured full professor of psychology at NYU. Can't lose her job, gets paid as well as anyone in academia, and, on top of that, she can walk to work. She's published scads of stuff. There's an instrument named for her, some kind of depression index."

"Instrument?" I asked. "Like an astrolabe or a speculum? For measuring depression?"

"No, silly, like a test."

I knew that. I was just jerking her chain.

"She's written a lot about depression in women," said Barbara, scrolling. "She has impressive feminist credentials."

"Depression and addictions can go hand in hand," Jimmy commented.

"Go together like a horse and carriage," I said.

"You'd think she would have had compassion for her alcoholic brother," said Barbara, "if she really knows about addictions."

"It usually doesn't work that way, my sweet," said Jimmy. While Barbara used the computer, he wandered restlessly through the room, looking indecisive and oddly naked.

"I know, I know," Barbara said. "I have a theory—don't groan, either of you!—that mental health professionals choose their field based on whatever way they happen to be screwed up, so that they can try to fathom the problem without having to admit they need help. That accounts for the prevailing belief, unfortunately based on reality, that many therapists are more or less nuts."

"So what's Lucinda's loony state? Depression?"

"We might know if we met her. She studies, she doesn't treat. Distances herself, but I don't know if that means she doesn't have to wallow in psychopathology or that she avoids personal connections. She could be schizoid, or a highly empowered woman with a healthy ego who doesn't give a hoot about her dysfunctional family. Since she's a feminist, I'd like to think she's cool. Like me." Barbara grinned. "But it doesn't necessarily follow."

"It could mean that she's mad at men," Jimmy pointed out. "That might color her feelings about her brother and his addiction."

"I want to meet her," Barbara said, "and not through Emmie. I don't want to blow my cover."

"Right," said Jimmy. "You don't want the Kettleworths connecting the dots."

Barbara had her elbows on the keyboard and was enjoying the conversation. When Jimmy noticed, he shoved her out of his chair and took over. He could search about a hundred times as fast as either Barbara or I could.

Like her sisters, Lucinda did a lot with fashionable charities. I don't quite get these thousand-bucks-a-plate dinners. Sure, they raise money for good causes. Why can't the rich folks just give the money to the causes? Anyhow, small world—Lucinda was on the board of BURS, for Bowery Urban Rehabilitation Services, the parent agency of our detox. Barbara had been doing her internship when they chose the name. They had tried a competition, with staff and clients suggesting alternatives and everybody voting. But the contest was hastily canceled when it became clear it was going to be a landslide in favor of Bowery Agency for Rehabilitation

Services—BARS. I wondered whether Lucinda's connection with BURS had anything to do with Guff ending up there. They weren't supposed to be speaking, but the Bowery is in walking distance of the Village. Lucinda was also on the board of ARFSU.

"What's ARFSU, Jimmy? Animal rights? It sounds like a dog sneezing."

"Let's Google it and see. Australian rugby, can't be that—oh, here it is. Aid to Refugees of the Former Soviet Union. Wonder why she's interested in that? BURS, I can understand, with alcoholism in the family. And they're both below Fourteenth Street."

A Manhattan urban legend: People who live in the Village never go uptown.

"What else is she involved in?"

"Feminist stuff, psychology stuff. And art museums."

"There's a lot of Russian art floating around these days. That could be the connection."

"I wish that thing could tell us if she saw her brother on January second," Barbara complained.

" 'That thing'?" said Jimmy, miffed, or at least mock-miffed. "It's a computer, not an oracle."

We had both heard that before.

Jimmy really could find anything in cyberspace. It took him no time at all to find a way for us to see Lucinda. She would be giving a public lecture in a few days. In the meantime, he managed to get some information about her finances. Gleaning information from an investment chat he dropped in on periodically, as well as a couple of academic bulletin boards, some on-line real estate contacts, and what he called "a little hacking that you don't want to know about," he ascertained that Lucinda Kettleworth was strapped for cash. Academic salaries were not so great, even for full professors, if their expenses were high enough. And having tenure just meant that she had job security, at the price of being stuck at NYU forever.

Lucinda had been there for a long time, accumulating pension money all those years. This would have been great if the economy were soaring, but it wasn't. Jimmy said her equities had slid badly, and one fund she was in was in trouble with the SEC.

"She's due for a sabbatical," Jimmy told us, "but according to my professor friends, that's not a free vacation nowadays. You go on something like half salary, which means you can't afford your life unless you work. The best solution is to get a grant for some kind of research. Lucinda was just turned down by two foundations, and she's trying to get a second mortgage on her house."

"Houses in the West Village are worth a lot," Barbara said. "I've seen some gorgeous ones walking through that neighborhood and peeking in windows. High ceilings, elaborate moldings, parquet floors."

"Only guess what. It isn't hers. It belongs to the family trust."

Oops.

Barbara and I actually had a fight—well, a squabble—about which of us would go to Lucinda's lecture and check her out.

"It's a feminist event, you goop," Barbara said. "The audience will be all women."

"Not necessarily," I said.

I hadn't been down to the Village sober. Jimmy and I had had some riotous times there in our youth. I wanted to see if any of our old haunts were still there, including the lesbian bar on Eleventh Street where Jimmy and Barbara had had their first date. I was there. And don't ask. That was what our lives were like back then.

In the end, Barbara and I went to the lecture together.

We took the C train down to the West Fourth Street station and walked east from Sixth Avenue to NYU. Lucinda's topic was family dynamics. I bet she had no intention of mentioning her own family. But maybe her professional armor would slip and she'd say something revealing.

"I love walking through the Village," Barbara said happily. "I used to think the Square was so romantic." She was talking about Washington Square. The "Washington" is silent.

"You did drugs back then?" I asked, surprised.

"Before then. I caught the tail end of the folkies, and I used to imagine the beatniks and bohemians before that."

"Ah, the good old days."

"Don't laugh. Look at that. It's a shame."

She nodded at what looked to me like a normal lively scene: big crowds around rappers and late-blooming break-dancers with boom boxes; drug dealers hawking their wares with one eye out for the cops. One forlorn youth sat all alone on a bench, strumming his acoustic guitar.

"What's wrong with it?"

"Every performer's passing the hat. People used to play for free."

She swept a hand to indicate the brick and white row houses that rimmed the Square. They oozed charm. Someone was always using them in a movie.

"They all belong to NYU. Nobody else can afford them."

"The university that ate the Village," I agreed. "And?"

"My mother's dentist had his office in one of those," Barbara said. "My dad had a buddy from law school who lived across the Square. He wasn't particularly rich, either. My parents didn't do rich."

"They still have a few coffeehouses on Bleecker Street and Macdougal," I offered.

"Yeah, but Beat poets and folkie wannabes don't hang out in them," she said. "They're more like places where you can get a four-dollar latte if you don't feel like walking another couple of blocks to Starbucks."

"You can still get your nipple pierced or buy a sex toy," I consoled her.

"And what does it say about our society," she retorted, "that so much is gone but the Pink Pussycat remains?"

The crowd on the street still looked like they were enjoying themselves. I said so.

"But where is that overimaginative teenager from Queens?" Barbara laughed. "I'm being silly, huh?"

"Not so terribly," I said. "Now they're underimaginative teenagers from Queens."

"And Long Island and New Jersey."

"Talking big about how they plan to score."

"Plan? They don't score?" she asked.

"Nah, they settle for a beer and a slice of pizza."

"Is that what you and Jimmy did?"

"Hell no," I said. More like a twelve-pack each and forget the pizza. "But we were alcoholics."

By the time we arrived at the lecture, the room was packed. To my secret relief, I was not the only guy. Lucinda was a tall, bony woman with a powerful jaw, an exceptionally resonant voice, and an emphatic delivery. She sounded as if she had never had a doubt in her life. She used all the buzzwords: *patriarchy, developmental perspectives, attachment model, self-in-relation, family systems, neurotransmitters*. Barbara kept nodding her head, so I guess Lucinda knew her stuff. At the end came a question period. I didn't understand most of the questions. Barbara raised her hand, but she didn't get called on.

"She knows all their names," Barbara murmured in my ear. "She's calling on her own students."

"So what do you want to do?"

"Look, she's leaving." The great woman passed us, processing down the aisle with admirers swimming in her wake like pilot fish. "Let's follow her home."

Barbara hooked her arm through mine and set a pace that looked leisurely but took us along at a good clip. We never lost sight of Lucinda's back. And by scooting a bit at the avenues, we made all her green lights—or at least didn't let the red ones stop us.

Lucinda lived on one of the quiet side streets west of Seventh Avenue. These were mostly residential, with a few understated restaurants and chichi shops nestled into blocks of Federal-style row houses and a surviving wooden house or two. The tangled streets were almost impossible not to get lost in. Good thing we were following Lucinda.

Lucinda turned in at a little jewel of a house. The West Village was pricey to move into, though it still housed some families that couldn't afford to move out, old Italians from when it was an ethnic neighborhood and WASPs like Guff's family.

"I bet she's had it since the Flood," Barbara said.

"The family did. They probably had their own ark, too."

We hung out on the corner till she unlocked the door. Then we strolled down the block arm in arm. I tried to look like I belonged. The facade was clean red brick with sparkling white trim. In the tall windows, gold drapes with tiebacks and swags framed glimpses of gilt mirrors and crystal chandeliers in a long parlor with elaborate moldings on the high ceilings. When Lucinda closed the door behind her, we moved forward for a better view. Lights went on in the windows on the next floor up. A hand, presumably hers, pulled curtains across the windows of what must be a bedroom. The lights were still on in the parlor.

"Let's see what's on the walls," I said. A wrought-iron railing blocked the small patch of concrete in front of the house, but she'd left the gate open. It didn't even creak when I pushed it with one finger. I walked right up to the house and kind of chinned on the sill of the nearest window.

"Don't," Barbara said nervously. "We'll get caught."

"I'm the one who'll get arrested as a burglar," I said. "If anyone comes, all you have to do is take a giant step backward and look like a Jewish girl from Queens." I might not jump turnstiles anymore, but I hadn't turned into a total wimp. I hoped. "I want to see what she has on the walls. Oh, wow!"

"What?" Barbara performed a series of contortions.

"Is that a Maori haka or a kung fu kata?" I asked.

"Shh. I can't jump up far enough to see."

"Stop trying to do it on tiptoe," I advised, trying to laugh quietly. "Stand on the railing. Looks like she's got a spectacular collection of Russian icons."

"They could be worth a lot," she said.

"And I'm not so sure you can just go out and buy them," I added.

"Let me see! I want a closer look." She tried to clamber up the wrought-iron fence, but she slipped. Her foot dislodged the cover of a metal garbage can. It clattered to the pavement with a noise like clashing cymbals.

"Who's there!" Lucinda's voice called out sharply from upstairs.

"Shit! Let's go!" I hissed. I was back out the gate in a flash. "Come on!"

Barbara growled at me under her breath as she struggled to extricate her foot from between two wrought-iron rails. I grabbed her hand and whisked her past the house next door to Lucinda's. Then I put on the brakes.

"Easy now. Let's just stroll. We're innocent bystanders who had nothing to do with the disturbance."

Luckily, the street remained quiet. Lucinda didn't come downstairs, open the door, or even peer through the upstairs curtains. A real New Yorker. When we hear an alarming noise, we might check for a second to make sure we're not in actual danger. But then we tend to shrug and go back to whatever we were doing.

Barbara whimpered and held back as I started to move on.

"What's the matter?"

She hung from my arm like a twenty-pound pocketbook.

"My ankle. I twisted it."

"Badly?" I let her lean her whole weight on me, hopping on one foot, as I bent down to feel it.

"Ow!"

"Big ow or little ow?"

"Little ow. I'm okay. Really." She put the damaged foot down gingerly. Nothing bad happened. "Just let me lean a little." The deadweight gradually eased off.

"Good to go?"

"Yeah." She limped a little, but we made it to the corner. "Now let me rest just a second."

It was brighter on the corner. The cross street had restaurants and shops in between the residential buildings. I looked around, checking once more for any signs of pursuit. A bulky figure turned the corner on the other side of the street. I grunted softly in surprise.

"Look, Barb. Across the street. Is that Boris?"

"Boris who?"

"Boris Goudonov. Don't stare! The Russian counselor from the detox."

She looked in the direction I was looking. He was as big as a dancing bear in a heavy black wool overcoat and one of those massive fur hats. Could it be some other Russian? I wondered. I didn't think so.

"Yes, it is Boris," she said. "What's he doing on Lucinda's block?"

"A coincidence?"

"There are no coincidences."

"Thank you, Dr. Freud," I said. "Hmm. He could be one of Lucinda's Russian refugees."

"Maybe," Barbara said. "But does that explain what he's doing on her block at ten o'clock at night?"

"I don't know, Dr. Freud. What do *you* think?"

"Maybe they're having an affair," Barbara said.

"Or maybe he's casing the joint. Like us."

"Let's wait and see if he rings her bell," she suggested.

And so we would have. But an oil truck too big for the street chose that moment to get stuck turning the corner. By the time we could see Lucinda's house again, Boris had disappeared.

EIGHTEEN

I had another pink-collar temp job. Even in what Barbara calls the postfeminist era, a guy being a secretary is still considered cute. If it had been a permanent job, I could have joined the secretaries' union. That would have been even cuter. The women in the office considered me harmless. They tended to treat me like one of the girls. This could have been a great preliminary to getting inside their underwear if I had been the slightest bit interested. My night with Laura notwithstanding, my libido was still in very early sobriety. So I was perfectly happy to share their tuna fish sandwiches and tell them comforting lies on their bad hair days and hear all about their boss. Especially since their boss was Guff's nephew, Charles G. Standish.

They all called him Chuckie, but not to his face. If I had to describe him in one word, the word would be "tightass." Not much over thirty, he was one of those men who seemed to have been born middle-aged. He skated as close to old-fashioned sexism as he could get away with in a union shop. He was finicky about the work. When he wasn't taking a client out, he ate the same thing for lunch every day: half a lean pastrami on rye with mustard with extra pickle and a diet Sprite. He never got the mustard on his tie. He had an annoying tendency to micromanage. When he got on the intercom, which he did dozens of times a day, he would never tell you if it was to give you a rocket or just a task. He would say, "I'd like to see you in my office." Never by name. I didn't care, but the permanent staff resented it. In retaliation, they snooped in his desk and gossiped about him and his family whenever he wasn't around.

Beverly, the office manager, reigned as queen of the office. She was in her forties. Her figure was lush. Her hair had an identity crisis every other week. Her pouty, squashed-together face made her look like Tweety Bird, and she had a squeaky voice to go with it. She wore tight skirts, high heels, and about a pound of makeup. Beverly knew the location of every ballpoint pen and yellow pad that she had ever ordered. It didn't take much to get her going about Chuckie. She'd been there forever, but she was not one of those loyal clerical slaves. In fact, she had been instrumental in getting the union in. She had been shop steward until she got promoted into management. While she did her job with fierce rectitude, she had no scruples about responding to an innocent leading question with a flood of information. When Chuckie got a call from his uncle, Dr. Samson Weill, I let Beverly tell me all about it.

"That's Uncle Sam. Chuckie is actually his wife's nephew. They have lunch together about once a month. Dr. Weill does face-lifts and tummy tucks; he does very well for himself. Though like everyone else, he's taken a few hits in the past year as far as investments go. He's a good client, and Chuckie gets upset if he isn't happy."

"Why wouldn't he be happy?"

"Oh, money, it's always money, isn't it? They both belong to an expensive golf club, they go to the Caribbean every winter and the Hamptons every summer, their wives spend a fortune on their clothes, and the kids go to expensive schools."

"It costs a lot to keep up the perfect family, huh?"

"Perfect! Ha! You can't buy a perfect family."

"Trouble in paradise?"

"Uncle Sam's wife has a black sheep brother," she said with relish. "Chuckie's other uncle. They've shelled out plenty in *that* direction over the years."

"Bailing him out?" Beverly didn't seem to know that Uncle Guffy was dead. Talk about a news blackout.

"And paying him to go away. Not that it's ever worked for long."

"So where's the black sheep now?" I made the question sound as idle as I could.

"I don't know," said Beverly, "but I can tell you where he was at Christmas—in here, asking for a handout. He crashed the office Christmas party and went through half a bottle of Chivas Regal before Chuckie managed to hustle him out of here."

"Christmas?" I said, startled. I knew where Guff had been on Christmas Day.

"A few days before," Beverly elaborated. "The party is always before, so many people take off around the holiday. I thought Chuckie would turn purple, he was so embarrassed. You know how he likes to present himself to top management especially as never having a hair out of place. This uncle was a wild hair all right."

So Guff had visited his nephew in the course of his final bender, the one that landed him in detox. Had he made a return visit on his last pass?

"Did he give him money?"

"Took it right out of the office safe. He had me guarding Uncle Black Sheep out here while he was in there, didn't want to risk anyone seeing the combination."

"And was that the last of Uncle Black Sheep?"

"No, he was back right after New Year's. That time, Chuckie sent him off to Uncle Sam. Didn't give him anything but a cup of coffee."

The next day, I got to see Dr. Sam Weill for myself. He arrived at 11:45 for his lunch date with the boss. Beverly told me to go out and get him from reception. Of course I was invisible to him, just the retriever bringing back the game. He was a stubby little guy running to paunch and jowls. Vertical bad-temper lines had worn deep grooves into his face. Chuckie stood in the doorway of his office, looking as close to jovial as he ever did, which wasn't very.

"Sam," he said. He waved the doctor into his office. They both ignored me. Once the door had closed behind them, I picked up a couple of letters I had typed for Chuckie's signature and applied myself to loitering. My ear snuggled up as close to the door as it could manage. It didn't take long for the doctor to start getting loud.

"Damn it," I heard, "just put it in something that's going up!"

There was a pause—I assumed for a tight-lipped reply from Chuckie.

"What the hell do I pay you for?" the doc's grating voice demanded. Sounded like he was expecting his nephew to turn a bear market into a bull for his personal benefit. Good luck.

Inaudible interpolation from Chuckie, then a tirade from the doc that ended with ". . . kids' teeth!" After that, I couldn't catch anything for a while. When I did, it was right on target.

". . . Emmie's goddamn loser of a brother!" grated the doc. The voice fell slightly, and I wondered if I'd do better going in. If I knocked on the door and asked for the signatures I needed, I'd hear

— 154 —

better. But it would interrupt the flow. I decided to let well enough alone.

"... two thousand dollars in cash!" the doctor howled. I strained my ears, as if better hearing on my part would help him be explicit. "And where is it, damn it? ... returned with his effects, hell no!" The doc directed some explosive and comprehensive cursing at the detox, the morgue, the police force, and the City of New York in general. Eventually, it stopped, as Chuckie presumably spoke soothingly. By the time the door opened, Dr. Weill had pulled himself together. I was back at my desk, my eyes glued to the monitor and my fingers playing a scherzo on the keyboard.

"Back at two," the boss said curtly. The two of them strode away toward reception and the elevators. The moment they were out of sight, I hit my high-speed connection to the Internet. Staff rumor claimed that management read our e-mails. So I kept it short and cryptic. I typed in Jimmy's screen name and left the subject blank.

"Unc S pd G to go away," I wrote. "2K msng. Who?"

I was still stalling on asking Glenn to be my sponsor, but I made myself go out for coffee after the meeting. I sat in a greasy spoon with Glenn, the guy Gary, who did the coffee at what I guessed had become my home group, and two other guys, Roger and Mike. Roger asked me how long I'd been sober.

"Day One was Christmas Day."

"You must have had one helluva Christmas Eve."

"I probably did."

Everybody laughed. They'd all had blackouts, too.

"Bruce was in detox with a friend of yours," Gary piped up. "You don't mind, do you?" he hastily added, turning to me.

"Be my guest," I said resignedly. "It's all in the family."

"Who?" Roger asked.

"Your ex-business partner," said Gary.

"Oh God," said Roger. "That bastard. Don't remind me."

"I heard he died," said Mike.

"You mean I don't need to pray for him every day anymore?" said Roger.

Glenn looked faintly scandalized. Roger caught the look.

"I know, I know, I can't afford resentments. It's just that I wanted to kill the guy."

"You were ready to." Gary grinned. "I thought we'd have to pull you off him."

"Tell them," Mike said. "That guy really screwed Roger good."

"I should have known better," said Roger bitterly. "Don't get into deals involving money with people from the program."

"Bill W. was always lending money to drunks," said Glenn, referring to the legendary founder of AA. "It never got them sober. We're supposed to have learned a thing or two in more than fifty years."

"It wasn't lending money to a drunk," said Roger. "It was trusting someone I thought was in recovery to keep up his end of a deal that was really important to me. I also thought he had plenty. Doesn't he—didn't he have some kind of trust fund?"

"That's what they say," said Gary.

"That didn't stop him," said Roger angrily, "from defaulting on the loan he cosigned on. I ended up losing the business I'd been dreaming of for years, just when it was about to take off. Now I'm working a day job that I hate and I may never get back to where I was before that bastard practically begged me to be partners with him and swore he'd never let me down. I was stupid, but I still wish I'd beat the shit out of him when I had the chance."

"You'd only be feeling remorseful now," Glenn said. "The guy's dead."

"I wouldn't give a rat's ass if I had," said Roger stubbornly. "I hope he suffered."

There was a charged silence. Then we all started talking very fast about other things.

I ran into Mo again at a meeting down in the Village. It happened to be a gay and lesbian meeting. That wasn't my bag. But any meeting is open to anyone with a desire to stop drinking, and I was in the neighborhood. I guess my Higher Power wanted me to be there. Or to put it in less spiritual terms, my damn train went out of service at the Christopher Street station and I could either stand on a crowded platform for half an hour or get out of the subway and make the best of it.

Anyhow, I walked in late, and Mo was qualifying. I hadn't known that Mo was into women. She'd been involved enough with Guff to get hurt. I didn't see how she could have meant anyone but him when she told the group about the guy who was the first person she'd had sex with in sobriety. So she was humiliated when he had the bad taste to have trouble performing, refused to talk about it, and ran away.

The rejection triggered massive feelings of abandonment because it echoed her childhood in an alcoholic family, blah blah blah. After that, Mo concluded that men sucked. And then Guff conveniently up and died.

"Would you call a sexual rejection like that a motive for murder?" I asked Barbara later.

Asking Barbara a simple question yielded an information dump, as usual. The short answer was yes. Or maybe.

"Okay, I get it," I said. "They were both fucked up about sex and newly sober. He humiliated her. But to kill him?"

"It does sound far-fetched," Barbara conceded. "Also, how did they get together the day he died? Unless he looked her up with some harebrained idea of making amends."

I shook my head. Guff had definitely not been in an amends kind of mood that day.

They asked me to stay on another week at Chuckie Standish's firm. The secretaries and paralegals were going down like ninepins with the flu, and Beverly liked me. I figured my Higher Power was telling me to snoop some more. I wanted a look at Chuckie's files, which I couldn't get by listening at the door. I decided to work late one night. The fact that I got paid by the hour could have been a problem. I had to tell Beverly that I had a dinner date in the neighborhood and didn't mind finishing up some filing on my own dime. She looked incredulous, as well she might. But she finally left me alone. Luckily, Chuckie had had to rush out to some date or meeting. He hadn't had time to put his office in its usual finicky order. My offer to put away the books and papers on his desk induced her to trust me with access to his sanctum when she left with her duplicate key.

"Just don't forget to lock that door from the inside before you close it," she warned. "And he doesn't need to know I let you in there."

"I'll wipe off every fingerprint," I promised.

It took me only fifteen minutes to do the work I'd deliberately left undone. Chuckie's office beckoned. The first thing I did was to sink into his luxurious burgundy leather chair and put my feet up on his rosewood desk. Ahhhhhh. The chair swiveled fluidly. The deep bay below the window let me prop up my legs at an even more convenient height. He had left the burgundy velvet drapes pulled back on a spectacular unobstructed view of New York Harbor and the Statue of Liberty. I doubted I would have wanted to pay the price of three years' grind at law school and the eighty-hour weeks that fledgling corporate associates put in if they wanted to make partner. But it was fun pretending. I let myself space out for a while.

When daydreams of career success shifted toward visualizing Chivas Regal, it was time to get up and do some work. After some internal debate, I cracked the door open. If the cleaning team that went through the offices at night came this way, I figured I would hear them. Just in case, I started by putting away the things he had left out. Once those were out of sight, no one could tell that anyone but Beverly had come in there once Chuckie left.

I looked at everything before I filed it. Nothing personal showed up. The drawers in the rosewood desk were all locked. He had a laptop, but he always took it with him. Well, I'd be damned. He must have been in one helluva hurry. The laptop in its padded leather case stood on the floor near the door, half-hidden by a gray suit in a plastic dry cleaner's bag that hung from an elaborate brass coat stand. Well, well, well. I gently lifted the case onto the nearest flat surface, a small refrigerator that looked like a hotel minibar, and zipped it open.

To boot or not to boot, that was the question. If the cleaning people came through, I figured I would just seem to be doing my job. It sure would look suspicious if I was playing with the boss's computer. I thought about it for a while, prowling around the office. I stuck my head out the door. Nothing there but mute computers in their cubes. Not even the muffled roar of vacuuming in the distance.

I opened the minibar door and stared into it awhile. Refrigerator trance. No Chivas. I guess they'd finished it off at the Christmas party. He did have a bottle of Glenlivet single malt. Had he offered Guff a real drink? Inducing relapse is an awfully haphazard way of killing someone. Putting something toxic in their drink is not. But we knew Guff had made it back to the detox sober. The little fridge held a few small bottles of mixers, too—Perrier, ginger ale, tonic—as well as a lemon and three limes, an open pint container of half-and-half, and one of those little insulated brown paper sacks of fresh-ground coffee. The guy had his own espresso machine, complete with frother. Beverly had said "a cup of coffee." Pretty fancy cup of coffee. Not much room for pills or poison in the little cup. Hardly a mouthful, but strong espresso might disguise a peculiar taste.

How badly had Chuckie wanted Uncle Guffy out of the way? Maybe the laptop held something that would tell me. I lacked Jimmy's skills, but you couldn't do office work these days without knowing computer basics. I pressed the power button. The laptop whirred, and the screen lit up and started going through its routine. Good. The battery worked. As soon as the icons popped up, I right clicked and checked the charge. Sixty percent remaining. Good. Not having to plug it in meant I could leave it in the case, ready to zip up fast if I heard someone coming.

What should I look at first? Financial? Legal? Personal? I decided to go with e-mail. If Chuckie had said anything to Dr. Weill or anyone else in the family at the time of Guff's visit to his office, it should leap right out at me. I couldn't get on-line without plugging in, even if I figured out his passwords. But I didn't need to. Old e-mails would be downloaded to his hard drive. I opened AOL. His primary screen name was Chaz. At least his computer didn't call him Chuckie. I opened up "Filing Cabinet" and started scrolling back.

January 2. Well, well, well. A cry for help to Dr. Sam. Oh, this was cute. The good doctor called himself FriarTuck on-line. He wasn't fat or, as far as I knew, religious, so that had to be a reference to the tummy tucks that were his brioche and butter. I liked the

Robin Hood association. You could call plastic surgery robbing the rich. However, neither of these bozos had any intention of giving to the poor. Or tithing, either.

"Uncle G just showed up again," Chuckie had written. "Your turn to buy him off. I did my bit at Xmas. Sending him uptown."

The next one said, "So don't tell Aunt Em. This can't go on. We need a more permanent solution."

That had to be in response to one from Sam Weill. I scrolled down, and there it was.

"Don't do that! Emmie will want to take him in."

When I clicked open the next one, I read the bottom first to see what Weill had said.

"Is he on anything? What do you expect me to do?"

Chuckie's answer appeared above it.

"No, but he's still a nasty piece of work. He's not going to cooperate about the property. Give him something to get rid of him. Just make sure it's enough."

There was one more exchange.

Uncle Sam said, "Screw you, Charles. Don't send him."

Chuckie's read, "Too late. Screw you, too."

All that was suggestive, to say the least. But I didn't get a chance to think about it. I had had my ear cocked for the vacuum cleaner all this time. Now a different sound, the multiple dinging of the elevator bell, startled me. It meant a car had stopped at this floor. I heard a single person walking quickly. The footsteps clicked on the marble floor around the elevators. When they passed onto the silence of thick carpet, I risked a quick peek through the crack in the door. Damn! Chuckie had come back for his laptop.

I slapped the cover of the laptop down and drew the zipper all around with one quick movement. I eased the case gently to the floor. The man was so compulsive that he'd remember to a millimeter where he'd set it down. No way to get out of the office before he got here. No way I could explain my presence. I had no objection to getting fired, but I sure didn't want him calling the cops. Behind the door? For a second, I considered it. He would enter the room in a hurry, pushing the door inward as he came. That would conceal me all right, but only until he bent down to pick up the laptop that stood on the floor. Then, unless he was wearing blinders, he'd see me flattened against the wall.

The little private rest room contained nothing but a toilet. Couldn't hide there. If he needed to take a leak, I'd be busted. And that door opened outward. There was only one option left. As the door to the office opened, I slid behind the burgundy velvet drapes. Luckily, they were generously cut and fell to the floor. The fact that they were pulled back was in my favor. The bunched effect disguised my bulk. At least I hoped it would. I breathed through my nose as shallowly as I could.

I sensed rather than heard his footsteps on the even thicker carpet in his office. He checked, exclaimed, picked up the case. Just clicking his tongue, the guy managed to sound pompous. I heard faint chinking sounds from his desk. Straightening his pens. He started out, then changed his mind. He did need to take a leak. Didn't bother to close the bathroom door. Why should he? There wasn't anyone there. The guy's bladder must be a magnum. The fountain sound effects went on and on.

Finally, the sound stopped. There was a pause, during which, I assumed, he was giving his dick a shake. *Zip.* I heard the bathroom door close. He started out again. Stopped. Uttered another of those wordless exclamations. Headed, oh shit, in my direction. With dread, I heard him pull the cord. The heavy curtains started to move slowly inward. I held my breath.

If he closed the drapes all the way, he couldn't possibly miss my shape bulging out behind them. I did my best to flatten myself against the wall without actually moving any part of my body. Now I had to piss. Power of suggestion. The plush velvet fabric caressed my face as it passed slowly by. My nose twitched. I couldn't hold my breath much longer. I didn't have the faintest idea how I was going to get out of this. When the drapes reached a point precisely halfway closed, they stopped.

"Hah!" This time, the wordless little noise sounded satisfied. If Chuckie wasn't a diagnosable obsessive compulsive, he was enough of a neat freak to be pleased when he got the curtains exactly the way he left them every night—precisely halfway across. I waited behind the curtain for at least five minutes after he left, sweating but grateful to be undiscovered and very glad to breathe. Then I got my ass out of there. I did not pass Go, I did not collect two hundred dollars, and I did not risk visiting his bathroom. I actually used the men's room in the subway station, which, if you know New York, just goes to show how desperate I was. I was pissing copiously and with gratitude when I realized I had never turned off the laptop. With any luck, the battery would run down before he opened the case again. Next time he used it, chances were he'd plug it in. He'd never know.

That night, Barbara convened another council of war. She made Jimmy come out from behind the computer, brought in a pot of coffee, and settled us on the couch. She curled up in an armchair, facing us, with a lined yellow pad and a determined expression.

"So. What have we got?" Evidently, the question was rhetorical. "I've got it all divided into categories. One, his family. Two, people he knew from the program. Three, staff and clients at the detox."

Her face fell. "And four, everybody else in the world he might have known or might have seen, and we have no idea who they are. Oh, I don't know. Maybe it's crazy for us even to be doing this."

Jimmy got up, sat on the arm of her chair, and put his arm around her.

"No, baby, it's great. You're doing fine." He gave me a "Say something encouraging" glare.

"Go on," I said. "Even if we never find out what happened, I'd rather feel as if we're doing something. Really." As I said it, I realized with some surprise that it was true. We might be floundering around. We might even be the world's most aimless amateur detectives. But trying to draw the threads of Guff's life together was helping me get past his death. Tracking down people who'd known him, asking questions, it all gave it a kind of structure. It made the flatness of reality without a drink or drug a little more bearable. I imagined running into some old acquaintance who would ask what I was doing these days. "Staying clean and sober one day at a time." Yuck. "Working as a temp." Blech. "Trying to track down a murderer." Hmm. Tolerable. I tuned back in to Barbara.

"We know that everyone in the family gains financially by Guff's death. We know that Emmie and her kids saw him that last day, and that something could have been slipped into the tea he drank there. I can't believe Emmie would have hurt him, though. She was the one who loved him and had such a hard time not enabling him. Besides, I've gotten to know her a bit, and I've heard her share at meetings. She's so . . . sincere. It sounds awful, but she really is. Can you imagine a sincere murderer?"

Jimmy and I dutifully shook our heads.

"Let's not forget Emmie's husband, the plastic surgeon."

"Uncle Sam," I said.

Barbara made a face. "I still haven't forgiven him for reaming out that poor Marlene."

"Don't forget the nephew," I said. "It looks like Chuckie paid Guff off when he showed up drunk before Christmas. Whatever Chuckie gave him, he spent on booze and drugs. And got sick enough to end up in detox."

"When Guff went back there after New Year's, Chuckie sent him up to Sam. Sam gave him two thousand dollars. We do agree on that?"

"It sure sounded like it." Jimmy frowned. His fingers, which could never keep still and were usually playing over a computer keyboard, twiddled with the tassels on a cushion.

"The day after New Year's, Sam and Chuckie told each other they had to do something about Guff. They didn't want him coming back to the well every few days. But we don't know if they simply paid him to go away or egged each other on to do something drastic."

Barbara shook her head. "If you were going to kill one of your relatives, would you tell your nephew?"

"I don't have a nephew."

"Bruce!" She made it two exasperated syllables.

"Well, I don't," I said. "But no. If I planned to kill somebody, I wouldn't tell a soul."

"I have nephews." Jimmy moved restlessly back to the computer. "And no."

"Suppose Guff was getting in the way," I said. "Some family business scheme. Something he wouldn't sign or change. Like letting Lucinda sell her house." He had sounded gleefully vindictive that last day.

"But Lucinda wasn't the one who paid him off."

"Maybe the trust owns all their assets. I'll see what I can find out." Jimmy made a note, his fingers flying on the keyboard. "The more money involved, the more just throwing him a few thousand bucks to get out of town would not have been enough."

"When did Guff see Sam?" Barbara asked. "You say the nephew sent him up there. When he visited Emmie, Sam wasn't there. She said so."

"Before or after," I said. "Does it matter? He must have known they didn't talk to each other, at least about him. He could have stopped by to see Sam, gotten what he could out of him, and just not mentioned it when he went on upstairs to see his sister and the kids. He wasn't about to say, 'Oh, by the way, dear, I just extorted two grand from your husband.'"

Barbara nodded. "And Emmie didn't tell him Guff had visited, because he had ordered her not to let him anywhere near the kids."

"What was that about?" Jimmy asked.

"Sam being controlling," Barbara suggested.

"I wonder."

"Follow the money," I said. It was great advice, the kind I frequently wished I'd taken in my own life.

"So what happened to the money?" Barbara asked. "If he had two thousand on him when he got back to the detox, where did it go after he died?"

"Good question. They had a problem with a sneak thief." I had forgotten all about it. "They gave us the Talk. You know, about the code of the streets not applying in recovery."

"Charmaine mentioned it to me," said Barbara. "She worried that the men might be feeling sensitive about being accused."

"None of the guys I talked to admitted knowing anything about it. But yes, a patient could have taken that money."

"You two know the staff," Jimmy said. "What about them?"

Barbara and I looked at each other. Simultaneously, we said, "Darryl."

"Who's he?"

"One of the counselors. Used to be a dealer."

"A sleazebucket," I told him. "And he hated Guff."

"I didn't know that," Barbara said.

"Yeah, they had a nasty little head butt in group, and things went downhill from there."

"What if Guff caught him taking it?"

I thought about that. The code of the streets had sure as hell not applied to the relationship between Guff and Darryl. No loyalty there.

"If Darryl was the thief, it would have been a lot easier to take the money from Guff's pockets after he died. Especially if he already knew it was there."

"Would Darryl kill for two thousand dollars?"

"People kill for a pair of Nikes or a Mets jacket."

"Kids," Barbara objected, as if that made more sense. Killer kids. What a world.

"Ask yourself if he'd kill not to be exposed and prosecuted for theft. Or not to lose his job, if he was using it as a cover for dealing drugs."

"And a nice little market," Barbara added. "I hate to think that might be happening there. Some of those guys are trying so hard to get clean."

"Darryl was a repeat offender," I pointed out. "If he gets in any kind of trouble, it's big trouble."

"Anyone else you'd suspect?" Jimmy asked. "Counselors? The Russian guy? Security guard?"

"Security guard would have to wake up first."

"And Boris is a sweetie," Barbara added. "We still don't know how come we saw him near Lucinda's in the Village the other night. But as far as I can tell, that doesn't have anything to do with this."

"Darryl's the only real badass in the whole bunch."

"That may be true," Jimmy said, "but everybody has a vulnerable spot. If it isn't about the stolen money, what else could have been going on?"

"Something else that wasn't kosher, you mean?"

"Yeah. Who had a secret? Anything Guff might have seen or heard or made some kind of trouble about?"

"There's Bark's gambling," Barbara said. "A senior counselor doesn't make that much, and Bark is always going to Atlantic City. He won't admit he has a problem, but I think he's a compulsive gambler."

"Does Boris have a green card?" I had met my share of Russian immigrants, out drinking and in AA. Getting a green card was a big deal.

"He's going for his CASAC. You can't get the state counseling credential if you're illegal."

"He could have a fake." I had seen plenty of forged documentation—green cards, Social Security cards, you name it. I knew guys with two Medicaid cards.

"Lucinda's on the board of this Russian refugee organization. Maybe she helped him get into the States. Though as far as the credential goes, people will try anything, especially to get a job. Charmaine once told me about a guy she interviewed, sent her a great-looking résumé that listed lots of experience in psych clinics, gave psychiatrists as references. Turned out he'd been a mental patient. He was convinced that qualified him, too."

"What about Charmaine? Has she got a tragic secret?"

"Don't joke! Her little girl has Down's. It's not a secret, but it's a vulnerable spot. But you can't suspect my friends!"

"Okay, keep your shirt on. Then who else? What about the other nephew?" Jimmy asked. "Miles Standish."

"Robert. I forgot to tell you," Barbara said. "Emmie and I were coming out of a meeting the other night, and the AA meeting was letting out at the same time. So all of a sudden, Emmie lights up like a Christmas tree, gets this big grin on her face, and says, 'Stop a moment. It's my nephew!' And it was Robert. Of course I didn't let on I had heard of him. I let her introduce him to me—first name only, of course. Bobby. He's a nice guy. And he's been sober awhile, you could tell by the way he talked about the Steps."

"Sober doesn't necessarily mean above suspicion," Jimmy pointed out.

"Less likely, though," said Barbara.

"Guff never said a word," I said thoughtfully, "about anybody else in the family being in recovery."

"Didn't want to hear about recovery," said Barbara. "I gather Guff was still in pretty much of an active alcoholic head, wouldn't you say, Bruce?"

"Yeah. Maybe it would have changed. He didn't have the time."

Barbara was looking at me with compassion, damn it. She could spot sad at a hundred paces. The whole thing confused me—where I was at, where Guff would have been, where I might be. All I knew was I didn't know anything about anything.

"I think I've had enough for one night." My tone verged on the pathetic, but I couldn't help it.

"Fifteen minutes, sweetie," Barbara promised. "You met those people from the meeting who knew Guff. If sober doesn't equal innocent, we need to hear about them."

I groaned. "Okay, okay. I already told you about Mo, Maureen. She was in the middle of trying to figure out her sexual orientation when they had a fling that went badly. I don't know if she was more hurt or more angry. But since then, she's come out. If she's a lesbian, why would she care if Guff could get it up or not?"

"It doesn't necessarily work that way," said Barbara. "People can hold on to sexual grudges for a long time. Reason has nothing to do with it. Someone rejects you in bed, it's a narcissistic wound."

"If you say so. Then there's this guy Roger who got into some sort of business venture with Guff and got screwed when he didn't come through."

"Mistake," said Jimmy. "You should never try to do business with people from program. Too complicated. Ends badly."

Another of the thousand and one excuses for drinking.

"He knows that now. But in the meantime, he was ready to kill the guy, or at least beat the shit out of him. It sounded like his friends were barely holding him back at the time it happened."

"You think someone struggling with impulse control like that," said Barbara, "would even think of poison?"

"You never know. There could be more to the story than we know about."

"That's the trouble with this whole thing." Barbara looked discouraged again.

"Hey." Jimmy ruffled her hair. "One step at a time. That's all we can do."

"You can talk. You don't really care if we find out or not."

"I care!"

"No you don't, you're just humoring the children. It's okay."

"Are we through?" I asked plaintively.

Barbara looked at her notes. "The other sister."

"She's in Ohio. How are we going to do anything about her?"

"Frequent flier miles." Barbara looked pleased with herself. "Those conferences I went to last year? The time I went to Hawaii when you wouldn't go?"

"You're going to Ohio?" Jimmy sounded shocked.

Barbara started laughing. "You sound like one of those old Nero Wolfe mysteries where the detective never leaves his brownstone. " 'Out? Out the door and down the stoop?' Yes, Jimmy, I'm going out the door, down the stoop—or rather, since we don't have a stoop, down in the elevator, into a taxi, onto a plane, and to Ohio."

"Where in Ohio?" I asked.

"One of those C cities," Barbara said. "Jimmy looked it up. Cincinnati? Columbus? Cleveland?"

"Dayton," said Jimmy.

"Right. That's what I meant. Frances's husband teaches history at the university. I can stay over near the airport, look the sister up the next morning, and come back that afternoon."

"Ohio." Jimmy shuddered. City boys, both of us.

"She might know something that would help," Barbara said. "I have a feeling about it."

"That line," said Jimmy, "is supposed to be, 'I have a *bad* feeling about it.'"

NINETEEN

The best-laid plans, as the poet said, can get fucked up. Barbara's burning desire to visit Ohio got scotched when her boss, Dr. Arnold, announced an imminent audit, which meant the whole staff needed to work overtime for the next few days.

"It's a surprise visit," Barbara told us. "Very big deal. The charts all have to be perfect."

"If it's a surprise, how come you know about it?"

"Someone at the state office tipped Dr. Arnold off. They always do."

"Silly me!" I whacked the side of my head with my open palm. "Why did I even ask? It's so logical!" I raised one eyebrow like Spock in the original *Star Trek* and spread my fingers, two on a side, in the Vulcan peace sign.

"You'll have to go to Ohio, Bruce," she said.

That stopped my clowning.

"Who, me?"

Barbara made a big show of looking all around their living

room. I seemed to be spending as much time in their apartment as the gang on *Seinfeld* did at Jerry's.

"I don't see any other unemployed people here, do you?"

"Jimmy's schedule is just as flexible as mine," I protested.

"I assessed the relative difficulty," Barbara said, "of getting Jimmy out from behind his computer versus getting you onto a plane, and guess who won."

"She got that right, dude," said Jimmy, tilting his chair way back and sounding smug.

"Oh, go hit your head on the radiator," I said.

"Be glad it's not Cincinnati, son," Jimmy said cheerfully. "The airport there is in Kentucky." Knowing history means he knows geography. Have I mentioned what a pain in the ass he can be?

"Ohio, yes. Kentucky, no," I said. When the words were out, I realized I'd just capitulated.

Jimmy grinned. So did Barbara. But then her face fell.

"What about the frequent flier miles? I can't transfer them to Bruce."

"No problem," Jimmy said. "My treat."

Growing up in Yorkville, Jimmy, like me, had never had a dime. But that changed when he discovered computers and how willingly they opened up for him. As soon as he had money, Jimmy became the world's most generous guy. Usually, I admired that quality in him. This time, I was screwed.

There are over two hundred flights a day from New York to Dayton. Air travel being what it is in our cockamamie times, all the nonstops were booked. In the end, I had to change planes in Detroit. I wanted to visit Detroit even less than I wanted to go to Dayton. I reminded myself never to go anywhere near Ohio again. Or Michigan.

We flew into a pretty good sunset. When we got above the

clouds, it flattened out to a single line of blazing red-gold rimming an endless bowl of blue. I spent the whole trip looking at it. Good thing I had the window seat and the middle seat was empty. The businessman on the aisle spent the whole trip drinking bourbon. My only diversion was half a can of Coke in a plastic glass and a microscopic bag of salted peanuts.

Night fell quickly as I made my way through the unfamiliar airport. I hopped on a bus to the nearest low-end chain motel. Jimmy had suggested I call AA World Service and get contact numbers for the Dayton meetings. But I declined. I was still not so sure the New Yorkers in our own meetings were my brothers and sisters the way they thought they were. Instead, I went out for the native cuisine: an overcooked burger and greasy fries. In spite of all those amber waves of grain, midwesterners didn't have much time for vegetables. Maybe we were kindred spirits after all.

In the morning, since I was still in the heartland, I had a heart attack breakfast: fried eggs with bacon and sausage, toasted bagel dripping with butter. I regretted nothing but the bagel, an imposter that any New Yorker would have seen right through. Then I went in search of a map.

Frances Standish and her husband lived near the university. The bus I took let me off in a neighborhood that gave me the willies. I don't actually see water every day. But water surrounds Manhattan in all directions, and its absence gave me claustrophobia. This Dayton, Ohio, didn't have any water at all. Just row after row of houses and lawns and trees and stretches of sidewalk. Call it a cross between a cornfield without the corn and a Monopoly board. Landlocked.

Looking for Frances Standish's address, I got to see a lot of lawns and big trees marching down the streets. I mean we all marched: me and the lawns and trees and Monopoly houses. It probably was pretty in the summer. Fresh snow might have improved it, too, on the ground and on the bare branches of the elms, or whatever the big trees were. But there had obviously been a thaw and then a freeze. The lawns were dry and brown, the crossings a repository of frozen slush. We do frozen slush in New York, too. I should have felt right at home. It was cold. I could see my breath. Each time a gust of wind hit, the chill made my eyes water. The ground was frozen solid. When I stepped on a lawn, it crunched.

I finally found the house, a two-story white frame affair with the kind of front porch that's made for rocking chairs. If the Standishes had any, they had taken them inside for the winter. There was a two-car garage and one car, a biggish sedan in a discreet dark blue, in the driveway. Good. Someone was home. I hoped that it was Frances. God grant me the serenity to get this over with. I mounted the porch steps, took a deep breath, and rang the bell.

After a nerve-racking wait, a woman who had to be Frances opened the door. She looked at me inquiringly. She was tall, like her sisters, but with an entirely different face. She wore a tweed jacket, gray wool slacks, and a silky pink turtleneck, with a strand of pearls around her neck. Nice shoes.

"Mrs. Standish?" Well trained by Barbara, I usually said "Ms.," but west of the Hudson, the "Mrs." just slipped out. I talked fast. I needed to persuade her I was not the Fuller Brush man before she slammed the door on me. "My name is Bruce Kohler. I was a friend of your brother Godfrey. I happened to be in town. I had some business at the university, and I thought I'd take the chance of coming by to say how sorry I am."

I shivered involuntarily. It was cold on the porch. If Barbara had made this trip instead, the woman would surely have invited her in. I wasn't sure she'd trust a strange man that far. I produced what I hoped did not come across as a shit-eating grin and tried to look trustworthy. I figured I'd better add some corroborating detail.

"I know he'd been through some hard times. But I saw him just before he died, and he sincerely meant to turn his life around. I was close enough to know." Right there in the next bed, lady.

"I suppose you'd better come in," she said unsmilingly. She turned and led the way into the living room. The furniture looked well-worn and very sturdy, as if meant to be passed down to the next generation. A faded, probably authentic Persian carpet covered most of the floor.

She nodded toward a chair. I perched on the edge of it. Now I had to get her to talk. Barbara would have known how to pour a never-ending stream of words into her silence. I couldn't do that. We'd worked out an outline of what I should say. "I know he'd had some trouble with his family in the past. So I thought you might be interested to hear that he got help. We're planning an informal memorial gathering in New York." I'd rehearsed that lie on the plane. "We hoped you'd be willing to share some kind of positive memory. I don't mean to intrude. But some small anecdote? Maybe when he was younger?"

Her continued silence was unnerving.

"Mrs. Standish," I said, "I lost a brother once myself." That lie wasn't in the script. It just tumbled out. "I found I had all sorts of mixed feelings that made me very uncomfortable and didn't start to go away until I'd talked about them with someone." That felt more phony than claiming the nonexistent brother, considering I'd never been in therapy. But Barbara would have been proud of me. In New York, if I'd mentioned therapy, maybe eight people out of ten would have rolled the welcome mat right out. But this was not New York. "And I knew Godfrey."

"I doubt it," she said bitterly.

She hesitated, but maybe Barbara was right. Everybody needs to talk to someone sometime. I might be this uptight woman's only opportunity.

"You say he was getting help. I believe that there is no way to help a person with that particular problem, short of locking him up or warning everyone who has to deal with him. No amount of talking is going to change it, no matter what they say. In the Middle Ages, lepers had to ring a bell so people would know to get out of their way."

Another codependent, I thought. I was catching Barbara's habit of seeing them everywhere. Her husband taught history, and she scraped crumbs off his crisp conversation and added them to hers for flavor.

"I don't know what they did with my brother's kind then," she said, "but what we did was to keep the children far away from him."

Whoa, wait a minute. That kind? We alkies aren't that bad, lady. What the hell was she talking about?

"You want to know something my brother did that wasn't evil?" Rhetorical question. "He saved my nephew Brandy from drowning when he was eleven. But do you want to know why Brandy was in danger of drowning?" Definitely rhetorical. "He fell off the pier backing away from my brother, who wanted something unspeakable. Luckily, it was enough of a shock that Brandy admitted to us what had been going on. We didn't let the younger children near him after that. My sons were grown; they made their own choices. But if my sister let her younger boy and girl be in the same room with him after what happened, she's a fool."

"Are you sure?" I asked faintly. She didn't bother answering that.

"You say you were his friend. What kind of a person are you to have that kind of monster for a friend?" She regarded me with contempt.

"I didn't know."

I had no trouble looking and sounding horrified. She had just told me my friend had been a child molester. A pedophile. A monster. Barbara had described Emmie's son Brandy as looking frail and otherworldly. I suddenly remembered that Guff had called for brandy in his delirium. Brandy, short for Brandon. I guessed Brandy was now old enough not to be of interest. I'd heard they usually fixate on kids of a certain age, and go on to someone else when the kid outgrows their fantasy. I felt completely weird just thinking about it. Complete disconnect between "they" and the buddy I knew. And what about the younger ones? Would he have approached the girl, or just the other little boy? Duncan, the ballet dancer. He was only eight.

Frances regarded me impatiently. "How could you know? They never look like monsters."

"Did the parents know?" I blurted. Barbara would have a fit. I was Guff's friend, but she was Emmie's. Emmie! Would she turn out to be one of those women who cultivate denial and let the abuse go on? She hadn't stopped sneaking her brother into the house. She'd fed him Earl Grey and scones the day before his death. But she'd known he shouldn't be alone with the kids. She'd stopped it, but too late. And what about Sam Weill? He had to have known. He had made a rule not to let Guff near the children. He had not condoned it once he knew.

"Of course they did." Frances's thin voice dripped contempt, whether for me or for Sam and Emmie, I couldn't tell. Probably all of us.

"I just knew about the problem with alcohol and drugs. He really did get clean and sober right before he died."

"Do you believe in evil, Mr. Kohler?"

She remembered my name. She probably never forgot or forgave anything.

I temporized. "That's a hard question." I wished someone could have beamed me up back to New York. Immediately. I had the information I'd come to Ohio for. Beyond my wildest dreams. And I'd had enough. "Some people think it's an illness. But no one could excuse or condone it. And of course the most important thing is to protect the children." I hoped she couldn't take exception to that. I apologized profusely and got the hell out of there.

Back in New York, Barbara was just as upset as I knew she'd be.

"How could she? How could she!" She meant Emmie.

"How could Guff?" I said. "I'd have sworn he was a good guy. I didn't have a clue. He shut down when I tried to talk about the family. But I thought that just meant the break with them was painful. We all have people we're ashamed to face or think about."

I intercepted a meaningful look between Jimmy and Barbara. They knew they were on my amends list all right. But this thing made me feel like a saint by comparison. My worst day drinking, I'd never harmed a child.

"I don't get," Barbara said, "why Guff's chart didn't have a hint of this."

"You think he'd have told them *that*? No way!"

"You'd be surprised," she said. "You know, the state requires us now to ask all those sexual-abuse questions right away."

"That's ridiculous," Jimmy said.

"And intrusive," Barbara agreed. "You're right, Bruce, it's unlikely anyone would tell at that point. But the questions do get asked, because if not, the program could lose its license and funding. And when you ask the same tough questions day in and day out, you get a feel for when there's a story. So you persist. And you'd be surprised how many of them tell sooner or later. They do come to trust us, you know. Once they figure out we really care. At least the ones who actually want recovery do."

"Guff was smarter than most of those guys. He'd have made sure he didn't drop any hints."

"Smart don't cut it for an alcoholic," Jimmy said.

"Yeah, yeah," I said. "But he wasn't brain-fried."

"So maybe smarter meant he had a guilty conscience. He might have needed to confess."

"Amen," said Jimmy softly. You could never quite take the Catholic Church out of the boy.

"So maybe one of the counselors suppressed the information," I said. "What better way to protect confidentiality than not to write it down."

"You're not supposed to do that," Barbara said. "You're supposed to document everything and then guard the paperwork like the crown jewels."

But we'd already proved that we could get at the charts. If we could, so could others.

"It would feel like a betrayal," I said.

"For the client or the counselor?"

"Both."

"Not writing down the hot stuff would be a kind of enabling," Barbara said, "protecting the alcoholic from consequences."

"So we're back at codependency again, huh?"

"Well, we are," Barbara said. "It's an occupational hazard. The more intimate you are with an alcoholic or addict, the more you tend to rescue and enable. And what could be more intimate than a relationship that actually requires you to ask the person if he's a child molester?"

"I'm stumped," I said.

We all were. Who did this information point the finger at? It could have been a motive for anyone in the family. Brandy was

Emmie and Sam's son. Frances had said "we." The family all knew. How many of them subscribed to Frances's view that he was "evil"? What did that mean to any of them? Not fit to live? Undeserving of the family money? Hadn't they already hated how he squandered that in the course of going to hell?

"It's all suggestive," said Jimmy, summing up. "But we've still got questions, not answers."

TWENTY

Barbara slammed the apartment door, stormed into the
living room, and banged her backpack down on the coffee table so
hard, I jumped. I was having a little nap on the couch while Jimmy
improved his already-encyclopedic knowledge of archery on-line.
Had he ever shot an arrow from a bow? No, but he had designed
more than one computer game about medieval warfare. If you
asked him whether he liked Agincourt or the Norman Conquest
better, he got the same ravaged look on his face that he used to as a
kid if you told him he could choose between a Snickers bar and a
Baby Ruth. How could you *choose*?

"Do you live here now?" Barbara snarled.

"Whoa, don't shoot! I'm innocent! Do you want me to go
home?"

"Hey, peanut, did you have a bad day? Sit down and tell us
about it," Jimmy urged pacifically. In real life, where he spends
hardly any time, he's the world's most peaceful guy. "Bruce will get
you a diet Coke." She lived on the stuff. I was so busy wondering

how she could stand the chemical taste and lack of any interesting ingredients, such as hops or barley, that it took me a moment to realize he'd volunteered me. Jimmy could be sneaky.

"Double whoa," I said. "I'm resting from a long day staying sober."

Barbara laughed, thank goodness, and shoved me upright so she could plump herself down next to me on the couch. Our shtick entertains her almost more than it does Jimmy and me.

"No, it's okay," she said. "You don't have to make the Long March to the kitchen. I'm just tired and cranky from my own long day."

"More than usual?"

"Oh, I wasn't at work. After needing us so badly that I couldn't go to Ohio—"

"Scenic Ohio," I interjected.

"Right, scenic Ohio. Anyhow, somehow they found the time to send us all to this ethics workshop. I couldn't say no because I need the continuing-education hours for my counselor credential renewal."

"You don't like ethics?" I asked. "That sounds more like me."

"Of course I like ethics—silly, I mean I take my professional ethics seriously and it can be interesting to talk about and definitely relevant to stuff that actually happens at work. But as a rule, I care more about the relational aspect of these workshops than the content."

"She means she really goes to these things to see her friends and schmooze," Jimmy explained.

"I did know most of the people there," she said. "And that part was fun."

"Anyone we know?"

"Bruce knows Charmaine from the Bowery. And Jimmy, you've met my friends Ruth and Eileen. They both work in outpatient programs like mine," she said.

"What did they talk about?" Jimmy asked.

"It was a whole day! Actually, the part about Tarasoff was kind of interesting."

"What's that? Sounds like a number the Rockettes would do. Or a dish they'd serve at the Russian Tea Room."

"Closed," Jimmy pointed out.

"While I languished in the gutter, life on the planet went on," I intoned. "Seas dried up. Mountains rose."

"Goofball," said Barbara. "Duty to warn."

"Warn me to shut up or you'll do what?"

"No, idiot! Tarasoff. The therapist's duty to warn a murder victim."

"That would make it awfully easy to catch the murderer," I remarked. "Much easier than how we're doing it, running all over the city and going to Ohio and all."

"Before, dodo. You're the therapist. The client tells you in a session he plans to kill his ex-wife. You have to break confidentiality and warn the wife. There was a case in California where the family sued the therapist."

"I know there's a catch in there somewhere, but I can't think what it is."

"Well, it's an ethical dilemma, which is why we spent more than half an hour discussing it. They also talked about child abuse. And sex offenders."

"Did you bring up the thing about Guff?"

"I did. I fudged the details, said it was a case in my agency a couple of years ago."

"And did the others think it was plausible a counselor might have kept that information secret, not put it in the chart?"

Barbara waggled her hand from side to side.

"Some did; some didn't. The whole point of a workshop like this is to stir up controversy and discussion. Ethics is all about gray areas, really. Or at least you have to think harder about the gray areas than the black-and-white ones."

"What would be black or white?"

"Oh, sex with a client."

"Not like in the movies?"

"Definitely not like in the movies!"

"One of her pet peeves," Jimmy added. "Anything else interesting?"

"Yeah, at lunch Charmaine got to talking about your corpse, Bruce—don't look at me that way, I meant the old man in the laundry room, not Guff. I said we'd had a couple of unexpected deaths. And Ruth and Eileen said they'd had some in their programs, too, clients who unexpectedly developed symptoms and didn't make it, in spite of every effort. Eileen was there when they did CPR. She made it quite a story, with Sister Agnes from her unit doing the mouth part and the janitor, who luckily had taken the training along with the clinicians, doing the chest compressions. She said he's this stocky, very hairy guy and the sweat was pouring off his forehead onto his hairy arms, and he cracked two ribs—the client's, not his. Eileen said they popped. And the client died anyway."

"I wish you hadn't shared that," I said.

"Oh, no, Bruce, I'm sorry, I forgot you went through that with Guff."

"It's okay. I didn't do the CPR, I was just there."

"So was Eileen. She was terrified it would be up to her, because she hadn't had the training for almost a year and she wasn't sure she would have remembered what to do. I could imagine. They make us take it, too, and I always wonder if I'd rise to the occasion."

"Not everyone can be a hero," Jimmy said.

"Yeah, and in the training film, the real-life CPR stories all have happy endings. I guess they don't want to scare us. Anyhow, I don't mind not being a hero as long as I'm not the damsel in distress."

"Not much chance of that," said Jimmy comfortably.

"I take that as a compliment," Barbara said. "Oh, I almost forgot. Another client died at my place over the weekend. They told me when I called in. This is getting monotonous. He's another old-timer who came in drunk on Friday."

"One of your own clients?" Jimmy asked.

"Carlo and I both worked with him," she said, "and we referred him to the detox in our own hospital. Jeremiah—another alcoholic who outlived his liver. He got someone to sneak him in a fifth of vodka and managed to kill himself while the nurses' backs were turned. Acute alcohol poisoning, cirrhosis, and kidney failure."

"Three in your program," Jimmy said, "two on the Bowery, and now your friends tell you other agencies are losing clients over the odds as well."

"You say that as if it means something," Barbara said. "Does it? And if so, what?"

"Let's make a list," Jimmy said.

Barbara and I went over and looked at the computer screen over his broad shoulders. He doodled on a graphics program as we talked. We watched him draw a little cartoon of a man dead in bed with a bottle lying beside him.

"We'll use a spreadsheet," he said. He clicked the mouse. A grid popped up, and he typed in "Dead Clients" in bold at the top of the first row. "Tell me the names you know."

"Nick, in the Dumpster up at work," Barbara said. "Old Daniel the following week, and this new one, Jeremiah, this past weekend."

"On the Bowery," I added, "Elwood and then Guff."

"Eileen had one, when the janitor did CPR but it didn't work, and Ruth said one at her program, I think, maybe more. I can call and ask."

"Wait a sec. I'm filling in the agencies. If you can get me just a bit more data, we may see a pattern. How about age?"

"I can't give you numbers there. But except for Guff, all of them were old."

"Not that old," I objected. When I was twenty, I thought everybody over thirty should be dead. But sobriety was giving me a new perspective.

"At the hospital," Barbara said, "they've started calling fifty-five and over geriatric. You should have heard Carlo on the subject, he's fifty-six, and he had a fit. I learned a few Italian words I wouldn't use in the Vatican."

Jimmy gave her one of his Catholic looks.

"How about cause of death?" I asked.

"I'm thinking," Barbara said. "Oh, they found alcohol and barbiturates in Nick. I didn't mention it because we didn't consider it as murder. We know he had a bottle, and he probably crawled in there to drink it in peace and then sleep it off."

"Alcohol and barbiturates will kill you all right," I said. "He did OD? Kind of old-fashioned combo these days, what with crack and the designer drugs."

"Easy to get in a hospital, though," she said. "Dilantin is a barb, and I bet three-quarters of our folks have been on it at one time or another. Plenty of seizure disorders, whether they're epileptics or have alcoholic seizures. And so are Fiorinal and Fioricet, which are migraine drugs—caffeine and aspirin or Tylenol with a barbiturate. They figure he got them on the street, but I bet they started out in the hospital. He didn't have a prescription, that's for sure."

"All this fancy medical info," I complained, "makes my head spin. Where I come from, we just said, 'Gimme the blue pills. Gimme the red pills. Gimme the ones that'll mellow me out and the ones that'll blow my mind.'"

"Long ago and far away," said Jimmy.

"Stop showing off," Barbara said. "This is serious. Cause of death, overdose. He did have cirrhosis of the liver. Make a column for life-threatening illness. Let's see if it's separate from the cause of death for any of the others."

"Didn't you just say he had liver failure?" Jimmy asked.

"No, that was Jeremiah. Although his cause of death was acute alcohol poisoning. It is confusing, that's why we're writing it down."

"Okay, okay, I'm getting it," Jimmy said. "And Daniel?"

"He had a seizure disorder," Barbara said. "He would have had a prescription for barbiturates. In fact, he had a seizure on the unit on Friday. But they say he died of acute and chronic alcoholism. His organ systems collapsed. He drank on top of his Dilantin, too."

"How about the old man on the Bowery?" Jimmy asked.

"Terminal cancer," I said. "He was about to go to hospice."

"Charmaine assumed he died of that," Barbara said. "Maybe I should take a look at his chart, too. They can't screw up every Bowery autopsy, can they?"

Jimmy looked worried. "I don't know if you should be wandering around there yammering about murder to all and sundry."

"'Yammering'? *Yammering?* James F. X. Cullen, you are about to get your head handed to you."

Jimmy did his imitation of a monolith. It's as close as he gets to cowering.

"Okay, okay, unfreeze, I'll let you live this time. Will you please restate your concern?"

"Yes, dear," he said meekly. "Because I love you so very much, I feel anxious when you investigate possible felonious acts in the very workplace of the possible felons. While I understand that you take every precaution, and that you are not only awesomely discreet but fully capable of protecting yourself from any possible menace, I wish to hell you'd take a bodyguard."

Some days I'm glad I'm single. Most days.

We finished the spreadsheet after Barbara phoned Ruth and Eileen and got the missing information. Multiple deaths had occurred recently in both their agencies. And they'd heard of others from friends in other programs. These folks all tended to know each other. We could see a pattern. People who were expected to die eventually—except for Guff—had died unexpectedly, many of them from drinking and drug overdoses or some kind of lethal bellyache.

"What they really have in common," said Jimmy, frowning, "is that they all died in the hospital or some kind of alcohol clinic. I know hospitals kill thousands of Americans every year, but it's still a little odd."

"I think so," Barbara said. "Clients die all right, but it used to happen when they *weren't* in treatment. They'd relapse and disappear from the program. Usually, they don't want to know us as long as they're drinking."

That still hit home painfully. Jimmy and Barbara hadn't exactly thrown me away. They had backed off, and I had carefully avoided them. Or as carefully as I could while stumbling around yawing between blackouts, the shakes, and the remedial hair of the dog.

"And while they're drunk or high and far from medical help," Barbara went on, "that's when they get run over or OD or get stabbed in a fight or their liver finally gives out."

"Can you see any other patterns?" asked Jimmy.

"That's not enough?" I asked.

"Nothing is random. Chaos is just order that we haven't figured out yet."

"Thanks for sharing," I said.

"Wait a minute," Barbara said. "This is really weird. In every one of those programs, there's a sister on staff from Sister Angel's community."

"Avenging angels?" Jimmy joked. "Communal poisoning?"

"It is absurd. They're Catholics. The whole pro-life thing. Going to Hell for suicide, or is it Purgatory?"

"Hell," said Jimmy. "Unless you say you're sorry at the last moment."

"Which is probably physically impossible a lot of the time," Barbara pointed out.

"Homicide's a mortal sin, too, my pet. And with these particular sisters, the idea of them giving clients booze is even more bizarre."

"Forget the nuns," I said. "What I really want to know is this: Were all those people murdered?"

"Good question," said Jimmy.

The phone rang at that point. Jimmy scooped up the receiver with a long swipe of the arm without taking his other hand from the keyboard until he'd listened for a while. Then he put it over the mouthpiece.

"It's for you, Barbara. I think it's your friend Emmie, and she sounds upset."

"Oh!" said Barbara, pleased. "She's never called me before." She took the phone, and as she listened, her smile crumpled.

"Emmie, I'm so sorry! What happened?" To us, she mouthed, "Her sister died."

"Frances?" Jimmy asked.

"Lucinda," she whispered. "Shh."

While Barbara made condoling noises and asked if there was anything she could do, Jimmy turned to the computer. It took him only a moment to find the story on-line.

"The police think she interrupted a robbery," he said softly, so the woman on the other end of the line couldn't hear. "She was beaten and some valuable art she had was gone."

"The icons!" I exclaimed.

"Of course I'll come to the funeral," Barbara said into the phone.

She wrote down the information and said good-bye with many soothing noises.

"Poor thing! She could hardly talk for crying. You'll go with me, won't you?"

"To the funeral? I will, but Bruce had better not," Jimmy said.

I got his point immediately. Frances would probably fly in. I doubted she would be pleased to see me again.

"Now aren't you glad I went to Ohio instead of you?"

"Now aren't *you* glad you went to Ohio instead of me," Barbara retorted. "I can't say I love a funeral, but that poor woman. I'm not sure why I like her so much, knowing that she may have stood by while her son got abused."

"Denial," Jimmy said. "Hers, not yours. It's like with the alcoholic—you can't bear to know, so you don't know." He was still keyboarding and clicking away. "Listen to this. Lucinda had a fabulous collection of Russian icons, not necessarily of known provenance."

"Meaning she may have gotten them under the table?" I asked.

"Now I feel guilty," Barbara said. "Sherlocking when her body is hardly cold."

"It could be connected, pigeon," Jimmy said. "We'll give her a moment of silence if you want. And I said I'd go to the funeral with you. But it won't help Emmie or anyone else not to know who killed her, and we're the only ones who can see the whole picture."

"If we're right," Barbara said. "Okay, okay, carry on. What does it say?"

"Not all of the icons were on display. The ones you guys saw when you peeked through the living room window were only the tip of the iceberg. But her closest friends had seen them all. It sounds like she had one of those shady collection rooms where she could show them off, and they obviously thought it was wiser to come clean."

"So where does Boris fit in?" I asked.

"I knew there was something fishy about his showing up there," Barbara said.

"Whoa, let's not leap to conclusions," Jimmy said. "But—"

"But if he already had a relationship with her," Barbara said, "and he knew how valuable the icons were—"

"Or," I added, "if he might even have been involved in helping her acquire them—"

"A counselor's salary," Barbara pointed out, "is not the greatest. And he didn't even have his credential, so he's making less than I am."

"What did Boris do before he came here?" I asked.

"A lot of immigrants have to give up professions or skilled occupations because their English isn't up to it or they just can't get the jobs," Jimmy said. "Like our elevator man from Albania."

"He wasn't a professional comedian?" I asked.

"Biologist," Barbara said. "Boris's English is okay, but let's find out. Give me the phone."

She dialed from memory.

"Charmaine? Hi, just fine, how about you? Glad to hear it. I have a quick, dumb question for you. What did Boris do for a living in Russia? Yeah, our Boris, Boris the counselor."

"Really? Wow, that's interesting. Oh, for a paper I'm writing about who goes into counseling."

She shrugged at us. She had no reason to write a paper, since she wasn't in school. Thinking on her feet. But Charmaine wasn't looking for flaws in her story.

"He hasn't? And he didn't call? . . . I know, making sure you've got coverage is the pits. Glad I'm not an administrator! . . . Sure, sure, just let me know when you need me. I'm always glad to get some work and see you all—two birds, right? Take care. Yeah, I will, too."

She hung up and turned triumphantly to us.

"Well! Boris was a curator in an art museum, or maybe just a security guard—there's a faction on the staff that thinks he inflated his job history—but either way, he would know icons and might have had access. And that's not all. He hasn't been in for two days, and he hasn't called. She tried his home number, but the phone's been disconnected. And he needed money because he was hoping to bring over his wife's family."

"So do we tell the police," Jimmy asked, "that you guys saw him near Lucinda's?"

"Oh, Jimmy, sometimes you're no fun since you stopped drinking." Barbara pouted. "Just kidding, just kidding."

"Well, do we tell?" Jimmy persisted. "They probably have no idea he exists."

"They have no idea we exist, either," I said, "and I'd like to keep it that way. I don't much care to put myself at a murder scene."

"Good point," Barbara admitted. "Anyhow, maybe he had nothing to do with it."

"Then why did he disappear?" Jimmy asked. "Unless he did it."

"The police could find him," Barbara said. "I mean find a documented connection with Lucinda, if he was a protégé of hers through this immigrant foundation."

"She had an in on the Bowery, too," I said. "She might have gotten him the job."

"I can't ask Charmaine that," Barbara said. "I'd have to look at the personnel files."

"Hasn't it occurred to you yet," Jimmy demanded, "that it might not be safe wandering around down there looking at things you're not supposed to be seeing?"

"Oh, Jimmy, don't be silly. Anyhow, they're short a counselor again. I couldn't tell her I wouldn't help. She knows you're no company when you're doing your on-line thing."

"Yeah, yeah, blame it on me," he said. "Great maneuver—feint, counterattack."

"I learned it from you," Barbara reminded him.

"What? When? You're not interested in military strategy."

"When you were drinking. 'Don't be silly, Barbara,' you would say. 'It's just a beer. If you didn't nag, I wouldn't have to drink.'"

"Oh, that."

"I never knew how lucky I was," I remarked, "doing all my drinking single."

"Son, you have no idea," Jimmy said.

"I still don't see, though, what Boris has to do with Guff." Barbara was ready to stop fooling around. "I just don't see a connection."

"Unless Guff caught him doing something at the detox," Jimmy said.

"Something that wasn't kosher," Barbara added.

"Like stealing money from people's desks," I said. "You should have heard the lecture they gave us. They were oh so fair-minded, but they obviously suspected the patients. Maybe they were wrong. Though I'd have thought," I added, feeling slightly hurt as I said it, "that Guffy would have told me, whether or not he went to Bark or Charmaine about it."

"It didn't have to be the stealing," Jimmy said. "It could be anything."

"Like Darryl with the drug dealing," I said. "If he is dealing drugs. He could be operating out of the detox."

"The Russian could be trafficking in stolen art on company time," said Jimmy.

"Highly unlikely, even bizarre," said Barbara. "Anyhow, where would he hide it? There isn't a whole lot of extra space. In the laundry room? The client storage room?"

"You two know the layout," Jimmy said. "I don't. They have a computer, don't they? He could have been doing the business part of it from there."

"So could Darryl," I reminded him.

"But Boris could do it in Russian," Jimmy pointed out. "He'd hardly even need a password. It would be like the Navajo signal guys in World War Two—a foreign language is a code no cryptographer can crack."

"Then Guff couldn't have cracked it, either," said Barbara, "unless he happened to speak Russian. And if Guff couldn't catch Boris doing anything wrong—"

"Then Boris had no reason to kill Guff," said Jimmy.

"But if Boris killed Lucinda," I demanded, "who killed Guff?"

"And if he didn't," Barbara said, "if he stole the icons but didn't kill her, or if he didn't steal the icons but did have something to do with them—"

"Smuggling them in," I suggested, "selling them to her on the black market."

"Or physically took them to the house," Barbara added. "That would put his fingerprints there, nice reason to run away, especially if he was illegal. Even legal immigrants get paranoid about the law."

"With good reason," I put in.

"But if Boris didn't," Jimmy asked, "who killed Lucinda?"

TWENTY-ONE

Having made up my mind I wasn't going to drink again, I was having a royal bitch of a time with the First Step. I was having trouble getting into the proper attitude of surrender. I had always had to rely on myself. My mother had been depressed and ineffectual. My father had been too busy slowly dying of the booze himself as his ambitions got smaller and smaller.

After I met Jimmy, we backed each other up. We stood together whether we were wading into a ritual Saturday-night fistfight with the crowd on the next block or playing one of the historical war games Jimmy pushed us into with endless inventiveness. Our block boasted probably the only group of urban white-trash kids in New York who had heard of the Duke of Wellington's Peninsular Campaign or the Carthaginians' attempt on Rome. We fought them all over the neighborhood, complete with elephants.

But Jimmy and I couldn't always protect each other. In our world, admitting powerlessness could be fatal. Surrendering even to God was dangerous. Jimmy went to Catholic school and got chased around the school yard by a horny priest. After that, he decided he didn't want to be a missionary after all, though it sure would have gotten him out of the neighborhood. My dad's family were kind of half-assed Presbyterians. They seemed to view religion as an endless procession of rummage sales and good works.

A lot of people had told me first-step surrender was a paradox. Not Jimmy—he usually said, "Don't worry about it. Just don't drink and go to meetings." Sometimes admitting powerlessness and unmanageability made a glimmer of sense to me. Sometimes it sounded like pure and total hooey. I tried to keep it simple the way they said. Go to work, eat real food, watch TV. Don't drink, go to meetings, investigate a murder.

I had gotten into the habit of going out for coffee with Glenn and his friends, though I had yet to use his number. The phone was willing, but I was powerless over my fingers. I usually got to the coffee shop first. The others all had people to talk to, smoke with, and exchange those interminable hugs with when the meeting let out. Those hugs still embarrassed the hell out of my inner John Wayne. So far, nobody had said I couldn't be sober without them. So I wasn't having any truck with them.

On this particular evening, Glenn arrived five minutes after I did. It turned out that no one else was coming. Glenn was a savvy dude. He knew I would have bolted if I'd known it would be just him and me. So there I was, one-on-one with a potential sponsor. Talk about powerless and unmanageable.

Glenn grinned at me. "Looks like HP wanted us to be alone together tonight."

I looked around again to make sure nobody was within earshot. I'd rather be arrested for drunk and disorderly than let anybody catch me talking about a Higher Power in public. We were in a booth, and the place wasn't crowded. No escape there.

"How's your sobriety going?"

"We-e-ell," I drawled, "I'm not drinking."

"Sucks, doesn't it." Not what I expected him to say.

"Hell yes," I said. "When I hear someone in the meeting say their worst day sober is better than their best day drinking, I want to smack them."

Glenn laughed. "It's all a matter of perspective. I remember the first day I heard the words *grateful recovering alcoholic* come out of my mouth, I thought I'd been invaded by the body snatchers. It scared the shit out of me."

"Being sober scares the shit out of me," I admitted.

"You ever see that T-shirt that says 'Reality is for people who can't handle drugs'? I sometimes wonder why only active addicts wear it. It's true in recovery, too."

"It's humiliating," I complained, "thinking of myself as someone who can't handle drugs."

"Beats me," he said musingly, not at all in an argumentative way, but as if he really wanted to know, "how come we find it so much more humiliating to admit chemicals have us licked—only partly our fault, when you consider most of us got stuck with the genetic programming—than to be caught pissing against a wall in full view of dozens of strangers."

"Oh, you know that wall, too?" I cracked.

"Intimately." He grinned. "Have you found a sponsor yet?"

"I know I should. I know, I know, famous last words."

"What do you think is holding you back?" He still sounded as if he just really wanted to know.

"Sheer orneriness. I've been a maverick my whole life. Seems like that's harder to give up than the actual chemicals."

"I've got good news and bad news for you, fella. Every single one of us is a maverick."

"Is that the good news or the bad news?"

"Both." As I thought about that, he added, "I'd be glad to be your sponsor. Honored, in fact." He didn't make it a question. Just reeled me in with no further ado.

Two days later, by appointment, Glenn arrived at my apartment with a copy of the Big Book under his arm. I broke into a sweat the moment I saw it.

Glenn intercepted my aversive glance. "It's not gonna bite you," he said mildly. "I just thought maybe I'd pick out some of the good parts for you. Have you ever read any of it?"

"Not if I saw it coming. I've heard bits and pieces at meetings, but never anything to convince me it could ever be my bag."

"Maybe I'll manage to surprise you," Glenn said easily. "Ever heard the Promises?"

"No," I said warily. "I have to promise not to take another drink? I thought the whole program was all just suggestions."

"It is. Even the Twelve Steps are just suggested. Take what you like and leave the rest. One of the best arguments that AA is nothing like a cult, if you ask me. No, these are promises the program makes to you. Here, listen. It comes just after the Ninth Step."

" 'We are going to know a new freedom and a new happiness. We will not regret the past nor wish to shut the door on it.' " He went on. There were about a dozen of them. I didn't hear anything I could say I didn't want for myself, and it was oddly moving. When he finished, he closed the book and raised one eyebrow at me. He let the silence speak for him. I didn't know a damn thing about this guy. Yet he might end up telling me the most embarrassing and evil things he'd ever done, just to prove to me that I wasn't the only one. What a weird program. But it works.

We talked about the Steps for a while. I pissed and moaned about surrender. Glenn made some suggestions that weren't too terrible. We discussed what meetings I would go to every week. We drank a lot of coffee. Finally, he looked at his watch.

"I have to go soon," he said, "but there's one more thing I think we should talk about."

"And that is?" I asked, pretty relaxed by now.

"Prayer," he said, and then cracked up at the horrified expression on my face. "Sorry for laughing, but it's so predictable."

"Damn! Gotta work on that poker face. Okay, what do I have to do? Is this where we kill the chicken?"

"Shoot, I knew I forgot to bring something! Sorry to disappoint you. No chicken. No speaking in tongues. What I do is get on my knees."

"I'd rather have the chicken," I said.

"It's not required. It just kind of sets the stage. Helps me remember this is something I take seriously. How about trying it once? If it doesn't work for you, that's okay."

"Please say you don't mean now."

"I'll close my eyes." He was humoring me.

"Just don't tell anybody," I said.

Glenn mimed locking his lips and throwing away the key. I slid out of my chair. My joints creaked, protesting. The uncarpeted floor was hard against my knees.

"This isn't going to hurt," Glenn said. "And if you're a good boy, you can have a lollipop afterward."

After all that buildup, all he did was have me repeat the Serenity Prayer. That's the one about accepting the things I can't change, the courage to change the things I can, and the wisdom to know the difference. I couldn't argue about the sentiments. I couldn't even argue about the simple elegance of the prose.

"See?" said Glenn. "You do know how to pray."

"That's it?"

"It'll grow on you," he promised.

"I don't know about the knee thing,"

"Not a deal breaker."

"How long do I have to do it?" I demanded.

"One day at a time." He grinned.

"Just the Serenity Prayer?"

"Come back when you've mastered it," said Glenn, "and I'll give you another. We probably met in a previous life, and I'm sure we'll be able to find each other in the next one."

I disentangled that more slowly than I would have if I'd fed my neurons more spinach and fewer hallucinogens. "You mean it's not just days to perfect wisdom?"

"Nope. Takes a lifetime of practice to achieve a spiritually sound state of imperfection."

"Oh, if that's all!" I said, getting my wind back.

Glenn looked around for his jacket, found it slung over a chair, and put it on.

"So you're all set for now, huh?"

"Just peachy," I assured him.

"Oh, before I forget. You know what's the biggest problem a recovering alcoholic faces after making ninety days?"

"Never got close enough to think about it, but I'm sure you're about to tell me."

"For most of us, it's what the hell to do on day ninety-one."

"Makes sense," I admitted. "I've met a number of guys in detox who had a brilliant idea about how to celebrate."

"Exactly. We don't want you to be one of them, so I'm going to make it easy for you. Once you have your ninety days, I'd like you to join my men's group."

"Men's group? Real men or quiche-eating men?"

"I'd say we hit the golden mean between macho and wimpy. Sober guys, in other words. You know some of them already."

"The guys we have coffee with? Mike, Gary, Roger?"

"And a few others. We don't talk about it much because it's not a meeting, just a private thing we do. I didn't mention it to you before because for a while there, I wasn't sure if you were just resting between slips or really going for it this time. But I think you're serious, don't you?"

"Good Lord, a compliment. Be still, my heart." All right, I didn't know how to handle feeling an unaccustomed pleasure and pride. But that was okay. Glenn saw right through me. It confirmed my awful suspicion that he just might be the right sponsor for me.

"I do appreciate it," I managed to get out. I didn't want to come off like a total dork. "Hold on a sec. I'll walk you out." I had run out of cigarettes, and I wasn't about to turn in my smoke rings for a halo quite yet.

"We didn't use to be so careful," Glenn explained as we clumped down the stairs. "But we learned something from that unfortunate dustup with your friend."

"Guff was in that group?" I said, surprised. "The guy you called 'God.'"

"He called himself that," Glenn said. "Mostly, we tried not to call him anything. He asked, and as I said, we weren't screening new guys all that carefully. The fight with Roger that you heard about? That actually happened in the group. The other fellows had to pull them off each other, literally. It almost broke up the group, and every one of them hated him by the end. He had what my shrink calls 'boundary issues,' and he also tended to act as if he thought his money made him . . . well, God."

"Well, you won't have that problem with me," I said. "I only knew the guy in detox, and I didn't see that side of him at all."

"He was only human," Glenn said, "and we all know how deflated you feel the first few days sober."

"Tell me about it," I said in ironic tones.

"He would have gotten over it soon enough. Just go easy on

mentioning him to the other guys." I might have mentioned once or twice that I was poking around on the subject of Guff in general. "Some of them still have very short fuses where he's concerned, and you don't want to set them off."

"I'll be careful."

"In their minds, he's the proverbial drunken son of a bitch. Know what you get when a guy like that gets sober?"

I paused in the doorway of the bodega where I usually got my cigarettes.

"I give up." I knew, but I knew he wanted to tell me. "What?"

"You get a sober son of a bitch."

TWENTY-TWO

"So how was the funeral?" I asked.

"Crowded," Jimmy said. "Episcopalian."

"I hardly even got to speak to Emmie," Barbara said. "A quick hug and a few words. I didn't want to foist myself on her, even if I could have, but I'm glad I showed up. All the Lucinda groupies we saw at the lecture were there. Two of them talked about how brilliant she was, and one read a poem that nobody understood."

"I understood it," Jimmy said. "Death is scary, but if you're an intellectual, it's okay, because the afterlife blows your mind like a 'Eureka!' moment."

"How does he do it?" I asked Barbara.

"Beats me. Oh, we saw your Frances—"

"She's not my Frances," I objected. "And it's not my Ohio."

"Whatever. She had a man with her," Barbara said. "We haven't even talked about the husband."

"Professor Henry Standish," I supplied.

"You didn't even try to make contact with him while you were in Dayton."

"I couldn't think of a good excuse."

"Not after you'd established yourself with Frances as Guff's friend," Jimmy helped me out.

"Besides," I said, "I don't see how he could have had anything to do with it. He lived six hundred miles away."

"Unlike his brother-in-law," Barbara said, "the nasty Dr. Weill."

"You've really got it in for the guy, haven't you," I said.

"At least I know what he looks like now," Barbara said. "He was there. His nose is bigger than mine."

"You've got a beautiful nose, my puffin," Jimmy said tenderly.

Barbara's face went through a lot of changes as she considered how to respond to this dubious compliment. I decided to divert her.

"You know, guys, right after New Year's, the university was probably still on winter break. Jimmy, check the airlines. See if we can catch the professor flying to New York around the holidays."

"You want me to hack into the airline computers," he said. "Why am I not overjoyed?"

"We need that information," Barbara said. "Can't you go around them?"

"We have complete confidence in your abilities," I chipped in.

"*Et tu, Brute?*"

Of course Jimmy found a way. He remembered that Henry Standish was a historian. It took him only seven minutes to find out that Standish had presented a paper at an academic conference in San Diego on January 2.

"Hmm, this is interesting. Want to hear what his paper was about?"

"Not really," Barbara said.

He told us anyway. He told us all about the politics and economics of relations between England and Scotland in the 1590s. That was during the reign of Queen Elizabeth I of England and King James VI of Scotland, who lucked out and also became James I of England when Elizabeth died.

"Especially," Jimmy said enthusiastically, "the perennially shifting Border. He's written a ton of scholarly work; it's all listed here. Oh, and a biography of this guy who was a kind of supercop who ran around bashing heads and chasing cattle thieves on the Border. The whole population on both sides was into stealing cows and horses from one another whenever they could. It's way out of my period," he admitted, "but I have a certain fondness for fellow Celts with a flexible attitude toward larceny."

"I can identify with that," I said. "Is any of this relevant?"

"Actually, yes. That biography might have made money. Academics don't usually get rich, but this sounds like more of a pop thing. If he was getting decent royalties, maybe the Standishes didn't need Guff's trust fund."

"The definition of *need* is highly elastic," I said cynically. "But it's moot. He wasn't there. Neither of them was in New York when Guff got killed."

The next day, we checked the news again. They still hadn't found the icons or the murderer. Boris was still missing. And we still didn't want to tell the police about Boris. The sticking point was that if we said anything, then we were involved. We all agreed, fervently in my case, that it was better not to be involved. We also talked about my discovery that Guff had had not one or two but numerous ill-wishers among the people who had known him in AA. And another point I'd forgotten.

"I saw what looked like a lovely little Russian icon in Boris's office one day."

"I never saw anything like that when I was there," Barbara said.

"He was kind of worshiping it when I happened to look in," I said. "He probably kept it in a locked drawer most of the time. It looked valuable."

"And everybody knew there was a sneak thief lurking some-where," she reminded us.

"So what next?" Jimmy asked. "Are we getting somewhere? Any-where? Nowhere?"

"I need to go back to the detox," Barbara said. "I've got to take one more look at that chart."

"I could go," I said. "I could have a few drinks and get myself readmitted."

"No!" Jimmy and Barbara said simultaneously. Loudly.

"Keep your doublets on. I was just kidding," I said.

"Boris is still missing. Bark and Charmaine are going nuts trying to keep the unit covered," Barbara said. "I can work any shift I want. Anyhow, I thought the whole point of this," she had to add, "was to keep you from picking up a drink over it."

"And here I thought it was to keep you amused when keeping the focus on yourself gets too boring."

She threw a cushion at me. Her aim wasn't bad.

"I'm sorry, I'm sorry," I yelped. "I didn't mean it." I fired a cush-ion back at her. Then we had a little pillow fight.

Jimmy looked on benignly. When we ran out of steam, he in-quired, "Have we reached the end of the line here?"

We were both disheveled and out of breath. I sat down firmly on the last cushion so Barbara couldn't throw it at me.

"I'm going to give Ed Bark a call," she said, "and ask for a night shift. One more little peek at the chart, just to see if anything pops out at me. And maybe a look at the computer. I know I can get onto the computer in the nursing station."

"Looking for what?" I asked.

"I'm not sure, but I'll know it if I see it. Maybe."

"And then you'll be ready to let this thing go?" Jimmy asked, his tone making it clear what he wanted the answer to be.

"And then we'll see."

TWENTY-THREE

A week later, Barbara spotted Emmie at a meeting, looking a little paler and a little thinner and dressed in well cut black.

"Emmie!" Barbara put her arms around her, noting with pleasure that she barely stiffened before hugging her back. "How are you doing?"

"Fairly well, thank you," she said. Barbara reminded herself that Emmie might never pour out her heart and guts the way she and most people in the program did. "Thank you so much for attending the funeral. It was a lovely service, wasn't it? Her graduate students insisted on doing everything. The flowers and music were lovely, weren't they? Lucinda and I were not close. It's just that after Guffy"—her voice cracked a little—"it was a bit overwhelming." She smiled tremulously. "The children were adorable. At least Duncan and Lucille—it didn't touch them very deeply—they're too young, and Lucinda wasn't good with children. They dressed up beautifully and were so good through the whole affair. Brandy wouldn't go." She sighed. "I so feel I've failed him."

Barbara agreed but would certainly not say so. She gave Emmie's shoulder a little squeeze.

"Come on, I'll walk you home."

They set out, walking slowly, through the icy streets. It had thawed, rained, and then frozen again, and the sidewalk was treacherously slick. Barbara was more than ready for spring.

"Please come in for a cup of tea," Emmie begged. "You mustn't say no. I'd like you to meet my husband. If he's working late in the office, we'll stop in. It's just downstairs from the apartment."

Barbara caught herself about to blurt, "I know." She reminded herself that Dr. Weill had never met her. She had left his waiting room before he saw her face-to-face. Marlene, who had seen her, would be long gone this evening. It might still be awkward meeting him. She rehearsed polite opening lines in her head as they walked.

The light in the first-floor window on the street leaked out around the edges of the blinds. This was supposed to be her first time in the doctor's office. She stood back to let Emmie buzz and, when there was no answer, fish out a couple of keys.

"I know he's there," Emmie commented over her shoulder, "or this second lock would be locked. He needs it open to buzz the patients in, and he locks it with his own key last thing before he comes upstairs." She pushed the door open. "Sam? Are you there?"

Barbara need not have worried about about what to say. Sam Weill lay in a heap on the waiting room floor. He was dead. The condition of the side of his head made that beyond debate.

Emmie went as pale as the body and started to shake.

Barbara felt nauseous and panicky. She found herself repeating the Serenity Prayer over and over in her head.

"We have to call nine one one," she said.

"The phone is on his desk."

Surprised to find herself both thinking and coping, Barbara said,

"We'd better not. It's a crime scene; there might be fingerprints." Barbara doubted that Emmie watched *CSI* or *Law & Order.*

"Whatever you say," she said faintly. "Use the phone upstairs. Oh! Brandy. He's upstairs baby-sitting with the little ones. I don't know if he should see—"

"You need someone to hang on to," Barbara said with more confidence than she felt. "I'll go up and call nine one one and send him down."

Brandy, told that his mother needed him, raced down the carpeted stairs after showing Barbara to the phone. Emmie waited at the foot, her white face looking up. Feeling guiltily grateful not to have to break the news to the boy, Barbara could hear the murmur of their voices as she talked to the 911 operator. When she got back, they were locked in each other's arms. Brandy, with an unchildlike gravity, seemed to be doing the comforting. Parentified child, Barbara thought grimly. If he had any childhood left, there it goes.

Between them, they persuaded Emmie to wait in the apartment. She wanted Barbara to leave, reluctant to inconvenience a friend who need not be involved.

"I should stay with him," she said faintly.

It took both of them to get her up the stairs.

"Come on, Mother," Brandy coaxed. "I'll make you a cup of tea."

"I'd better go back down," Barbara said. The unspoken words "and stay with the body" echoed between them.

"I'll bring you a cup of tea," Brandy offered.

He brought the tea downstairs in a thin porcelain cup, the pale brew slopping into the saucer. His hand shook a little. He showed no other visible reaction to the sight of his father on the floor.

"Thanks, Brandy." Barbara sipped gratefully, the hot liquid making a trickle of impact on the sliver of ice in her heart. "Is there something we could, um, put over him?"

"Oh, yes," the boy said. "I'll get a blanket." He whirled and galloped up the stairs, moving, Barbara thought, more like a real boy this time. He brought a hand-embroidered throw, featherweight and exquisitely made. They spread it over the body. As they flapped it and let it float gently to rest, neither looking as Sam Weill became a series of lumps beneath the fabric, Brandy gave her an odd look or two. That prep school training keeps him very polite, Barbara thought. When he had first come down, Emmie had mentioned almost immediately that she'd come from a meeting. Brandy asked Barbara no awkward questions about how she knew his mother. Nor did he remark that they had met before.

Barbara had no doubt that it was murder. She looked around for a weapon. One of a pair of marble bookends lay on the carpet near the door. They looked like the kind of reproduction sculpture Barbara had seen in museum gift shops. The Museum of Modern Art, she thought, Arp or Brancusi. Or maybe they were originals. If so, they were more expensive than many doctors would use to decorate a waiting room. But since the building housed his family, Dr. Weill must consider—have considered—that the office was part of his home. The bookends were too heavy for anybody's pocket and too bulky for most purses. You could fit one in a backpack, but why would you? Someone had almost certainly found it at hand, given the doctor a lethal bash on the head with it, and dropped it where it lay. Luckily for all of them, she thought, it was the proverbial blunt instrument. The back of his head looked crushed, but nothing had oozed out.

The police, when they arrived, were more insistent than Brandy in their need to know where Barbara fit in. Barbara finally explained with some embarrassment to the most sympathetic-looking woman cop that they knew each other from a twelve-step program.

"I walked her home purely by chance," Barbara said, quaking

inwardly and thinking that her free-floating guilt had never been more inconvenient.

"Oh, yes, Officer," Emmie concurred anxiously. "We've recently had another death in the family, and she's been most kind." Barbara noticed that she made it sound as if they were mere acquaintances. She was grateful, though her heart thumped with the stress that the sin of omission produced. The police officer had gone alert like a pointer at Emmie's mention of another death. She lost interest in Barbara, who was allowed to go within an hour, after giving her name, address, and phone number, along with her description of how they had found the body.

"Do you want me to stay?" she asked Emmie. "I'll be glad to if you need me."

"No, no, Barbara, go. You've been wonderful already. I'll call my sis—" She checked abruptly, obviously stricken as she remembered that Lucinda was dead. No doubt Frances would fly in from Ohio for the funeral, but she'd be no use tonight.

"It's all right, Mother," Brandy said quietly. "I called Cousin Robert."

"Oh, Brandy, you are so good!" Her face lit up. "Robert is my nephew. Oh! You met him." Of course, Barbara thought, Frances's son in AA. "He lives in Westchester, but I'm sure he'll come. And his wife is lovely."

"He said he and Cousin Martha would be here in forty minutes," Brandy confirmed.

Cousin Martha, married to a recovering alcoholic, Barbara realized, might be a plus. Codependents made wonderful caregivers. She would probably get Emmie into bed with hot milk and a sleeping pill, stay over to keep her company, organize the funeral, and envelop Emmie in love. She looked a little better already.

"Are you *sure*?" She addressed the question to Brandy as well as to Emmie. "I feel guilty about leaving you."

"Positive," said Brandy firmly.

Emmie nodded, then offered with a hesitant smile, "Better to feel guilty than resentful," an Al-Anon saying she had learned from Barbara.

"We'll make sure she's taken care of," the woman cop put in. Moving toward the door with Barbara, she added softly, "Let go and let God." Barbara grinned delightedly at this verbal twelve-step secret handshake. It seemed the police officer was in recovery, too.

TWENTY-FOUR

Jimmy and I both went to the funeral with Barbara. I tried to wriggle out of it.

"I don't like funerals," I whined.

"Nobody does, old son," Jimmy said. "Barbara needs us."

"I do," she said without her usual breeziness. "I broke down when I got home last night."

"She cried for about an hour," said Jimmy proudly. Couples!

I tried another tack.

"What happened to not wanting Frances to see me? Besides, Chuckie, the nephew, will be there. I worked for him for two whole weeks. He's going to wonder what the hell I'm doing there."

"At this point, we're both too involved to hide," Barbara said. "Marlene, the secretary, will be there, too. As far as she knows, I'm a disgruntled prospective patient who didn't even stick around long enough to keep my appointment. She'll wonder what the hell I'm doing there, too."

"But you won't seem ubiquitous. And Marlene's not part of the Kettleworth clan. What she thinks won't matter."

"Wiggle, wiggle, little worm," Barbara said. "You're not getting off the hook." She laughed.

"Glad you're feeling better," I said sourly.

"Honestly," she said, "I need a lift. You didn't see Sam with his head dented like a cheap car after a fender bender, or Emmie and that poor kid."

"All right, all right, I'll come," I said. "Just stop. You're breaking my heart."

"I tell you what," said Barbara with a gleam in her eye. "If we have to, we'll explain I'm Emmie's friend and you're married to me and exclaim over what a small world it is."

"Married?" Jimmy and I chorused.

"It's easier to say than 'significant other,'" she explained.

"Why not me?" Jimmy demanded.

"Lucinda's funeral was so crowded that none of them knew you were with me, Jimmy. You can pretend you came alone and don't even notice us."

"Like Winnie-the-Pooh strolling along humming, talking about a little cloud, and wondering if it will rain."

"Exactly." She beamed, ignoring his ironic tone. "It's going to go just fine."

When we reached the church, a classy high Episcopal one that Jimmy whispered hosted a lot of meetings, Emmie was surrounded. She was the chief mourner, so we had to pay our respects. Jimmy and I hung back, looking solemn while Barbara gave her an air kiss, a hug, and a practiced but genuine "Sorry" or two. Emmie squeezed her hand and cast her a grateful look, her eyes brimming. Then, obeying Barbara's imperious jerk of the head, we stepped up and shook her hand and mumbled something. Considering how Barbara probably shared in meetings, Emmie had to know exactly who we were, though maybe not which was which. Luckily, thinking about us was not her top priority right now. She murmured a civil "Thank you," then turned courteously to the next well-wisher.

As we stood wondering what to do with ourselves, a young woman with hair, makeup, and clothing quite a few decibels louder than anybody else's entered the room.

"Marlene?" I asked.

"Right on the first guess."

She spotted Barbara almost at once and came right over. Barbara gave Jimmy a little nudge—he later called it a shove—to cut him loose. But I stayed right beside her. I was curious and surprisingly attracted. The wrapping might be a little gaudy, but she was a firm little package. In the 1920s, just barely long enough ago for Jimmy to consider history, they called it "It." The word has gone out of fashion, but Marlene had it. Also, I felt sorry for her. She looked so outclassed. Barbara claimed I'd been the worst kind of handsome devil with women until the drinking got so bad that I lost interest in anything else. I'm not proud of it. But since getting sober, I'd waited anxiously for the slightest stirring of attraction. I didn't expect it to crop up at an Episcopalian funeral. But it was hard to ignore.

She was a trusting soul. She didn't even ask what Barbara was doing there. She gave me a shy smile that sat oddly on her heavily made-up face when Barbara introduced me with a grudging "This is Bruce. Marlene," realizing I wouldn't go away. I read her as a nice and pretty insecure kid peering through a brassy mask. Marlene launched immediately into a running commentary on the eulogy, the flowers, her sympathy for the widow, and what was going to happen to her job. As she talked, she dabbed at her mascara with a wad of tissues. Considering how he had reamed her out, it was nice of her to grieve for her boss at all. Barbara listened with her counselor face on. It made me want to kick her. A few weeks sober, and I was turning into Sir Galahad. I didn't understand myself.

When I entered the conversation, Marlene perked right up.

"I've been doing temp work lately," I offered. "All the agencies want to know if I have medical office experience. If you've done insurance billing, they'll snap you up."

"I sure have." Her inch-long lashes fluttered. I guessed that they came off at night, along with her lipstick red nails. But so what? "I've never done temp. Is it nice? Do you know how much they pay?"

I was glad Barbara hadn't introduced me as her husband or even her boyfriend. She cast me a meaningful look. I read it as an instruction to chat her up and find out if she knew anything that might be relevant. Barbara accused me later of ratcheting up the charm, as if I did it by turning a crank. I was just trying to be nice. And do what Barbara wanted.

"Would you like to go out for coffee? Maybe I can help you get hooked up."

"I'd love to!"

Barbara looked disgusted. What was wrong with her? She couldn't have it both ways. I had a sudden burning desire, as they say in meetings, for her to go away.

"Go find Jimmy," I said. "Her boyfriend," I explained to Marlene. "And let's get out of here."

We went back to my place. Maybe I did get carried away. The eyelashes weren't supposed to come off, but things got so moist and steamy that they did. I was grateful everything on my side worked the way it was supposed to. I would put it on my gratitude list.

I didn't plan to date Marlene for long. We both agreed we were too different to get serious. But she was affectionate, especially if bellowing like a banshee and scoring my back with trenches I could still see in the mirror three days later counts. I was glad to help her out with my favorite temp agency. I offered to meet her there the next Monday morning. I was due for a new assignment myself. What would really get her the jobs was her résumé and her word-processing test. But I could probably get her in to see my most loyal placement counselor without a three-hour wait. When Monday came, I was even willing to give her a call when she hadn't shown up an hour after the time she'd said she'd meet me.

The bad part started when the police answered the phone. They wouldn't tell me what had happened, but I deduced it wasn't good. I tried to minimize their interest in me, saying I was just a temp-agency acquaintance. It didn't work. They told me to stay right there. Someone would come and talk to me.

A pair of cops showed up half an hour later. I had persuaded the detective on the phone to let me meet them in the lobby. I didn't want to blow my relationship with the temp agency. It didn't take much to make them put your résumé on the bottom of the pile. The cops were one of those unmatched pairs the police go in for in the age of diversity, a big bulky woman who looked Polish and a short café au lait guy who was probably a blend of African-American and Hispanic.

They told me right away that Marlene was dead. Her roommate—I didn't know she had a roommate, it hadn't come up— had found her strangled in her apartment. I hoped they would accept me as no more than a casual job-market acquaintance. But when I gave my name, which I certainly couldn't refuse to do, they exchanged a glance that turned my bowels to water. Marlene had told her roommate about me. At least they couldn't prove I'd made love to her right before her death. I hadn't even seen her for a week. They took a swab of my cheek cells for comparison with something I didn't want to think about. At least they didn't send me to the rest

— 221 —

room with a copy of *Playboy* and a paper cup. That really would have been the low point of my day.

On the bright side, the roommate's story matched mine. I had met Marlene by chance at her boss's funeral, which I'd attended with a friend of mine who was also a friend of his wife. We had impulsively gone to my apartment together. We hadn't seen each other since, but we were friendly enough that I'd offered to help her with temping. And that was it. Marlene had told the roommate just what I'd told the cops. She'd added enough salacious detail about our afternoon in bed that it was hard to look the detective who interviewed me at the precinct in the eye. They also ran my name through the computer. They uncovered some turnstile jumping and a couple of drunk and disorderlies. I was lucky it wasn't worse. If I still sometimes regretted every wild night and outrageous act I'd missed, at that moment I was glad I hadn't tried them all. Especially any that, if I had, would have showed up in the police computer. I told them I was in AA, hoping that would improve the impression I made. I also said "sir" a lot. Finally, they let me go. They warned me not to leave town. Just like the movies. As if. And go where? Scenic Ohio?

When I got home, I called first Jimmy, then my sponsor. It felt great to get two phone calls—the precious privilege of a free man. If they'd arrested me, I'd have used up my one call on Jimmy. He would do anything to help me, now that I'm sober. And if he had to bail me out, Barbara would be breathing down his neck, consumed with guilt because she'd roped me into this and given me a hard time on top of it. Just as well I called Glenn, too. Turned out he was a criminal lawyer. That gave me a warm fuzzy feeling right away. My risk-taking days just might be over. Please, Lord, I prayed. Just get me out of this, and I'll never work without a net again. My sponsor was right. If the stakes are high enough, anyone can learn to pray.

TWENTY-FIVE

Barbara got off the subway at Astor Place. She mingled with a crowd of playgoers heading for the Public Theater over on Lafayette and walked down past Cooper Union, where Abraham Lincoln had once made a speech. She felt nervous and forlorn. She had pooh-poohed Jimmy's advice to cancel her night shift at the detox, insisting that she couldn't go back on her promise to help Ed Bark out. But if she hadn't been so furious at Bruce, she might have had his company tonight. She shouldn't have accused him of thinking with his gonads. He was already freaked out enough by Marlene's death and the police questioning. Nor could she forget, no matter how they all walked around it, the elephant in the living room: the time Bruce's regrettable impulsiveness had led him to her own bed. It would have served her right if that incendiary piece of ancient history had come out in front of Jimmy.

Squaring her shoulders, she marched down the Bowery. One day at a time. She'd better focus on her two tasks for the evening, the one they'd pay her for and the next step in the investigation.

With two members of Emmie's family dead in addition to Guff, as well as an in-law's employee, suspicion focused on the Kettleworths. If Jimmy really thought it was a family affair, she'd pointed out, they had nothing to fear in her going to the detox for one last look at the files. The trouble was, Jimmy argued, they weren't sure. If the killer wasn't in the family, her snooping in the detox could put her in danger.

"I'm going so we can be sure," she'd said, too caught up in the argument to listen to the flutter in the pit of her stomach. "We've got to rule it out."

As usual, the elevator wasn't working. She took the stairs up, thinking about all the stories she had heard, some but by no means all of them apocryphal. Those stairs had been the stage for a fair amount of mayhem over the years. The building was owned by the city, and not everyone who had business there was clean and sober. There had been shootings, stabbings, and countless muggings. Illicit drugs had been smuggled up those stairs, and computers and other portable equipment with good resale value down them and out the door. The lights were never bright enough, and at least half of them were out at any one time.

The night security man gave her a drowsy greeting and promptly disappeared. Barbara remembered he spent most of his shift either napping in the subbasement or drinking coffee and playing the numbers at a hole-in-the-wall bodega down the block. That would be the last she saw of him that night. She had meant to borrow Sister Angel's office again, but the door was locked, and the master key was probably in the security man's pocket. The key box in Charmaine's office was also locked. Bark had probably taken his master key home with him. After making the rounds and exchanging a few words with those patients who were not already asleep, she settled down in the nursing station. She booted up the computer. She had not yet checked any of the electronic files. But first, she wanted to look at Guff's chart one more time.

First, she had to find the chart. Last time, it had been on Sister Angel's desk. If that were the case tonight, her mission had already failed. But no, a stack of charts lay heaped in a haphazard pile in a corner behind the copier. A sticky note on the topmost chart read, "Closed—file in dead storage." Barbara blessed the blend of overwork and inefficiency that left the staff perennially weeks behind on filing. Dead storage was in the subbasement, where stacks of file boxes piled up to the ceiling; it would take a derrick or a couple of weight lifters to shift them.

She took the chart to her desk and started to read. Instead of being overwhelmed by information, as she had on first reading, she now found the chart sketchy. She had learned more about Guff and his family in the interim than he had revealed in detox. She had little hope of finding anything new. Keeping her expectations low, she told herself, would spare her disappointment. So when she came upon a squeezed-in note in what she recognized as Charmaine's handwriting, she felt an unanticipated flicker of excitement. It looked as if Charmaine had written it in later. Editing formal chart notes after the fact was against the rules—against the law, in fact. But the note had not been there when she had read the chart before.

Charmaine had used a lot of medical abbreviations: hx for history, sx for symptoms, tx for treatment. Barbara frowned at "hx sx sx, ⊖ tx." History, symptoms, symptoms, a Greek theta—what did that mean?—treatment. Huh? She puzzled it out. That second "sx" wasn't for symptoms; Charmaine had meant sex or sexual. And the theta wasn't a theta; it was a sloppy rendering of a minus sign enclosed in a circle, which meant something was negative or denied. Guff had a history of sexual symptoms for which he had denied ever getting treatment. She read on. Charmaine had written, as cryptically as possible, that a staff member had reported Guff's admission of ideation—thinking about—sex with juveniles.

Had he also admitted to acting on his fantasies? Why hadn't she blown the whistle on him? Health professionals were supposed to report suspected child abuse. If she hadn't been sure, she wouldn't have wanted to stigmatize someone on the brink of turning his life around. In that case, why had she gone back and added it? Barbara suspected that the seminar on ethics they had both attended had prodded Charmaine's conscience. The omission had weighed on her, and in the end she had done the professional thing by putting it on the record. "Staff member reported . . ." Guff had talked about this not to Charmaine, but to someone else.

Who could the unnamed staff member be? Sister Angel? He might have associated a nun with confession, absolution, and confidentiality. On the other hand, Barbara had trouble imagining Sister Angel, that model of rectitude, failing to chart child molestation. What about Darryl? He was no stickler when it came to charting and reporting. But he and Guff had hated each other, according to Bruce. Darryl would surely have been the last person to whom Guff would admit his most shameful failing. Bark, then? All the patients talked to him. But he and Guff came from very different worlds. Guff would have had no particular reason to trust him. Or how about Boris? Clients trusted him, too. His teddy bear physique and tuba voice made them feel safe.

She flipped through the chart again, trying to find the final lab report. Instead, she found another added note. "Lab reports bloodwork January 2 lost, computer error." Whoever thought computers were going to solve all the problems of record keeping, she thought disgustedly, must be eating their words, and I hope they taste like iodine. They would never know now if Guff had picked up a drug, knowingly or not, on his last day out. This chart was not going to yield any more secrets.

Elwood's chart was even harder to find than Guff's had been. She finally located it in a drawer full of current patients' charts. She sat down again and flipped through it. Now this was interesting. This time, Dr. Bones had *not* signed the death certificate. Because Elwood had died unattended, they had done an autopsy. Even more interesting, the old man had not died of cancer. Nor had he had a stroke or heart attack. He had been smothered. They had found traces of fiber in his mouth and nostrils consistent with the rather coarse cotton sheets and pillowcases the detox used as bedding. That could not have happened by accident. Why had the police not followed up? Never underestimate bureaucratic incompetence, she thought.

The report indicated he had been given the usual sleeping pill. Barbara snorted, thinking of the hospital joke that sleeping pills are needed so the nurse on duty can sleep through the night. Someone in the detox had made sure he took it, maybe even given him an extra. No alcoholic or drug addict in any condition would ever refuse a pill. And then, that person put a pillow over his face. Or maybe a wad of laundry—Bruce had found him in the laundry room. It had looked like a natural death, so the murderer had to have stayed long enough—or come back—to rearrange his body.

Why did the detox staff not know this? The murderer must have gotten hold of the autopsy report when it arrived. An aide was supposed to sort the mail. But nobody, Barbara knew, had time to supervise the aide. In practice, the mail lay in a pile on the security guard's desk, and everyone on staff helped themselves to whatever was addressed to them. Sometimes, as in this case, even if it wasn't. The murderer had deliberately misfiled it. Why not just destroy it? Its survival suggested someone who had been in the field a long time. The more experienced the professional, the more ingrained the principle: Never, never, never throw out a piece of official paper.

This revelation put the murders squarely back in the detox. Only a staff member could have killed Elwood, arranged him to look natural, intercepted the autopsy report, and hidden the chart. But it still raised a lot more questions than it answered. Why would anyone kill Elwood? He was harmless, and he was dying anyway, liable to get moved to hospice soon, even if he survived longer than expected. And what did Elwood have to do with Guff? Barbara made a mental note to ask Bruce if he could think of anything—if he was still talking to her. But if someone in the detox had killed Elwood, who had killed the old men in all the other programs, including her own? And where did the Kettleworths fit in? Or had someone else altogether killed Lucinda, Sam, and Marlene?

She put both Elwood's chart and Guff's aside and turned to the computer. She wanted to see the personnel files and any personal files the staff members kept. Jimmy had held forth many times on how predictable most people were when it came to choosing passwords. The supervisors, Bark and Charmaine, had access to all staff records. She started playing with their names and what she knew of their personal history. She had better take her time, nervous though she was. If anybody came in at the wrong moment, what she was doing would be hard to explain away. She struck out enough times for a full nine innings before the word *casino* worked. Atlantic City was the only place Bark ever went beyond a mile radius of the Bowery.

Before diving into the files, Barbara made sure the Internet connection was up. If she found anything interesting, she could upload it and e-mail it to Jimmy. Printing would be too noisy. She glanced through the glass wall of the nursing station into the darkened ward. Everything was quiet. With luck, she would not be disturbed.

She found nothing about Bark and Charmaine that she didn't already know, except that Charmaine was a few years older than she admitted to, and Bark, the grand old man of the Bowery, was a few years younger. Boris had gotten his job through ARFSU, but if he'd had a personal recommendation from Lucinda, it was not on the computer. He had his green card, and if he had ever been in trouble, the agency didn't know about it. Darryl, on the other hand, had had to disclose his felony record to get hired, and it was worse than they had imagined. He had done time for manslaughter and aggravated assault as well as the inevitable drug-related charges.

As she stared at the screen, the door clicked open behind her. Her heart thudding, she grabbed the mouse. The usual home page leaped up onto the screen, covering the page she had been looking at. Swiveling her chair around, she found Darryl looming over her.

"What the hell do you think you're doing?" he demanded.

"Working the night shift," she faltered. "Bark asked me. What are you doing here?"

Could she close his personnel file without it appearing on the screen? If he realized she had looked at his private information, he would be angry. With Darryl, the violence pulsed just beneath the surface even at a staff or AA meeting. With trepidation, she forced herself to meet his eyes. If she locked his gaze, he couldn't focus on the computer screen. Her heart was pounding so loudly, she could hardly believe he wouldn't hear it.

"I work here." His voice dripped sarcasm.

"It's the middle of the night."

"Yes, it is. You really like snooping around here, don't you?"

It would probably be more productive to go on the attack. If only her blouse wasn't getting soaked with sweat. If only her hands weren't shaking and her voice threatening to soar up into a squeak. If only she didn't suddenly have to pee very badly.

"And what about you? Every time I cover a night shift, there you are. If you're supposed to be here, how come Bark has to bring me in?"

"None of your business." Ha! she thought. He wasn't supposed to be here. She was not sure putting him on the defensive would turn out to be a good idea, but she had nothing better to run with.

"It is if you've been messing around with the clients," she retorted. "What about Godfrey—the guy who died at New Year's? What were you up to there?" Oops. That had come out more baldly than she had intended.

"What the hell are you talking about?" His eyes flashed and his fists clenched.

She rolled her chair back until it slammed against the back of the desk. Her arm shot out, and her hand came down on the phone, fortuitously just within reach. Her sweaty hand grasped it gratefully. Darryl's eyes immediately went to the phone jack, which was within his reach. He'd only have to jerk the cord to pop it out of the wall. To her relief, he started pacing instead. The crowded little goldfish bowl of a room offered space for no more than a couple of strides. He moved like a caged tiger in an unmodernized zoo, lashing his figurative tail.

"What the fuck do you know about it?" he demanded. "Bourgeois little vanilla cupcake!"

Better than "bitch," she thought, sternly repressing the impulse to say it out loud. She must not forget for a second that this man was dangerous.

"Mommy and Daddy always bought you everything you wanted, I bet. Have you ever been on the streets? Have you ever been down-and-out?"

"You don't know anything about my life," she said hotly.

"I know enough, bitch," he said contemptuously. There it is, she thought, grimly amused even though she could feel her crotch melting with fear. "What are you going to tell me, the silver spoon in your mouth was plate instead of sterling?" How expressive, the dissociated, ironic part of her thought. Usually, it was a lot of "Fuck this, fuck that."

"Fuck that," he said. "That bastard didn't need the money, and I did, see. You want to fight with me about it?" He grinned, disclosing the diamond chip set into one of his terrifying teeth.

"So you're the one who's been stealing things. You're the one who took Guff's money."

"Who says I did? You weren't there, you couldn't know, and we didn't have this conversation." He bared his teeth again. The diamond glinted menacingly. "If you know what's good for you."

She hunched her shoulders and turned her back on him, whirling the swivel chair around. The lights provided some reflection from the screen. In it, she watched him warily. She still had one hand on the phone. She hoped he couldn't see her trembling. Darryl was a predator, and it would be better not to look too much like prey.

"Go away," she said, steeling herself to sound as rude as possible. "Since we didn't have this conversation, I have things to do."

If he attacked her, she could scream. There was a ward full of sleeping men out there. Of course, they had all had the sleeping pill, and most of them were weak as babies from detoxing. Besides, she would be embarrassed. A codependent was someone who would literally rather die than make a scene. She must remember that. It would get a big laugh at her Al-Anon meeting, if Darryl didn't kill her first.

"He didn't need it," he said sullenly. "Besides, the muh-fuh cops or the EMTs would have gotten it if I hadn't. You just make sure you keep your fucking mouth shut!" He slammed out, banging the door behind him.

Barbara breathed a shaky sigh. Her sweaty fingers were slick on the keyboard. She opened an e-mail window, typed in Jimmy's address, and wrote, "Help!" She hit *Save* and minimized the window.

If Darryl came back, she could send it in a second. Glancing over her shoulder, she brought Darryl's file back up and closed it. Thank heaven he hadn't seen that she had opened it. He would have gone right over the edge. Once it was safely off the screen, she was able to concentrate on what he had said. Evidently, Darryl had swiped the two thousand dollars in cash from Guff's body—or, more likely, his clothes—after he was dead. He had robbed him, but if he'd told the truth, he hadn't killed him.

She could tell Bark or Charmaine about the theft. They would probably believe her, and they could keep an eye on Darryl, hoping to catch him doing something else, if they chose not to confront him right away. Her safety, at least for now, depended on Darryl believing he had intimidated her enough that she wouldn't dare tell anyone. After that, all she had to do was stay far away from Darryl. That would be accomplished easily by not working any more per diem on the Bowery. Jimmy would be pleased, and it would be a relief to her, as well. She had only worked this last couple of times in order to snoop around, as Darryl had rightly concluded.

Thoroughly rattled, Barbara got up and paced the cramped space much as Darryl had. She didn't feel like a tiger, though—more like a gazelle with no place to bolt. That reminded her of one more precaution she could take. She locked the nursing station door. Her fingers still shook, but she didn't want to stop now. She sat back down and opened Sister Angel's file. She had never known the name of what the nun called "my community," but here it was: the Sisters of the Blood of the Lamb. She had listed other sisters as emergency contact and next of kin. With a start of recognition, Barbara read the name Perseverance. There couldn't be two of those. And Eileen's Sister Agnes, with a Brooklyn area code.

What a small world! Or was it? Connections clicked into place in her mind like a jigsaw worked by invisible hands. A rash of unexpected client deaths in hospitals. A flock of bloody lambs. Sisters everywhere. One in every program, all connected. It all pointed to a conclusion that still felt absurd. Back in Jimmy's drinking days, steeped in confusion and denial, she had said, "Sometimes I think the real problem is your drinking." When he said that was ridiculous, she'd thought he must be right. Her mind had told her to ignore her gut, and her mind had been wrong. Hadn't she better pay attention to her gut now? The "still small voice within" was just the spiritual term for a gut feeling.

She clicked open file after file. She scrolled down a list of trainings Sister Angel had taken or, in some cases, presented. Homeless, psychiatric, social services—abuse. She had participated in a panel on pedophilia. Next, a whole series of seminars on child sexual abuse. It seemed to be one of her specialties, even though she had worked for decades on the Bowery with men who had left their families far behind.

Besides the official personnel file, there might be personal files. Employees were not supposed to keep their updated résumés or half-written novels on the office computer, but everybody did. She had friends at work who kept their cover letters to other employers on the hard drive and didn't even have a password. More paranoid colleagues kept their personal material on something portable, like a CD, and took it home with them every day. The Bowery staff fell somewhere between the two. Everybody had a passworded folder. Once again, Barbara summoned up her ingenuity to figure out their passwords. Bark's was "in a box"—the way he always described his drinking years on the Bowery. She skipped Darryl's. The thought of his coming back and finding her reading it frightened her too much to contemplate. She skipped Boris's, too. If he had any sense of self-preservation, it would be in Russian. Who next? Charmaine? No, Sister Angel. She struck out with religious associations but finally hit a homer with "Lucky." Part of Sister Angel's legend was the pack of cigarettes she used to whip out to gain a client's confidence in the days before smoke-free zones. Before filter cigarettes, she'd carried Luckies. Bark remembered and still occasionally teased her about it. She would say, "It's a message from God. With God, even these broken men can improve their luck."

To Barbara's relief, the file did not reveal a secret sex life. More lists of sister Sisters. Schedules of meetings with cryptic agendas. Medical and pharmaceutical information that would have looked perfectly normal on bookshelves in her office or bookmarks in her unpassworded files. And here was a file labeled "Mercy." Another Sister? It sounded like that kind of name. She clicked it open.

They say the power of life and death are Thine. But am I not a channel of Thy peace? What peace can those poor souls have who are racked with pain and offered no palliatives in their misery but the very drugs we have seen destroying minds and lives? The mercy that we bring to those in misery is our sacrifice, mine and my sisters', as Thy Son gave His blood upon the Cross to bestow the mercy of salvation upon all of us. I have sworn my life to Thy service, so how can I hold back, how can I not take upon myself for these unfortunates the cross of guilt, the sin of action? If they themselves raise a hand to end their agony, their souls are forfeit. We take it on ourselves, our mercy is the sacrifice, and we give it freely in the light of Thy love. This is not orthodoxy, but when have I ever been orthodox? Thou hast shown me favor all my life, giving me the strength to go among the lions in their very den, and the jackals and hyenas, too, and I believe with all my heart that Thou art with me. And I will go further, smiting evil on Thy behalf. I take upon myself what some would call sin, but Thou knowest I am but the sword in Thy hand. I come to them in darkness when my sisters guide me to them. And in mercy I strike them down. I give them to drink of the chalice of Thy perfect love. And thus in mercy I bring them to Thy light.

Thanks to the twelve-step programs, Barbara could recognize a spiritual meditation. And her counselor training and experience had given her a fairly good instinct for psychopathology.

"Nuts," she said aloud. "The woman's nuts."

At that moment, she heard a tap-tap-tapping down the hall behind her. Before she could react, the lock clicked, and the door creaked open. Sister Angel had a key.

TWENTY-SIX

"Bruce! Pick up the phone!"

I came to with a start. I'd fallen asleep in a chair. The video I'd been watching had switched itself off. I didn't know how late it was, but it was dark. I'd imagined Jimmy's voice.

"Bruce! *Bruce!* If you've chosen this moment to drink again, I will kill you with my bare hands! Jesus, Mary, and Joseph, *pick up the phone!*"

It was Jimmy. I looked muzzily around. The phone was ringing, shaking as it trilled, as if it had a life of its own. But Jimmy's voice was coming from the computer. He had fixed me up some kind of gadget, but I'd never bothered to let him teach me what it was or how to use it.

"Okay, okay," I mumbled, "keep your shirt on." I stumbled toward the phone. I picked up the receiver clumsily, dropped it once, nearly fell over picking it up again, and poked it in the general direction of my ear.

"Yeah," I said blearily. "I'm here."

"That's better. At least you get it that we're talking. Bruce, you didn't pick up, did you?" He meant pick up a drink.

"No, damn it!" I let myself sound as cross as I felt.

"Thank God! Now, listen. You've got to get to Barbara."

"What?"

"It's Barbara. She went down to the detox to take another look around. I can't reach her, and I just got an e-mail that said 'Help.'"

"Help? Help what? Help who?"

"Just 'Help.' Help Barbara, you moron."

"Barbara said a one-word sentence?" My brain was slowly waking up, but my tongue was still stupid.

"Never mind that," Jimmy growled. "You've got to get to her!"

Jimmy sounded desperate. He never sounded desperate. Jimmy had always been the cool one, even when we were seventeen and running from the cops across the Queensboro Bridge after ditching our one and only stolen car. They didn't catch us, but the chase scared the bejesus out of us. And so did our fathers when we got home. We never figured out how they found out. Suddenly, I was wide-awake.

"I'm on it. I'll grab a cab. Hop in one yourself. I'll meet you there."

"No!" Jimmy's cry of anguish knifed into my gut. "It's got to be you. I'm not home!"

"What? But you're always home," I said. "You're at your computer."

"Of course I'm at my computer, meathead," he snarled. "I took the laptop with me to my sister's. She's having a baby."

"But your sister lives in Patchogue."

"Now do you get the picture, you dunderheaded jerk? You've got to get to Barbara before anything happens to her."

"She went in without backup?" It was a dumb-ass thing to say, but we've all watched too many episodes of *Law & Order*.

"You know Barbara," Jimmy groaned. "She's so busy being a feminist. She always thinks nothing will happen to her."

"I know," I said as soothingly as I could. "Nothing will happen. I'm on my way."

"I'll come in," he babbled. "No, I'll stay here—wait! No, I'll call a limo; even the LIE can't be crowded at this hour."

The Long Island Expressway is always crowded.

"Jimmy, it's okay. I'm on it. Patchogue is what, an hour and a half by train? Forget it." I refrained from saying, "It'll be all over by the time you can get to the city." Instead, I said, "I'm on it. Listen, I'm putting on my shoes right now." I hopped around, the phone clenched between my jaw and my shoulder, suiting the action to the word. "I'll take my cell phone. Click. I've turned it on." I had finally paid the bill just last week.

"I'll be afraid to call you. It might ring at just the wrong moment," he said anxiously.

Jimmy, my man, my rock, was falling apart. It scared the shit out of me. And like him, I began to feel a gnawing worry about Barbara. Not only because Jimmy would be lost without her but because I'd be seriously devastated, too, if she got hurt. Or worse. We'd been playing at murder up till now. We'd never expected to get hurt.

"I'm leaving now, big guy. Just sit tight. I'll get her. I've got my jacket. My wallet. My father's bowie knife." I had snatched it up at random from the shelf it had been lying on for years. It had been a birthday gift one year, but he hadn't gone out and bought it for me. He'd probably won it in a poker game or traded it for a bottle from some hobo around a trash-barrel fire. "Stay by the phone, and I'll call you as soon as she's safe."

"Do you think I should call nine one one?" he asked helplessly.

"Jesus Christ, man, you haven't done that yet?" Truth: I hadn't thought of it myself. "Do it now. I'm going out the door. You get the cops. And tell them not to arrest the handsome dude with the bowie knife by mistake." Idiots in a crisis, that was us.

"Asshole."

"Creep."

When we hung up, I got out the door fast. I galloped down the stairs two at a time, shrugging on my jacket and dropping the bowie knife, loose in its battered leather sheath, into my pocket as I ran. I caught a cab headed downtown on the corner of Second Avenue with a piercing whistle, a burst of speed, and what I hoped was not my quota of good luck for the night. Ten minutes later, I was on the Bowery.

I didn't want to risk a frontal assault and the probability that I'd waste endless time talking my way in. I walked casually past the entrance, trying not to look furtive, and slipped past a couple of reeking garbage cans into the passage leading to the delivery entrance. The heavy door to the storage and maintenance areas on the floor just below ground level should have been locked. But it wasn't. I felt the jamb with a finger, not surprised to encounter a sticky wad of gum. A faint odor of cigarettes hung in the air.

The night security guy was nowhere to be seen. So what else was new? The elevator indicator informed me the car was in the subbasement. When I pressed the button, nothing happened. He had probably turned the automatic mechanism off so nobody would bother him. I ran to the stairs. I had to exert myself to open the door to the stairwell. It was heavy with some kind of electronic bolting mechanism, but it wasn't locked. I didn't know whether to be glad or sorry that no alarm pealed out as I dived into the stairwell.

I panted as I flew up the first two flights. I was still out of shape from all those years of sitting on my duff in bars. I'd have to do something about that. A crisis took a lot more out of me, I discovered, when I met it sober. On the other hand, my wits were working fine. I still wasn't used to that. I climbed with the bowie knife in my hand. Patients' knives were confiscated on admission, but I told myself I was not a patient anymore. The stairs were dangerous, with or without Barbara at stake. I'd rather stay alive to get arrested than get killed playing by the rules. My eyes darted from side to side. ACOA hypervigilance was a good tool in a crisis.

I forgot to look up. As I breasted the rise at the end of the second flight, I stubbed my toe on something soft. Darryl! What the hell had happened to him? He was either dead or unconscious. I didn't see any blood or any weapons sticking out or lying around. I thought of checking for a pulse or breathing. But I didn't stop. If I got arrested with a knife in my hand, I'd rather have been saving Barbara than looking as if I'd just killed Darryl. Barbara hated being saved. She was like a kid about doing it herself. I could imagine what that cry for help to Jimmy must have cost her. The situation must be dire, and finding Darryl on the stairs, knocked out or worse, confirmed it. I doubled my pace. Or tried to. Stairs are aerobic, and my wind was not great.

It got worse. Barbara lay sprawled like a rag doll on the next landing up. My heart clutched. I turned her over gently. A dribble of saliva ran from the corner of her mouth. Her eyes were closed. She was breathing, thank God.

"Barbara!" I called her name in a fierce and urgent whisper. I shook her shoulders, then remembered I shouldn't move a person who might have a spinal injury. "Hey, it's me. Wake up. What happened?" Had she fallen down the stairs? Who pushed her? I couldn't rouse her. But my efforts made her stir and squirm. It didn't look like she had broken anything major. Her hair fell over her face. As I pushed it back, I saw what I had missed before: a steel cord around her neck. Someone had tried to strangle her but hadn't finished the job. Darryl? Was he the murderer? Or had he interrupted the murderer? Holding Barbara's limp hand and trying to think, I realized that I knew that cord. It belonged to a highly functional rosary with a crucifix dangling from it. And I knew who always wore it around her neck.

One more flight and I'd reach the detox. I hated to leave Barbara lying there, but I stood between her and the menace above. I eased the chain from around her neck, uncovering the ridge where it had been pulled tight. Her neck was already turning a bruised blue. I stuck the chain in my pocket, where it clanked against the bowie knife. I couldn't remember shoving the knife into my pocket. I must have done it when I went to Barbara. I drew it out and held it in my hand. I'd never knifed anybody, but there was always a first time. I bounded up the last flight to the detox two or three steps at a clip.

An implacable figure stood at the top of the stairs, gazing down.

"Mr. Kohler," Sister Angel said. "We have to talk."

In my head, I heard Jimmy at his most pedantic saying, "The side that takes the high ground has a big advantage." He said it all the time, with illustrations ranging from Gettysburg to Waterloo to our own close encounter with a troop of mounted New York City cops in Central Park during the Vietnam protest era. At least she didn't have a horse.

I reached the landing, where I could meet her eye-to-eye. She looked the same as always: compassionate and steely at the same time, peaches and cream complexion. The bad guys didn't always look like monsters. It made Sister Angel all the more scary. I knew the force of character that made her a legend on the Bowery would dominate me if I let it.

"The police are on their way," I said.

"I don't believe you," she said calmly.

Teetering on the edge of the landing, I had nowhere to back up. She took my arm in a grip of iron. Those efficient little hands of hers were strong. I had to overcome conditioning I didn't know I had to grab her by the arms and start wrestling. I don't think

Jimmy could have done it. And I dropped the bowie knife, which skittered away and bounced down the whole flight of stairs. So much for stabbing a nun. I couldn't have done it anyway.

She didn't really want to talk. She wanted to kill me if she could. I saw her grab at her neck for the rosary, her fingers scrabbling as she realized she didn't have it.

"I've got it," I panted as we scuffled. "You didn't kill Barbara." Let her think that Barbara had gone for help. "And you can't strangle me."

That was the wrong thing to say. She immediately started trying to push me down the stairs. I shoved back, gaining ground half an inch at a time. I couldn't believe how strong she was. I would have to start working out. I maneuvered her a step or two downward. Locked in a weird embrace, we gripped each other's forearms. I had to get above her. She pivoted around me and blocked my upward route. I let go of one arm, grabbed the banister, and climbed fast, pulling myself along. She hung on with both hands and followed.

Breast-to-breast with her and two feet clear of the edge, I felt her check and change her strategy. She grabbed me by the ear. Ow, that hurt. Jimmy, who'd gone to Catholic schools, said they taught all the nuns ear grabbing when they were novices. The detox was home turf to her. Mayhem on the stairs was traditional, but the nursing station made a better killing ground. She marched me along, and somehow I let her do it. She still had the moral ascendancy.

A heavy door led from the stairwell into the detox. It was made of steel and weighed a ton. I got close enough to open it a crack and jam my hip and one foot into it. She was still between me and the stairs, but to get in, she'd have to go right through me. She had another idea. She tried to push it closed on me, using her whole body. If she didn't slice me in half, I'd have a black-and-blue mark right down my middle. I struggled to wrench the rest of my body through. All of me in the detox was a marginally better choice than half in and half out. I tucked the arm still on the landing side up close to my body so she couldn't slam the door on it. I didn't need a broken arm.

Sister Angel made little panting sounds and grunts as she fought me. Disgusting.

"His glory is invincible," she panted. "I am the angel of mercy, and I cannot fail. You must be the sacrifice, the blood of the lamb of God."

Now she was really giving me the creeps. The woman was crazy. It made me feel a little better about not being able to take her, though. Weren't mad people supposed to be exceptionally strong? Or was that a myth? I'd have to ask Barbara. As I thought of Barbara, I instinctively chose to take the fight farther from her, rather than closer. I squeezed through the door. Sister Angel slithered in before I could slam it. Now we were in the detox. We tussled our way down the hall. I hauled her one way; she chivied me the other. Now neither of us had the advantage.

Fixed to the wall about halfway along the corridor was a red metal bin marked SHARPS. They used it for discarded razor blades and hypodermic needles. As we swept by the bright red bin, Sister Angel plunged her hand into it and fished out a used syringe. She stabbed at my face with it. This was beyond hardball. I could end up with hepatitis C or HIV. I redoubled my efforts, trying to knock the syringe out of her hand without the needle scratching my face or piercing my clothing.

The nursing station door hung open. The place showed signs of a scuffle: chair overturned, the computer half off the desk with the keyboard dangling, papers everywhere. Barbara must have found something on the computer. I wanted to see it, but not with Sister Angel's death grip on me. Once she got me in there, I really wouldn't be able to get away. The whole fight had felt defensive on my part. Even fighting for my life, I couldn't make myself use force beyond what it would take to stop her. I set my heels and dragged in the other direction.

Momentarily, the momentum swung her way. We burst through the door of the nursing station together. I grabbed the phone. She got hold of the cord and jerked it out of my hand, but the syringe flew across the room. She looked wildly around for another weapon, relaxing her grip on me. Ha! I thought. Now I've got you! Then she got hold of the computer keyboard, ripped it off its cord, and started beating me over the head with it. She drove me down to my knees. I was clinging to her legs and wondering if I could bring myself to bite a nun when a strong blow to my head cracked the world open and I saw first stars, then nothing.

When I came to, Sister Angel lay unconscious on the floor. It looked as if she'd been snowed on. Shredded paper, I thought, then saw that it looked more like foam. The mystery was solved when I discovered Barbara lying just outside the door, not down the stairs, where I had left her. She had been knocked out again, or maybe fainted. But a small copper fire extinguisher lay a couple of inches beyond her slack fingers. It rolled slightly when I stubbed my toe on it.

A few minutes later, the police came pounding up the stairs. Jimmy had called 911 after all. Even better, he must have told them about me. They clearly didn't regard the guy kneeling over the girl as a suspect, but brushed past us into the nursing station. Barbara came to as I bathed her face with a cloth I'd found in the laundry room. I hadn't squeezed it dry enough. Water dripped onto her closed eyes.

"Did they get Sister Angel?" she asked.

"Yes, it's all right. The cops are here."

She didn't open her eyes.

"Bruce."

"I'm right here." Conscientiously, I added, "Jimmy is on his way. His sister had a girl out in Patchogue. Eight pounds, five ounces."

Suddenly, her eyes flew open and she sat bolt upright. She clutched frantically at my arm.

"You didn't rescue me! You didn't rescue me!"

I looked down at her with a tender expression that must have been a revelation to my face.

"Shh, it's okay. I didn't rescue you. You rescued yourself, and me, too."

"Ahhh." She sank back onto the floor with a wince of pain. "I remember. She was killing you. So I bopped her on the head with the fire extinguisher and sprayed her."

"You did a great job," I said. "Lie down."

She lay down.

"I'm not a damsel in distress." She sat up again, grabbing my arm with both hands and pulling at it like a chinning bar. She looked anxiously into my eyes. "I'm not, right? Promise?"

"Promise. You did it all by yourself."

I reached out and stroked her hair. She gathered me against her, letting go of my arm to lock her arms around my torso. For a moment, the old attraction between us was so strong that I was afraid we might have to do something about it sometime. And here I'd thought on my side it was just the booze. For a moment, we breathed heavily and in unison. Then she let me go. After that she winked at me, and it was okay.

"Why didn't you scream?" Jimmy asked. He had come to drive us home from the hospital. We had both spent the night there while they monitored our matching slight concussions.

"Too busy," I said. "And I know from personal experience how hard it is to wake up anyone who's had one of Charmaine's sleeping pills."

But he meant Barbara.

"I should have screamed," she said. "*Someone* would have come running. But you know what? I was too embarrassed."

"You were alone with a murderer, choking to death, and you went with *embarrassed?*"

"Crazy, isn't it?" Barbara agreed. "I've never been so scared in my life. I felt a kind of flooding along my arms and a watery sensation in—well, never mind. I keep telling you codependency's a killer, and you never believe me. I didn't want to make a scene—I just couldn't."

"Then why didn't you make a break for the elevator?" asked Jimmy practically.

"It wasn't working," I chipped in.

"Or kicked her in the shins and slammed the door? Or pulled away from her and run?"

"I tried." She waved a hand at me. "Bruce tried, too. Tell him."

"The woman really had abnormal strength, dude. If Barbara hadn't clobbered her, she would have killed me. As it was, she knocked me out cold."

Jimmy was still dissatisfied.

"You could have thrown whatever was close at hand and tried to smash the wall of the nursing station. You said it's glass. Surely someone would have come to see what was the matter."

"Give it a rest, bro," I advised. "You're just still stewing because you weren't there. Anyhow, what happened there is yesterday. It's over. One day at a time." I grinned. Usually, that reminder went the other way.

TWENTY-SEVEN

As we learned later, Darryl was okay, too. He got off with a concussion worse than ours and a broken leg. He was so glad not to be dead that, for probably the first time in his life, he cooperated with the police. Up to a point. He didn't say a word about dealing drugs. But he told them he'd become suspicious of Sister Angel's activities. To hear him tell it, he had also become concerned about Barbara's safety. He claimed he was on his way to call 911 from the street when Sister Angel caught up with him. It might even have been true. If Barbara had ended up dead, the subsequent investigation would have opened up a can of worms that he had good reason to keep a lid on. His story did such a good job that whatever he wanted not scrutinized stayed hidden. He was lucky, too. Sister Angel had a lot of credibility in the bank.

We figured out a best guess as to what really happened. If we were right, he and Sister Angel, skulking around the ward at night, had each learned what the other was up to. Neither dared blow the whistle. They must have met between when Darryl left Barbara in the nursing station and when Sister Angel walked in on her. Whatever they said to each other, the nun got mad enough to give him a push down the stairs.

"I don't get it," Jimmy said. "Why didn't she just turn him in?"

"No hard evidence," Barbara said. "She couldn't prove it, and Darryl belonged to the union, which made it unbelievably hard to get rid of him. It's the bureaucracy. At my hospital, one counselor dealt drugs for months. Everybody knew it. And you know what they finally got to fire him for? Poor attendance."

"Like the G-men getting Al Capone for tax evasion," Jimmy said, his face lighting up. He always accuses Barbara of digressing. Well, we both do, because she does. But give Jimmy a whiff of a historical scent and he's off in full cry.

"Anyhow," I said with emphasis.

"Okay, okay," said Jimmy. "It does make sense. If she'd blown the whistle, he would have retaliated by telling the authorities about the detox deaths."

"Do you think he had evidence, or just suspicions?"

"No idea. But he could have used whatever he had to plea-bargain."

"She might have risked it," Barbara said. "Under the Saint Petunia Pig exterior, she was as cold as ice. With hindsight, it feels like I always knew that. Anyhow, she decided to trade silence for silence, until I arrived to complicate matters for her."

"That you did, p—uh—" Jimmy stopped short. He was running out of endearments beginning with *p*.

"Pork chop," I supplied. They both scowled at me. I was only trying to help.

Once they knew where to look, the police figured out how Sister Angel killed Sam Weill and Marlene. Dr. Weill had called the detox to complain that the money he had given Guff to leave his family alone had not been returned with his effects. Sister Angel happened to answer the call. She admitted that much, and the police put enough pressure on her that she admitted she'd gone to his office to see him. That connected the deaths of Sam and Marlene with the detox murders. We could only speculate on what happened next. Barbara thought, having seen the doc in action, that he must have tried to bully her. Maybe he'd threatened to go to the board of directors when it became clear that she could not return the money. Or they'd quarreled about Guff and the abuse. Or both. Sam Weill had tried to protect his kids, however belatedly. He could have seen in Sister Angel the symbol of the professionals who failed to "do something." She might equally have blamed him for not speaking up about the abuse.

"I can imagine Sam bellowing," Barbara said, "and Sister Angel becoming more steely and inflexible by the minute, until she finally snapped."

Or it might not have happened like that.

Charmaine told Barbara, who told us, that Sister Angel's community's lawyers considered having her plead self-defense in Sam Weill's death. She had evidently wiped the marble bookend she used on him, but they'd found Sam's fingerprints on the other one. And Emmie told Barbara how fond Sam had been of those bookends.

"They were a gift from a former patient," Barbara reported, "and he liked the heft of them. Emmie said he always picked them up." She turned her hand palm up and made a jouncing gesture, demonstrating. "She didn't tell the cops that when he got angry, he sometimes threw things."

"We knew he had a terrible temper," I said.

"Emmie said he was a good man who didn't really mean it," Barbara said. "But then she admitted that he could be terrifying when he got into a rage. She swore he wouldn't have thrown an object that heavy. But he might have picked it up and threatened Sister Angel with it."

Sister Angel's trail led from Sam to Marlene, thank heaven. I was completely off the hook. So it was just as well that Marlene and her roommate had liked to share all the details. The evening Sam got killed, Marlene had been the last one in the office. She finished up some paperwork and locked up when she left. But halfway between the doctor's office and the subway, she realized that she had forgotten her scarf. Coming back for it, she passed Sister Angel coming in. Why would a nun consult a plastic surgeon? If Sister Angel had worn her flea market clothes, Marlene would never have noticed her.

Sister Angel killed Marlene because she could place the nun at the scene of Sam's murder. She didn't know Marlene had already mentioned her to the roommate. She didn't even know who Marlene was when their paths crossed. But she must have taken a good look around the office before she left after bludgeoning Dr. Weill. She recognized Marlene from a family picture on her desk. Her name was on a bronze nameplate right next to it. And her address was in the phone book. She must have been totally panicked by that time. Thinking she had to kill Marlene was kind of paranoid. But she had gone around the bend when she decided she could justify mercy killing. From that point, things spiraled out of control.

Barbara swore Jimmy and me to silence before telling us that Darryl had more or less admitted to stealing the two thousand dollars.

"I promised, so I won't say a word," Jimmy said. "But why are you protecting him?"

"It is possible," Barbara said, "that he intended to try to save my life, the way he said. Besides, he'd make a dangerous enemy if we blew the whistle on him."

I considered it a waste of good something-for-nothing money. But I wouldn't tell. Shortly afterward, Darryl left the detox. To our chagrin, he got a much higher-paid job with the city's Human

Resources Administration. For all I know, he'll live happily ever after as a municipal bureaucrat.

In the end, they decided not to try Sister Angel. She ended up at Kirby Forensic Psychiatric Center on Wards Island. The DA didn't want to give the press the kind of field day they would have had with a nun on trial for murder, especially a saintly nun who had worked tirelessly with the homeless. They weren't even sure they'd get a conviction. Thanks to all the half-assed forensics on TV these days, juries are a lot more unreliable than they used to be. Besides, she really was out of her gourd. After her fight with me and Barbara, her ability to function and cover it up collapsed completely.

They couldn't prove, either, that the Sisters of the Blood of the Lamb had harbored a euthanasia ring. But a few nursing and counseling nuns, including Barbara's Sister Persistence, were quietly asked to retire. The little cabal had started out with patients who were never going to get better, sparing them increasing pain and a lonely death. They targeted the homeless and elderly at first, people with no family and no place to go. Alcoholics in particular were easy marks. We'd drink anything you gave us. No sipping, either. Even if it tasted odd or bitter, we'd never hesitate. Bottoms up.

The whole thing sounds crazy, doesn't it? Everybody but sociopaths knows murder is wrong. But it was Sister Angel's idea, and she convinced the rest. She could be very persuasive. Why did they go along with her? They couldn't all be sociopaths.

"I guess they got a little unbalanced," Barbara said, "after years and years trying to live the religious life in an increasingly secular world."

"That's putting it nicely," Jimmy snorted. Like a lot of lapsed Catholics, he could get quite caustic about the Church. "Unbalanced! It should come as no surprise."

Sister Angel was on her own when she decided that child molesters should also be helped along the way. The others didn't know. Guff may have been her first attempt. His bad luck. I thought about him a lot. I wondered if he would have stayed sober if he'd lived. If we would have stayed friends. How he and Jimmy would have liked each other. If we hadn't stopped her, there would have been others.

Boris came out of hiding to tell the police that art thieves, not nuns, killed Lucinda. One group had stolen the icons in order to supply art-loving customers like her. And unfortunately, she caught another group in the act of stealing them again. Boris had brought the icons into Lucinda's house in the first place. He disappeared because he feared he would be implicated in her murder. His AA sponsor convinced him to turn himself in. AA! There's nothing like it. He got off with a suspended sentence and five hundred hours of community service. They allowed him to do his service hours at the detox. His first day back on the job, he got a round of applause from the staff and patients.

Emmie knew Jimmy and me as Barbara's friends by now. I think she kind of had a special feeling for me because I'd known her brother sober. It meant a lot to her that I had liked him. Besides, I'd almost gotten myself killed, along with Barbara, catching her husband's murderer. So I went along with Barbara when she went to Emmie's to confess how come she'd gotten to know her in the first place, have a long, frank talk, and make amends. To tell the truth, I owed her amends myself, having taken advantage of several members of her family at least as badly as Barbara had deceived Emmie.

"It'll give you a head start on the Ninth Step," my sponsor told me when I tried to wriggle out of going. So we went.

Emmie was really nice about it. She hadn't been in love with Sam for many years. She blamed herself for his death. She thought it wouldn't have happened if they'd pooled their information. She wouldn't have let him try to buy Guff off or threaten Sister Angel about the money, if that's what he did.

"We never talked," she said, tears welling in her eyes. "About so many things. And we should have protected Brandy better."

"Emmie, what about the younger kids?" Barbara asked. When Barbara said a frank talk, she meant it. I just drank my tea and tried to look inconspicuous. "Especially Duncan, since boys seem to have been the problem. If he's been damaged, you need to get him help. Have you ever *asked* him?"

Emmie was silent so long that even Barbara, she admitted afterward, prepared her foot for transport to her mouth. Then Emmie's lips firmed up and her jaw set.

"We're going to ask him right now." The kids were doing homework in their rooms down the hall. "Duncan!"

"What, Mother?"

"Come in here a moment, please, I'd like to ask you something."

When he came, she held out her arms. He snuggled against her readily. He had just lost his father, after all. She stroked his hair.

"Sweetheart, you've met my friend Barbara before. And this is her friend Bruce." We nodded at each other. "Barbara is a counselor, someone who works with people who have problems, like Uncle Guffy."

"He was an alcoholic," Duncan said knowledgeably. Emmie and Barbara exchanged a look. I kept my face blank. I was just an observer, and I meant to keep it that way.

"That's true," she said. "But there was something else. Will you give Barbara your permission to ask you one or two questions?"

Duncan nodded, looking cooperative and tranquil.

"Duncan," Barbara said gently, leaning forward so their eyes were on a level, "it's okay if you're uncomfortable or don't feel like telling me anything. Please speak right up if you want to stop."

"Okay."

"Did your Uncle Guffy ever touch you on any part of your body that you felt uncomfortable about, or ask you to touch him?"

"He tried, but I didn't let him."

"What happened?" She put the question broadly, so as not to lead the witness.

"I ran away," said Duncan simply.

"What are your thoughts or feelings about why he did that?"

"He was a pedophile."

My eyebrows shot up, and I heard Emmie's sharp intake of breath. Barbara managed not to look surprised. As a counselor, she got a lot of practice. Duncan's face remained tranquil.

"Why do you say that?"

"He got off on little boys," said Duncan matter-of-factly. "All the kids who dance in *The Nutcracker* know about pedophiles. Some of the parents seem to think everyone in ballet is like that, but that's bu—uh, nonsense."

Emmie made an effort, visible to Barbara and me, if not to the kid, and controlled her face and voice. She gave him another kiss and sent him back to his homework.

"Helping Brandy will be a lot harder," Barbara said afterward. "Stop looking worried, Jimmy. You don't even have to remind me it's none of my business. I just encouraged Emmie to talk with him as soon as possible."

"I still have trouble," I said, "believing that Guff was a full-fledged pedophile."

"Whatever the connection was," Barbara said, "I guess it ended when the boy fell off the pier and Guff saved him from drowning. It wasn't Brandy's fault; that's the important thing. I told Emmie to call me if she needs help finding a therapist for him."

But she never did.

I made my ninety days. Barbara snuck into the closed AA meeting when I qualified for the first time. Barbara thought my story was hilarious. Jimmy laughed louder than anyone. Both Jimmy and my sponsor think that office temping is okay for a recovery job but that I should eventually go back to school and get myself a real career. The other day, I called Jimmy up to ask what he would think if I became a nurse. He had made Barbara get off the extension right away. But when I told him my idea, he bellowed with laughter, even louder than at my qualification. I could hear Barbara in the background, saying, "What? What?" the way she always does. She can't stand being left out. Jimmy could barely speak for laughing, but he told her. Then he had another fit of laughter.

In between snickers, he said, "Yeah, man, I can just see you in one of those starched white dresses with the little cap."

Barbara said, "Idiot. Nurses don't wear those caps and dresses anymore."

Between the two of them, they sure have one weird sense of humor.

After all the excitement was over, we all lay low for a while. Barbara and I both got headaches for a few weeks on account of our concussions. Jimmy settled back in behind his computer, happy as a clam. I temped and went to meetings and tried to walk the line between thinking about the future and living one day at a time. It wasn't boring, but it was quiet. Spring took its time coming that year. Easy does it, just like getting sober.

On the first warm day, near the end of April, the three of us got in the car and drove north. We went up along the Hudson River, with the Palisades on the other side. We passed through some little towns that Barbara thought were cute, with neo-country inns and craft shops and little restaurants with daffodils and grape hyacinths blooming all along their front walks. We kidded around and laughed a lot. We even sang "A Hundred Bottles of Beer on the Wall" and squabbled, still laughing, over which of us was the worst singer.

"How many kinds of laugh do you think there are?" Barbara asked.

"What do you mean?"

"When I was a kid, I used to read these girls' magazines. I once read an article about the different kinds of laughs—giggles, titters, snickers, guffaws, you know. Sometimes laughing comes from amusement, sometimes from malice; there are different motivations. But the best one, the laugh of laughs, according to the article, is the laugh for pure joy. I always wanted one. I wanted a perfect oval face, too, but I never got it."

Jimmy, at the wheel, grinned at me over Barbara's head.

"Women. They're a different breed."

"For sure."

"And thank goodness," Barbara said.

We found a state park with a brook and a classic swimming hole fringed with the pale, edible green of newborn leaves. There was even a little waterfall. The brook babbled away. The falls glinted in the sunlight. It was a weekday, and there wasn't a soul around but us. Barbara had taken a day off from work. Jimmy had even left his laptop home. We lay on a big rock that the sun was hot enough to bake to a comfortable warmth. Barbara had stripped down to shorts and T-shirt. Jimmy looked unusually relaxed with his pants rolled up to the knee and his legs getting pink in the sun.

"Are you admiring my legs?" he asked.

"I am," Barbara said.

"Me, too," I said. "They're very pink."

"I'm going swimming," Barbara announced.

"Won't it be cold?" I asked.

"There's one way to find out," she said. "Want to come?"

"No, thanks."

"Suit yourself." She slid off the rock into the water. "It's cold," she yelped, hopping up and down. "Not too deep, though."

Jimmy and I both sat up to watch her. The water came up to her waist.

"Watch out," Jimmy called, "it may be slippery."

She made her way across the little pool, stepping cautiously on the rocky bottom, until she stood almost under the waterfall.

"Come on in! It feels great!" She beckoned with a broad gesture of her arm.

"No, thank you," called Jimmy.

"Aw, c'mon, it'll be fun." She splashed to show us how much fun it was.

"You said it's cold," I objected.

"Not once you get used to it," she yelled back. "Come on, it's delicious."

"Delicious my frozen ass," said Jimmy. He gave me a poke, and we started roughhousing. We rolled around like little kids until we finally managed to tip each other into the water with a howl and an almighty splash.

I surfaced, spluttering. Jimmy's cheerful pink face and dripping hair bobbed up beside me. Barbara stood there in the water with the little waterfall sparkling and rushing at her back and the earthy green smell of growing things all around. She threw back her head, and there it came: a laugh for pure joy.

"I knew I'd know it if it ever happened," she called out.

For a giddy moment, I felt like Barbara. Joyful. Like a guy with a best friend. Like a guy with a future. She caught my eye. For a moment, the radiance already fading from my face was reflected in hers. I looked from her to Jimmy, who grinned like a loon at both of us. Across the plash of the falls, she said, "We're going to have a great summer."

4/2008